RISE
OF A
DARK THRONE

THE MŌSA CHRONICLES

THE GREAT LANDS OF TRANSEA

- GRIMERG RISE
- SANCTUM
- THE VENTANE WOODS
- HOUSE OF DO'RAMOS
- KINGGUARD'S REEF
- GALAMEDA BRIDGE
- MENELIK ATHENAEUM
- HOUSE OF PORTE
- MŌSA
- IRIS EXPANSE
- THE SANCTUARY

This book is a work of fiction. The characters and events are the product of the author's imagination or are used fictionally. Any resemblance to actual persons, living or dead, events, or locales is entirely coincidental.

Text and artwork copyright © 2022 Ligia Cushman

All rights reserved. No part of this book may be reproduced in any form or by any electronic or mechanical means, including information storage and retrieval systems, without permission in writing from the publisher, except by reviewers, who may quote brief passages in a review.

Published in the United States.

Visit me on the Web!
www.lnguzman.com

ISBN 979-8-9869869-1-3

Printed in the United States of America

CONTENT NOTE

This book contains classism, death/dying, drinking, discrimination, forced captivity, graphic sex, grief and loss, murder, racism, serious injury, slurs, swearing, violence, warfare, and weapons.

To Melissa, my very own Nisa Asha.
Rest easy, amiga.

PROLOGUE

"You must survive for our people," King Menelik III said as he ushered young Prince Axel through the dark corridors of the sand-colored castle. The prince didn't understand why his father was being cryptic, but he could hear the urgency in his tone. That was why he tried to match his father's quick footsteps as much as he could. He would be a king one day, and it would do him well to do as his father said.

The king's most trusted soldier moved ahead of them, leading them through the maze of passages that ran underneath the city streets, past the stone seawall that guarded the golden city of Sundom from the waters of Transea, and out onto the docks.

The sea was dark and Prince Axel could hardly see what was in front of him, trusting only his father's large hand at his back as it guided him forward. When they neared the edge, he saw his mother, Queen Amina, aboard a small ship designed more for speed than carrying the bulk of trade goods. Before he could wonder why its sails didn't bear the familiar quartered broad shield between two mermaids, the Porte family crest, his father got down on his knees in front of him, leveling him with a clear, steely gaze.

"There is an island on the Northwestern Coast of Transea," he said as he unfastened the golden clasps on his cloak and threw the plush garment over Axel's shoulders. Although his shoulders had broadened at the young age of eight, his father's long cloak still dwarfed him. "Its waters shine like an endless burst of sunsets. It is called Mōsa, and there you will guide our people, make a home for them, and establish our kingdom."

Axel's eyebrows drew together in confusion and he said, "Father, our home is here and our kingdom is here."

King Menelik III shook his head as he tucked in the loose ends of his cloak on his son's shoulders. Then he took off his signet ring, looped the cloak's clasp through it, and laid his large hand over it, right above his son's heart. He said, "Our kingdom is here," and tapped the prince's chest, "and our home is where our people are."

Just above his father's shoulders, Axel could see shadows of ships long departed for that island his father had spoken of. His father had sent his people to safety first. But what were they all running from?

"Father, why are we leaving Sundom?"

For a second, the king hesitated. But his signet ring

on his son's chest told him that his child was no longer a child, but was now a sovereign. He deserved to know the truth.

"A'Dien Alacor's hatred for our people has driven him to commit widespread violence against them, and tonight, he attempted to have your mother and I assassinated," he told his son in an even voice. "Sundom has grown too small for all of us, and our fate and fortune lie elsewhere. You, my son and my heir, will guide our people to better tides."

Fear and anguish gripped Axel's young heart. "You don't mean to join us?"

King Menelik III gave his son a small, sad smile. "I have survived all these years so I can get to this moment for our people. I have to buy enough time for you and our people to get as far away from Alacor's reach as you can," he said.

"But Father, you will be surrounded by the enemy."

"Yes."

Axel bit his lip to keep it from trembling. "You say there are remnants of magick in our blood, but those are all stories," he said with growing dread. "You are human. You have no magick. You will die!"

The king nodded, but his eyes shone bright. "I have no magick, that's true. But I won't die, son." He touched Axel's forehead with the tips of his fingers, a blessing, and his last moment of affection. "Because you shall live. As it has long been for fathers, mothers, and their children."

Axel fought the onslaught of tears as he received his father's unspoken demand for urgency. He could cry later. But first, he had to make sure his people could get to the island of Mōsa.

"What do we say, son?"

Axel looked down at his father's signet ring, held tight to his father's cloak, close to his heart. It flashed gold, even in the darkness. Then, he looked up to meet his father's eyes. Steadily, he repeated his family's motto for his father, "Here before, now, and after."

His father, the King of Mōsa for as long as Axel had known him, dipped his head in acknowledgment of their family's words. Then he rose and stepped aside so his son could board the last vessel out of Sundom. With one hand resting on the hilt of his sword by his side, he raised a hand in a wooden farewell to everything and everyone he had lived for, and now chose to die for.

Prince Axel held onto his mother's hand as they waved goodbye to the lone figure by the dock. Still, he fought the urge to cry. But as his father's figure drew smaller and smaller, he couldn't help the sad, desperate, scream that rang out from him, "I love you, Father!"

It was swallowed by the sudden flash of lightning that

streaked across the sky. The neon bolt looked like it was driven by some unknown wrathful power as it aimed down and hit the sea at the horizon. Half a millisecond later, thunder exploded all around them as the sea lit up with electrified veins of lightning. It began to rain.

But it didn't drown out the memory of the lightning.

CHAPTER 1

Thunderbolt and Lightning

The rose-colored waters of the Serena Sea glimmered under the light of its two moons. The waves, usually playful under the sun, had calmed down to such an extent that if one didn't know any better, the sea would have been mistaken for a lake. The trees swayed in the benevolent spring breeze, as if they were happy to take part at the union of two enigmatic lovers.

Owls cooed softly in the distance. Fireflies flew in spiraling patterns far above the garden of roses that surrounded the ancient home of the Porte family. It had served multiple generations, making it a landmark.

Nothing could eclipse the romance in the air, except for the upcoming union of Nasir Asha and Lia Soleidae Porte, the second daughter of King Axel Aquor Porte of Mōsa. It was a time of joyful celebration as Nasir and his bride, who was more known by the name of Sole, were to solemnize their bond. Even inside the Porte family home, their union was the only topic of discussion.

The King of Mōsa looked out over the land. Lanterns began to light up as people made their way to the celebration. From his balcony, he could see most of Mōsa and how it stretched out to the Serena Sea. His people knew peace and prosperity, and he wished, especially on days like these, that his father was here to see this. With a sigh, he turned away from the balcony and made his way back into his suite.

As soon as he slid the glass door shut behind him, he felt the unmistakable crackle in the air as the wind shifted. He glanced outside the window just as the clear night sky grew heavy with clouds and a dull fog crept around the edges of the island. It began to drizzle.

King Axel's eyes were fixed on the horizon through the large window of his quarters. "Never mind the rain," he murmured to himself. "The island's color becomes brighter under a little rainfall and everything will be all the more romantic."

He stepped back from the window, trying to ease low hum of trepidation in his senses. He sat on the edge of the settee near his bed, breathing slowly as he tried to shake off old childhood memories.

"We must make haste, my love," the voice of his

queen saved him from spiraling further into the past. Lygia Porte, the love of his life, entered their royal quarters in a haze of silk and the sweet scent of jasmine. She stopped when she saw her husband, still dressed in the casual tunic he preferred whenever he worked alongside his people. "You must be getting old, my love. You do know that your beloved Sole is getting married today and it's your job to make it official, right?" she said, a teasing glint in her eyes.

That brought a smile to the king's face. His wife always had a way with him. Distracted by his memories, he had almost forgotten about the occasion that required his presence. He was fortunate to have a wife who could pull him back from such a reverie. "Who are you calling old? Surely not me, my queen?" he said as he stood up and playfully puffed his chest.

His queen merely rolled her warm brown eyes at him and said, "All right, maybe old isn't quite the right word. Slowpoke is much more fitting." She then gestured with an elegant hand towards the ceremonial robes that hung in front of their massive closet. "Hurry up and get dressed."

His wife was right, as always. It was imperative that he was dressed and fully prepared for the ball that was to be held in honor of his daughter, Sole, and soon to be son-in-law Nasir's union by now. It was out of character for him to act this way. Usually, it was his wife Lygia who took too long in getting dressed and he would have been the one urging her to hurry.

Even though he was king of the people of Mōsa, he knew how to party, and on all past occasions, he was the one to initiate a good time. All the guests revered his presence as their king, but they also genuinely wanted to be around his light, joyous nature.

Today was one of those occasions when that side of him was needed, not just by the people, but by his own daughter. But there was something in the dark edges of the horizon that left him feeling quite unsettled.

Maybe this feeling was not new; maybe this feeling had something to do with how he had felt for the past three months. It had been too peaceful, too quiet, like the fates were simply biding their time before extracting their price for the prosperity they had been enjoying. He was unsure what was happening in his mind, but in his heart, he knew he had to be steadfast, averting any danger to his beloved queen, his precious daughters, and the people of Mōsa.

And so, with a steadying breath, he made his way to his dresser and began to dress for the celebration. Even when he heard the soft drizzle turn to a hard rainfall, he forced himself to keep moving, to fix his robes, to put on his shoes, and to don his crown. When at long last, he was ready, he turned to his wife with an outstretched hand, ready to accompany her to the ball.

Queen Lygia beamed at him, terms of endearment ready at her lips, but both were drowned out by the sudden flash of lighting, painfully visible through their large windows and the glass doors of their balcony. It streaked across the sky, looking like a neon bolt that was driven by an unknown wrathful power. It aimed down and hit the edge of their world where the sky met the sea.

Half a millisecond later, thunder exploded and the bioluminescent sea turned bright, almost radioactive, for a few precious seconds. Then it died down, and it began to rain in earnest.

And King Axel knew tonight was the same as that night so many years ago on his last day in Sundom. It held the same eeriness, the same rotten stench in the air, as if demanding a sacrifice not of the body but the soul. It wasn't a new feeling—it had been building inside him for the past three months, and now it had peaked with such fury that it shook even a man of his stature.

Heeding the uneasiness in the air, Axel looked at Lygia with worried eyes and said, "Dear love, maybe we should wait to celebrate Sole and Nasir's union. I know I should not be saying this, but I fear something isn't right."

Hearing the words of her beloved, she recognized the worry in his voice. This kind of recognition was not something ordinary or easily acquired. Instead, it was harnessed after a lifelong partnership, achieved by their immense love for each other. They were true mates in every sense of the word; it was amazing how they both understood each other with just a glance.

She approached and kissed him lovingly, soothingly. Axel hugged her and lifted her from the ground. Looking into his eyes, she adjusted his crown.

Gripping Axel tighter than ever, Lygia inquired, "How would you have felt if my father delayed us on our bonding night? I am sure it would not have been pleasant. In my opinion, my love, we shouldn't keep them waiting. I believe they have waited long enough as it is."

Her words took him back to their bonding night. He had hardly been able to wait, Lygia's beauty impossible to resist.

Lygia was a rare flower among all the women of Mōsa. She was a dazzling beauty often adorned in fine silk and ornaments that enhanced her athletic frame. However, there was a reason she was so different from her people; she was a foreigner and belonged to the city of Aivren, Sundom.

When Axel first laid eyes on her, it was impossible for him to look away. It was love at first sight. She excelled in her charm and beauty with dazzling champagne-brown eyes, lips of berry red, and a figure that made his heart skip a beat. Originally, she lived alone near the island's western coast, near the Serena Sea, relying on nature to sustain herself. She had no skill with the sword when she first arrived from Sundom all those years ago, unlike the women of Mōsa who were taught the blade arts from a young age. Yet, after more than twenty-four years on the island, it almost felt as if she had been born here.

Although she had initially been a fragile little girl, after training for ten seasons with the Misa Warriors, she had mastered the art of wielding two blades at a time, transforming her into the battle-hardened Queen of Mōsa. Her hardened leadership started and remained on the battlefield, and at home, she was wise, soft, and caring with her mate and her daughters, Lia, Sole, and Lola.

Before Lygia, he had been content with the home he had built for his people and the kingdom he had restored for his father. But Lygia had given him a family, his own home, and his own legacy. So, if she thought things were going to be all right, then they were going to be all right.

Queen Lygia took in the pensive look in his eyes, his fretful silence, and the shades of doubt that lingered. She cradled his cheek gently and said, "Come now, love. I imagine this is a difficult night for you. You and Sole have always been so close." She curled a hand around her husband's bicep and subtly nudged him towards the direction of the festivities. Then, she continued. "But know this. Sole cherishes you as much as you cherish her. So, please put all these dark feelings aside and come be a part of her dream; I know her happiness is what's most important for you."

He looked at Lygia in love and gratefulness. She always knew the right words to say. "I adore our girls," he told her, "as I adore you."

With tears filling her champagne eyes, she responded, "And I, you. You know Sole deserves this day to be perfect. And that is what we will make it."

It was time to steel his heart and put his past aside. So, he took a deep breath and set off to celebrate the union of his precious Sole with full fervor and heart.

He willed himself to smile, to look assured. Then, he took his wife's hand, placed it inside the crook of his arm, and led her out of their room.

Lygia had accomplished what she set out to do. Once again, like many before, she reassured her husband, as mates do, to move forward confidently.

He understood what he had to do. It was not a time to show weakness in his demeanor or resolve. It was a time to celebrate his second-born daughter's bonding ceremony.

As he walked beside his wife, Axel glanced at Lygia and took in the beauty of her profile. Her mahogany copper skin looked smooth as selenite in the dancing firelight, her coiled hair plunged over her shoulders in waves of midnight black, and her smile, even today, was spellbinding. She had given him everything a man could ever want and he was doing her a disservice by marring their present, and their daughter's future, with thoughts of his past.

He could only hope that all his worrying was nothing and the omens he saw in the sky, thunder, and lighting were simply figments of his vivid imagination's cruel creation, no doubt colored by his past. But that was all it ever was—the past. And there, his memories should stay. What better way was there to dispel a dark past than a ceremony that could assure the coming of a brighter future?

***

The tradition in Mōsa dictated that all bonding celebrations occur when the mauve moons were at their highest and the bioluminescent bay surrounding it glowed the brightest. However, all across Transea and its many islands and kingdoms, it was not tradition to allow the second daughter to marry before the first daughter. Being the second born was never a position of honor. For most families, the union of a second born child ahead of the first was unheard of, an absurdity, and in some far-flung regions, a curse.

But in Mōsa, they did away with this nonsense and broke with this tradition, the same way King Axel's father had broken away from the kingdom at Sundom. Here, they made their own kingdom, their own traditions, and followed only those from the old ways that still made sense. King Axel had seen that Sole and Nasir's love was as rare as Lygia's beauty and worth the risk. They publicly embraced each other, and there was nothing that could stop them from their bonding.

Besides, since Sole and Nasir's fathers were brothers in arms, Sole and Nasir's union was seen as fate and love at work. As children, they had been close friends, and as they had grown, so had their affection for each other. They were truly meant for each other, and this bonding ceremony was meant to celebrate that love.

It had been the start of the third uncommonly hot night in a row a few hours ago. Sole had hoped the evening would at least bring a cool breeze to their festivities. The immense heat was not typical of a Mōsian Spring. The weather had grown quite unpredictable over the last season.

So, when it began to rain, Sole had breathed a sigh of relief. Rain brought cooler temperatures and the island's colors always seemed brighter under a rainfall. Sole also knew the canopy of trees that grew over the Iris Expanse, where important Mōsian rituals were always held, was thick enough to protect them from getting wet.

Like all Mōsian rituals, their bonding ceremony started at dusk, timing their movements with the rise of the two mauve moons. From the window of Sole's room, she could see people making their way towards the Iris Expanse, tucked inside the bioluminescent bay in the center of Mōsa, ready to bear witness to and celebrate her union with Nasir.

A knock on her door startled Sole, but she quieted when Nisa's head popped into her room. She had her eyes closed and her apple-like cheeks, cute button nose, and pillowy lips were all scrunched up in an effort to keep them that way.

"What are you doing, Ni?" Sole asked, laughing at her dearest friend who also happened to be Nasir's only sister.

Nisa entered the room, slapping a hand over her eyes, and said, "I'm not supposed to see your dress right before your wedding."

That made Sole laugh even more. "But today is my wedding!"

"I'm still not supposed to see what you're wearing right before the actual ceremony!"

Sole rolled her eyes at Nisa and moved to stand directly in front of her best friend. "I'm pretty sure that only applies to the groom, and the last time I checked, I'm marrying your brother, not you," she said.

Nisa let out a little shriek. "Are you sure it's okay? You don't know how much of an effort this is for me to not see what you're wearing."

Sole smiled at that. Unlike her sisters, Luna and Lola, Sole had spent most of her free time in her father's library studying ancient ledgers and taking in as much knowledge as she could about her family's sordid history. Although she knew her sisters loved her, they never really spent much time around her because she was, in their opinion, boring.

Nisa never felt that way. She was always with Sole, prancing about in dresses and costumes, while Sole walked around the library looking for yet another book to read.

Nisa always loved beautiful dresses and ball gowns. When they were children, they had loved playing dress up. Well, Nisa loved it and loved the fact that Sole always agreed to wear anything Nisa put on her. Sole never cared much for dresses, but she cared a lot about Nisa.

"Oh, trust me," Sole laughed as she pried Nisa's hand

away from her eyes, "I do know. Come now, open your eyes. Besides, after today, you really will become my sister."

At that, Nisa finally gave in and opened her eyes.

Sole had expected her best friend to squeal or jump up and down as she did when she was excited. But all Nisa could do was look at her, tears gathering at the corners of her eyes, her gaping mouth covered by one delicate hand, while her other hand held Sole's.

"For the first time, something is more important than dresses," Nisa said in a whisper.

Sole's eyebrows shot up in surprise.

"You're marrying my brother, but, I mean, who cares about that? We're going to be real sisters!"

The pair collapsed in a fit of giggles. Sole's union with Nasir would undoubtedly bring joy to both their families. Through their laughter, Nisa managed to remember why she had barged into Sole's room in the first place.

"Come on," she said as she tugged on Sole's hand just as she had when they were children. "Let's go get you married to my ugly brother."

"He's not ugly! He's very handsome, actually. And very sexy."

Nisa made a face as if she would puke. "Yuck."

Sole only giggled at that and let her best friend lead her to the Iris Expanse.

The humble bay became luminously rich in vivid purples, pinks, greens, and blues as Transea's two moons peered over the horizon. Their glow lit the natural path to the ceremony. The dense canopy composed of pine, maple, and larch was only occasionally interrupted by small glimmers of the moonlight peeking through. A mishmash of shrubs were bustling with the flickering of fireflies, their backdrop the fertile grounds below.

At night even the damp wood gave off a soft glow of purple, lighting the passage ahead. Silent climbing plants clung to the trees as their vibrant flowers swayed in any open pockets they could find.

As was the tradition, women crafted an ornate gilded lantern once they reach the age of nine or ten. The lantern was a symbol of their position and talent and later became an integral part of their mating ceremony.

As the guests stood in anticipation of the bride and groom's arrival, Nisa Asha stepped out from the crowd in her violet tea length ball gown and began the wedding procession with her lantern, adorned with rainbows and flowers, as she loved all things bright. Next came Sole's sisters, Luna and Lola, who entered the passage in their flowing gowns of lilac, holding their own golden lanterns high. Luna, the eldest and most serious, had the fierce and territorial Northern Gorshawke, the red-eyed terror of the skies, carved around her lantern. Beside her was

Lola, the youngest of the Porte sisters, who probably spent more time in the water than on land. She had painstakingly carved the sleek body of the Sturgeorae fish on her own lantern. Sole's own lantern, adorned with stacks of books that she so loved, hung from an enormous tree veiled in vines at the end of the path. This was where Sole and Nasir were to exchange their vows.

Nasir's parents, Gira and Imed Asha, entered next in their stately attire with a royal blue sash, a symbol of their position within the kingdom of Mōsa. At the bottom of the sash, by their hips, was the Asha family crest—a shield with the mirror images of the Porte family's mermaids with a pair of swords crossed on top of it. The Asha family was known for its generations and generations of serving as advisors and protectors for the kings and queens of Mōsa.

Then, the people held their breath as their monarch, mother of Sole and beloved of King Axel, Lygia, Queen of Mōsa, entered the Iris Expanse, adorned in flowing layers of golden silk. Her neckline dashed toward her navel, intense yet refined. As always, she was a sight to behold.

Like all Mōsian mothers, it had been Lygia's responsibility to approve her daughter's choice of mate. Lygia knew Sole and Nasir would be mated when they were just younglings. Although Sole had always been enamored with Nasir as a young girl, it was Nasir himself who had declared to Lygia when he was just five that he planned to marry Sole. Although rare for true mates to discover their connection so early on, it wasn't unheard of.

When Queen Lygia reached the end of the path and made her way to the side, it was time for Sole and Nasir to make their grand entrance. As was tradition, the husband-to-be would enter first. Dressed in high fashion, he strode down the path lined with beautiful white flowers. His smile was bright and accented his glistening grey eyes.

Nasir wore a sleeveless white linen shirt that rested on his muscular chest and buttoned to the top. His matching sleeveless velvet navy jacket featured the rose gold embroidery of his family crest at the top right side. The jacket, also accented with rose gold thread, fit him well, revealing his muscular arms. He looked quite beautiful. His grey eyes seemed to shine brighter in the moonlight.

His white pants were fitted down to his ankles, revealing his black leather loafers. When he reached the end of the aisle, he turned and stood beside Sole's father, King Axel, who wore similar pants and a jacket of deep ivory.

Sole entered the Expanse by the bay, majestic in the moonlight. The crowd gasped at her fairy-like appearance, as Sole only wore glamourous gowns or golden body paint on rare occasions. Typically, Sole wore her hair up in a tight bun, never revealing its true length. Paired with her burgundy spectacles, many villagers didn't understand what Nasir saw in her. In this moment, the idea of a nerdy girl who would rather read a book beachside while the other children swam in the Serena Sea was gone. On this moonrise, before the people of Mōsa, stood the woman Nasir always saw. For him, she was forever beautiful.

Sole, now twenty and three, resembled Lygia in many ways. Her locks cascaded over her shoulders in braided rows of cinnamon-brown. Her glowing smile was captivating when paired with her piercing walnut-brown eyes. Like her mother, she had puffy, pouting lips that were soft like fresh blossoms, now painted pink to match her blush-colored gown.

She looked stunning with her warm brown skin, even warmer brown eyes, rounded nose, and a bright smile that captivated the entire island. The blush sleeveless gown exposing her toned arms and soft bronze skin flowed from her right shoulder across her ample bosom. It gathered at her waist before flowing like waves to the ground, covering her sateen champagne slippers.

Her subtle rose gold necklace hung on her chest, completing her breathtaking look.

As the Mōsian leader, it was tradition for her father to wed each couple. This particular ceremony was extra special because it was Sole. They were close. Part of their bond grew from their love of books. Both avid readers, Axel and Sole spent many moonrises in his study, learning about the Great War and the magicks long passed. Axel was fascinated with the idea of magick and wanted his girls to have his same passion. Only Sole was as captivated as he was about their rich history and the world that came before them.

"Repeat after me," he would tell a young Sole. "Magick lives in you and me." With her little alto voice, she would squeak out his words. Her chocolate eyes glistened whenever he sat her on his lap and say those words. Today too, King Axel had her repeat after him, but the magick today was her wedding vows.

Repeating after Axel, Sole and Nasir recited their vows as the rest of Mōsa fell away and it felt like it was just the two of them. Together, they said aloud, "Love, you are the sky and the clouds. You are the gentle river and the birds that sing. I feel you in the air, long for your touch, and would be lost without you."

King Axel took Nasir and Sole's hands and placed them on top of each other as they moved to the next part of their vows. Nasir and Sole's voices wrapped around each other as they said, "You are my medicine, light, laughter, and hope. I slipped my heart into your pocket some time ago, and there it has stayed, safe and sound."

Their clasped hands tightened, and King Axel encased them by placing one hand above theirs, and another below. This was the king, forging their union, blessing it.

Looking deep into each other's eyes, Nasir and Sole completed their vows in strong, reverent tones.

"I marry you with my eyes wide open, my heart in your hand, and my soul forever connected to yours. I marry you with all my heart and claim every future dream as ours together. I see all of you, your joys and your sorrows; you are my home."

The entire Iris Expanse exploded in thunderous applause. King Axel forced himself not to look out over the horizon once more to check for errant lightning. This union should be enough drown out the past and any ominous futures. He threw himself into the party- and people-loving monarch role he was known for.

Sole and Nasir's mating ceremony celebrated their love and those who came to share their joy. The grand feast was a garden party held beneath the pink moons at their peak. Love was in the air, as if it was a new kind of electricity, so palpable and real. Amid the flowers with their petals in romantic hues of pink and lavender, Sole felt renewed. As she and Nasir danced, a gentle, sweet harp played their favorite song while fireflies glowed around them.

Sole saw it all, but at the same time, felt blind to everything except for Nasir's eyes. She could only see him. There was so much joy in it, in them, and she couldn't help but wonder if it was normal to be this happy. As if the rest of the world could disappear and she would be all right, as long as she had Nasir.

Sole rested her head against Nasir's broad chest, closed her eyes as she took in his masculine scent, and whispered, "It all feels so unreal, like I'm in another place, another time. Like I'm another me."

Nasir bent his head, leaned in to close to her ear, and said, "When you're with the right person, wherever you are is the right place to be."

Sole's heart thudded in her chest as she let Nasir's words wash over her. His words were sweet and gentle, but nothing seemed to calm her agitated heart. Maybe it's just nerves, she thought to herself. After all, any bride would be nervous, most especially someone like Sole, who had never expected anyone to be interested in her, let alone marry her. She tried her best to will away her jitters as she let Nasir sweep her across the dance floor.

When the moons reached their absolute highest, and the land was lit the brightest, the crowd of guests slowly faded into the corners of the garden. As Sole and Nasir continued to dance, a ring of people formed around them. The crowd held hands and prayed to the Holy Mother that the union formed before them would remain strong forever. The circle broke as the crowd retrieved small woven baskets of flower petals to throw. The different colors transformed the ground below Sole and Nasir's dancing feet. The hues made it seem as if they were dancing on an artist's palette, causing ripples with each movement.

Queen Lygia and King Axel watched the couple from a distance until a Misa warrior appeared before them with an ornate rose gold box embossed with the Porte family crest on all its faces.

The Porte family crest was distinct. It featured a broad shield with a short, pointed top and a diamond-shaped bottom. Flanked by mermaids on either side, the center held a rose gold circlet atop four divisions, each holding a symbol of their lineage. A sail, an anchor, a helm, and three crowns. Finally, a majestic ribbon hung below the crest carrying their motto, "Here before, now, and after."

The Misa warrior raised the gilded box towards the queen. Lygia accepted it as she turned to face her king. As Lygia held the box, the king gently opened it. From within, he removed two ornamental antique circlets passed down through generations as heirlooms. The crowd grew silent as the ceremonial drums began their cadence, their echoing call signalling the music to recede. Sole and Nasir's dance ceased and, hand in hand, they turned towards the king.

King Axel made his way to the dance floor. With his right hand raised, he addressed the crowd and spoke with quiet intensity, "Thank you all for gathering here today. Our Sole and Nasir stand before the Holy Mother and all of us, reminding us what true love can be."

Raising the two circlets, he continued, "Sole, Nasir, kneel before your king." As Sole kneeled, Nasir held her hand until she was settled, then he followed and respectfully bowed his head. "Many will not understand why we broke tradition to allow our second daughter to marry before our first. I will continue to respond in the same manner. No one knows when the Holy Mother will send your mate to you. But, when she does, we must honor her wishes. Therefore, on this moonrise, I crown you, Nasir, as the first Prince of Mōsa and welcome you as my son."

The king passed the remaining circlet to Lygia with a smile. The queen made her way to Sole and placed the circlet on her head. With tear-filled eyes, she said,

"Sole, today I crown you the Princess of Mōsa, and I bid you to write the fortune of our people alongside your prince."

In unison, Axel and Lygia proclaimed, "We crown the future of Mōsa; may the Holy Mother bless their union, in life, loss, and in love."

The people of Mōsa repeated after them. Turning to the crowd, King Axel said, "People of Mōsa, it is time we let the young couple retire to their quarters. I believe they have waited long enough, haven't they?" Hearing the King's words, the crowd parted into equal halves, forming a path for Sole and Nasir and showering the royal couple with well wishes as they passed by on their way toward their chambers.

Sole could feel the heat within her rising with every step, her heart beating like never before. She clasped her hand around Nasir's rougher one, signaling to him that the time they had waited for, the time they have saved themselves for, was finally upon them. She felt him squeeze her hand back in silent affirmation of his own excitement.

Misa warriors stood at the entrance of their bedchambers. The Misa are the elite war maidens led by Queen Lygia. Also known as Maidens of the Shining Sea, King Axel's all-female military regiment went from daughters to soldiers, from wives to weapons, and they remain the only feared frontline female troops in Transea. Their regiment grew over the last four generations and now stood six thousand strong.

The female war maidens are structured parallel with the army, with a central elite wing acting as the royal family's bodyguards. Trained to be fierce in battle, the maidens were recruited at the early age of sixteen. Trained to fight, wielding two machetes, mastering a bow, and riding horseback saddle free were standard. Nevertheless, Sole recognizing Aurora, her sister Lola's best friend and a fierce Misa warrior, standing guard made her feel safe and embarrassed simultaneously.

"Hi, Rory," Princess Sole said shyly, eyes smiling.

In quiet tones, Rory replied, "Princess." Like all Misa, Rory was beautiful. Her long flowing braids almost fully cover her chiseled, radiant face. Piercing honey eyes, watched over the Princess she has protected all her life.

As was custom, a handmaid passed along a large glass of aged honey wine for after their mating. Then the warriors pulled open the large wooden doors, revealing a wide corridor strewn with rose petals that led to their canopied bed.

Once inside, they heard the loud click of their door shutting, a signal that they would not be disturbed until the sun shone on the door at sunrise.

Sole bent down to pick up some petals with the full

intent to tease Nasir by throwing them at him. Nasir, on the other hand, had other plans. He leaned forward, grabbed Sole's waist, and tossed her over his shoulder, giving her an unobstructed view of his muscular back. Sole shrieked playfully after realizing that she had been outplayed. In jest, she tried to escape, a graceful yet fruitless attempt.

Nasir carried his beloved as he made his way deeper into their bedchamber. The room was decorated with hundreds of candles, carrying the subtle scent of lavender that Sole so loved. Their dancing flames cast a warm glow over the room and Nasir's eyes flashed at the thought of how the flickering shadows would tease Sole's bare, golden skin.

Their enormous, gilded bed was adorned with overlapping layers of gossamer tule for its canopy, while silken ivory sheets covered the mattress that was fit for a king and his queen. Nasir gently placed Sole on the waves of silk and took his time, gazing down at her.

Taking advantage of the moment, she tossed the petals she had been hiding toward his face. Seeing her child-like act, he smiled and said, "Do you really want to mess with the Big Bad Wolf?"

"I am the wolf here; you will never take me," Sole replied in a comical voice. She pushed herself back and rested her head on the pillows in the middle of their bed.

With the intent to tease Nasir some more, Sole slid the sleeve of her right shoulder down, all the while looking at Nasir coyly from underneath her lashes.

Nasir climbed onto the bed and kissed Sole's exposed shoulder and said, "This is mine to undress. Don't you dare take what's mine."

Giggling nervously, Sole slid her hands up to his face and pulled it in towards her own, kissing him on the lips. Nasir could feel the heat radiating from her body, and unable to resist the urge any longer, he began fondling her curves as gently as he could. His hands roamed hungrily over her thighs, her hips, the dip in her waist, and up and around her breasts. Her body tingled at the feel of his frame leaning on hers as one strong arm wrapped around her waist while his other hand searched for the button and zipper at her back that held her dress together. His touch nearly felt forbidden.

In a low rumble, Nasir whispered, "You can't imagine how long I have waited for this moment." Nasir poured his feelings into every word he spoke to her, sending electric chills through her body. He peppered her face down to neck with hot, open-mouthed kisses as he continued, "I wish our mating would last forever, for I fear it's the only thing that will sate my hunger."

She smiled between his kisses and countered, "My love, I feel the same. You are the first man who has tasted my lips, kissed my neck, and caressed my breasts."

Her fingers combed through the short crop of his hair as his lips teased the swell of her breasts, her dress barely clinging to her curves. "I want you to take me until I become a part of you. I have seen the hunger in your gaze; I have watched you undress me with your alluring eyes."

Hearing Sole's words of love for him sent a burst of fire into his soul. It gave him the encouragement he needed to proceed further into his exploration. He tugged the silk dress down her body, baring Sole to him for the first time.

Her breath hitched as she recognized that after tonight, she would be a changed woman.

Time moved slowly as Nasir entered Sole numerous times, his desire endless, and Sole reveled in it, craved every moment of it. She kissed his body all over and tasted his sweat, a sweet reminder of the fragrance in the gardens they used to play in when they were young.

Their love flourished throughout the night, the bed rocking from side to side until the last of the candles stopped burning. Exhausted, but not completely sated, Nasir wrapped himself around Sole from behind and entered Sole one last time, keeping himself tucked into her body as he succumbed to their bodies' demand for rest after the toil of making love through the night. They fell into blissful sleep in each other's loving embrace.

They had become one as they had always wanted, and they hoped it was just the beginning of many sweaty, steamy nights to come.

CHAPTER 2

Magick from Sorrow

With an acute feeling of uneasiness, Sole woke. An eerie breeze, cold as the mountain snow, crept in from the window, little chills emerging from underneath her spine. She wanted to blame the strange spring weather they had been having lately for the chill in the air. Yesterday had been too hot. But now, it was too cold. She also noticed a faint dark aura to the wind but gave no heed to it. She thought maybe it was all in her head.

Just a few hours earlier, she had been celebrating her mating ceremony. It was an intense feeling to be loved by someone who held her so dear. For Sole, that feeling was still fresh in her mind. She was now Nasir's wife, something she had forever longed for. Happiness bloomed in her heart, despite the chill in the air. The love they cherished, the bond they adored, fueled them in their earlier mating ritual. It was deep, raw, and full of lust, but above all, it was filled with love as they started their journey together as husband and wife. Sole's body still glistened, a reminder of her lover's intense attention from last night. After all the hours of lovemaking, she still felt the need for his comforting embrace.

She turned her head towards the faint early morning light and saw the only possible source for the chill in the room. The windows were open. Sole chuckled at the thought that now she would need more bedcovers, because Nasir appeared to love to sleep with the windows wide open. He must have thrown them open in the middle of the night, she thought, as she glanced over at his side of the bed. She smothered a small laugh as she saw he had all but buried himself under the covers, despite wanting the cold. Sole herself was not used to her bedroom air being so biting. She would have to get accustomed to having more blankets, a compromise she was willing to make. Anything for Nasir.

Grabbing her favorite plush white blanket, which had fallen to the floor during last night's activities, she wrapped it over her naked, dark brown shoulders and rose from the bed. As she tiptoed across the cold granite floor to close the window, an intense fear captured her. An unnerving silence seemed to have swept over Mōsa, and she could feel it pressing down on her. She caught a glimpse of the outside world while she struggled to close the large windows of their suite. The air was so still, even the early morning dark fog between the trees and above the ocean didn't seem to be moving.

"Why must there be a bitter wind in the middle of our Mōsian spring?" Sole again wondered to herself.

Turning to wake Nasir, she saw his hand poking out from under the covers. She knew it was his right hand because she could see the glow of the golden wedding band she had placed on his finger only hours before. Mōsian metal was bioluminescent, allowing it to radiate in the absence of light.

"Nasir, I think something is very wrong. Wake up, love," she said urgently as she made her way to his side of the bed. "We must go tell my fa—"

It wasn't until she touched him that she realized he was as cold as the granite throughout the citadel. In a panic, she reasoned that maybe the open window made his skin feel so icy. She grabbed a nearby candle and tried to light it with the match but her hands failed her, frozen, shaking, and numb. She seemed to be losing control of her own limbs. Abandoning the candle, she took a deep breath and tried to calm herself. Somehow, she found the strength to turn down the covers and look at her husband. What she saw would haunt her for the rest of her life.

Nasir lay lifeless. His grey skin resembled the sand on the shores near the Serena Sea. His hands were frozen, his fingertips consumed by blackness as if they had been dipped in a well of deep blue ink. Nasir's champagne grey eyes were gone; what remained was a black hole, no glimmer, no gleam, just a bottomless pit.

Sole tried to speak, make a sound, anything, but she was unable to even breathe. A slow, silent scream left her before she could find her voice again.

"No, no, no, please don't leave me alone, Nasir! Don't go! What happened? What happened, baby?" she said, frantically shaking his icy corpse.

Just when she thought this was the worst moment of her life, crippling darkness consumed her body. She didn't know if it she was about to die or pass out; she would have welcomed both at that moment. But she fought against the nauseating pain, dressing herself before she ran towards the door. Somebody must have snuck into their room last night and poisoned her husband as he lay sleeping and she fully intended on alerting the guards and mobilizing all the Misa warriors to catch the culprit. This was an attack on the future of Mōsa!

Reaching the large oak doors, she pushed at them with what was left of her strength.

"Guards!"

But the command she was about to bark out died in a scream when she saw the two soldiers who had stood guard over them last night slumped in an ashen heap on the floor. They looked as dead as her husband.

Her hands itched, as if her veins had grown electric currents and they were sparking all at once. Then her palms began to glow with a violet fire raging to get out. Sole shook her hands, wondering if she could somehow just flick off the eerie violet waves of light emanating from her hands. Sparks flew from the tip of her fingers, went straight up in the air, and scattered in different directions. But the violet glow in her hands didn't go away. The tingling in her hands refused to stop, so she curled her hands into fists and began running towards the palace, just across the town square. She was sure this wasn't an assassin's work, it was something else.

Sole wasn't very athletic; it was usually Lola who was running around or swimming in the sea. But Sole pushed her legs to take her to her parents faster, to her sisters, and then to the library to figure out what was going on. She had an inkling about what this could be, but she wasn't absolutely sure. Maybe the old tomes had an answer for this.

However, the moment she reached the square in the middle of town, she stopped in her tracks. Mōsa's merchants, usually up and about at this hour to get ready for the day's trade, were strewn about on the streets, over their carts still filled with goods, and on top of their stall counters, as if they had decided to take a nap while in the middle of a task. Sole knew if she looked closer, she would find the same ink-black, dead eyes as her husband's.

There was kind old Dinorah, who had sold her and Nasir the sweetest star apples, slumped over her cart with her grey and black hair hanging limp over her pile of round shiny, burgundy-colored fruits. Sole hadn't realized she had moved towards her until the old woman's hair glowed violet. She was touching old Dinorah's hair, brushing it back gently. She didn't need to turn her head to know if the old woman had suffered the same fate as her husband. She knew. She didn't have to see her eyes to know they'd be the same as Nasir's.

At the thought of Nasir lying dead on their marital bed, a sob rose in Sole's throat. But she couldn't fully indulge in a breakdown right now, because out of the dead sleep of her people, a few seemed to be waking up. A very scant few.

And one of them was old Dinorah, who was stirring beneath the violet glow of her hands. The old woman groaned, and Sole pulled her hand back to hide the unusual glow. Dinorah looked like she was waking up from a long, deep sleep, very much unharmed. All around her was a faint purple glow, similar to the one in Sole's hands. It pulsed around the old woman, almost like it was a living being, helping her stand and regain her footing. When she was fully upright, the violet glow faded away.

Sole's eyebrows drew together in deep thought. She turned around and searched for the few lucky ones who had woken up from this strange illness. Some had the glow, some didn't. This confused her, but she couldn't help the small surge of hope that rose up within her. She needed to test a shaky theory that was forming in her head.

She looked around and spotted a pair of Misa warriors who had fallen at their designated spots at the corner of the street that led up to the castle. Hurriedly, she ran to one of the warriors, crouched over her, and laid one glowing hand over the woman's heart.

She didn't know what she was doing, or how it worked. But if it did work, then the people she loved might still have a chance to survive this. Concentrating without knowing exactly what she was concentrating on, she pulled on all the hope and prayer and despair within her and willed whatever illness had befallen the warrior to heal.

Sole nearly jumped when tiny sparks flew out of her fingertips and shot straight to the warrior's heart. For a few moments, she waited without breathing. When nothing happened, a frustrated half sob escaped Sole's lips and she rushed to the other Misa warrior. She extended a glowing purple hand once more over the warrior's chest and called on the Holy Mother for help.

She didn't know how she did it but when the Misa warrior began to stir, Sole threw a prayer of thanks to the Holy Mother. Then, she got up, readied herself to run once more, until her next thought froze her. If she somehow had been graced with the power to heal, albeit selectively as only the Holy Mother willed it, then who would she run to first? Her parents? Her sisters? Her husband? Choosing one over the other seemed impossible and unbearable. How could she decide whose life mattered to her more when she had loved them all for all her life?

She didn't know how long she stood there, immobilized by indecision. Then a frail hand touched her arm and brought her out of her haze.

"Princess Sole?"

It was a little boy. There was no purple glow all over him, so he was one of the lucky ones who hadn't needed her assistance to escape this sudden darkness. But his large, tear-filled eyes told a different story of luck.

"My father, please?"

The little boy tugged on her hand, unafraid of the bright purple flame, and pointed to man who looked only a few years older than her and Nasir. He must be a young father, she thought to herself, and her heart broke into a million pieces as she realized what choice she would have to make.

Her parents and sisters would have to wait. Her love, Nasir, would have to wait. Because on the same day she had married Nasir, she had also been crowned Princess of Mōsa.

Her people would have to come first. So, she turned away from the street that led up to the palace, and didn't go back to her bedchamber until she had attended to every last one of her people who had asked for her help.

When dusk fell, Sole finally found herself hurrying to the steps that led to the palace. While she had been about town, she found some Misa warriors who had survived, and some who had responded to her healing touch. She had instructed two of them to bring Nasir's body up to her parents' palace, so she wouldn't have to choose which place to go to first, or last.

Sole burst into the throne room of the kingdom of Mōsa, exhausted, but hopeful. Even as she knelt by the bodies of her parents and her husband, she told herself they weren't dead, they were just sleeping.

"Where are Luna and Lola?" she asked, looking around.

"We couldn't find their bo—them, princess," a Misa palace guard responded softly. "Perhaps they've been going around helping the people, as you have, and you simply missed each other on the way."

Sole nodded. That did seem possible. But right now, she had a task to do. Unsure if she still had enough to heal all three of them, Sole put out both of her hands, touched Nasir's chest, and sent out a prayer. Then came the familiar purple sparks, like little bolts of lightning. But Nasir didn't move.

Sole gritted her teeth and moved on to her mother. The same sparks, the same prayer. The same stillness from her mother. Fighting back sorrow, she moved to her beloved father. Hands, sparks, prayer.

But there was nothing but death and stillness.

Sole squeezed her hands into fists and pressed them to her lips, fighting back the sobs that threatened to overwhelm her. She refused to give in, so she held out her hands once more, spread out her fingers as wide as they could, and pulled on the magick her people had thought long gone. Then she sent a desperate cry to the Holy Mother.

Still, nothing.

Sole held out her hands for as long as she could, murmuring all the prayers she had ever learned, her despair rising in the same intensity as she fought to hold on to hope. The purple flame in her hands grew and grew and soon, the glow consumed the whole room.

A deep blackness swept her away. Her eyes closed, and she fell to the cool granite floor.

She lay lifeless like a doll, asleep, but even in that pitiful condition, her grief was visible from the sadness that had enveloped her face.

It would be another year before Sole could open her eyes again. She had survived being infected by the Darkness but not before it took everything from her, including her love, Nasir.

CHAPTER 3

Empty Thrones

At dawn, Sole stood on the terrace of the throne room where her parents had reigned, where she had been presented to the people of Mōsa when she was born, and where her family died. A year and a half ago, the Darkness, a mysterious plague that came once every few centuries, had claimed the lives of almost a quarter of the population of Transea. Mōsa, a thriving kingdom that sat in the middle of Serena Sea and separated from the rest of the continent, had been hit quite hard. Rebuilding her kingdom had been a slow, agonizing process that she had to balance with her private grief.

Her kingdom. The words didn't sit quite right with Sole, who was now crowned queen of Mōsa upon the death of her parents and the disappearance of her sisters. A lone queen, too. She had gone to bed with her husband and had woken up without him.

What she did wake up with was magick, the kind that

had the power to heal. In the ancient days, people had walked on the land of Transea with magick, until one day, perhaps after all the destruction and warmongering, the Holy Mother had stripped their world of magick. No one had been blessed with it for centuries until Sole woke up with it after the Darkness had fallen.

Before magick and the Darkness, whenever Sole was nervous, she would play with her hair, twisting it into tighter coils for hours. Now, Sole would whirl her right hand in circles and watch as the as the vibrant purple fire burn brighter, mesmerized by its beauty. Unfortunately, her purple haze made those around her nervous. To avoid making others feel uncomfortable, Sole found herself hiding her gift. If it weren't for her deep violet eyes, she could hide her magic from the world. Then, maybe the second-born prince of Sundom wouldn't have been sent to fetch her.

She knew it was a bad time to leave Mōsa, as they were only halfway through rebuilding and restructuring their kingdom after the Darkness. But news had quickly spread about her magick, and Sundom had come knocking just as quickly.

The missive they sent had said something about half of the country of Sundom needing her healing magick, although she suspected, given King A'Dien's reputation and stories from her own father, that the second-born prince coming to collect her was more for the monarch's benefit rather than his own people.

In the world her forebears had abandoned, second-born children were usually given the unwanted tasks that had to be carried out in secret. If her summoning had been for the benefit of the people, King A'Dien would have sent Prince Rill, the heir and firstborn, with all the pomp and circumstance involving the optics of a king coming in to save his people.

But no matter what their reasons were, Sole knew without a doubt that she had to make the journey. As Queen of Mōsa, diplomacy was now one of her responsibilities. For whatever reason, Sundom needed her, and she needed Sundom's trade routes opened to Mōsa in order to rebuild her kingdom. And if the tomes in her father's library were to be believed, then the Dark Wilds near Sundom could ease the ache in her heart.

The breeze was warm as sunlight kissed her dark brown skin. Would she ever hear the calming waves of the Serena Sea again? The same waves that carried memories of death crashed in like a flood that kept sweeping her under, making it harder and harder to breathe. Her night terrors came more frequently now. Every night, falling asleep was hard. Staying asleep was much more challenging, for every night she dreamt of them—her sisters, Lola and Luna. She wished she would see her parents, if only in her dreams, but all she ever saw were her sisters.

Sole had never cried like a child. Her young life on Mōsa was full of love, joy, and very few tears. She had only ever shed tears on this terrace twice, if she remembered correctly. Her memory had been quite foggy since magick entered her life, the night Nasir died, and the day she woke from the Darkness to find she was now orphaned and only left with magick.

Taking a deep breath, Sole made her way to the Great Hall. As Nisa was fretting with preparations for their trip, Sole walked past her. She needed to sit on her father's throne one last time.

A giant painting of Mōsa Island hung at the back of the throne room. In front of it was a stately throne of gold that was covered in symmetrical sacred carvings, with an abstract flower head fixed on each of the ornate legs. Engraved high on its back was a large mahogany tree with deep roots. The thick, light turquoise cushion had been embroidered with the twin mermaids of the Porte family crest. It had been her father's throne. And in many ways, it still was. She couldn't bring herself to call it hers.

Beside it was a smaller throne of gold that had all of the island's flora and fauna embossed all over its legs and arms—it had been her mother's. King Axel always made the decisions with his queen, which was why he had their thrones placed side by side, instead of having Lygia's behind his. As she and her sisters grew, her father had wanted them to learn how to lead the nation should the need arise.

Some of her father's counsel, still stuck in the old ways, had opposed teaching all his daughters about leadership as it was not the Transean way. The first born were to rule, while second and third born were to marry well, or were shipped off elsewhere to assure the firstborns a smooth ascension to the throne. But, her father had been different.

This was why King Axel had three simple chairs made from the most exquisite oak from the island's oldest trees, not quite thrones yet, but still regal. These were hers and her sisters' chairs and they flanked the pair of golden thrones, one on her father's side, and two on her mother's. She and her sisters had never cared which chairs had been theirs and her parents never assigned them any chair in particular. They just sat where they wanted. Sole trailed her hands over these chairs, committing to memory all the people who had sat there at some point. She remembered the last time they had all been together, at her mating ceremony. They had all drank, laughed, and danced. The Darkness had taken it all away from her and had gifted her with magick she never asked for, and a kingdom's survival to fight for, if only to keep the memory of her family alive.

"Sole! Are you listening to me?" Nisa called out to her and shook her arm gently. "They are ready for you." She gestured at all that lay before them.

Startled out of her trance, Sole nodded.

"Your travel trunks are on their way to the dock," Nisa prattled on, taking her role as Sole's adviser very seriously. "The Misa Warriors you selected only await your arrival to board the Radiant. We must make haste."

"Is Rory among the Misa?"

"Yes. She said she wouldn't stay behind and leave you defenseless." Sole healed Rory upon awakening. She knew that Rory, her sister Lola's dearest friend, would never agree to stay behind. Her decision to stay by Sole's side helped her feel as if Lola was with her somehow.

Nisa began checking tasks off of her long list before they set sail for Sundom. The Darkness had changed Nisa too. She seemed more serious now. As if every moment mattered. Before, Nisa had been a happy, free-spirited beauty, always ready for a good time. Now, she was quiet, task-driven, and focused. If Sole was being honest, the Darkness changed everything and everyone. Staring at her dearest friend, Sole hoped this new adventure to Sundom would help Nisa find her way back to herself.

What hadn't changed were Mōsa's most feared defenders, the Misa Warriors. These hand-selected female guards were led by the Queen of Mōsa. Lygia, Sole's mother, was their mighty leader for many moons. They were an army of women, once a thousand strong, who wore deep purple and gold armor made from an impenetrable mineral found in the bioluminescent bay. Although small in stature, the Misa warriors were mighty in battle. The key to their precise and effective movement was the lightweight but sturdy black mesh underneath their armor, allowing the Misa's agile movements to consume their enemy and giving them extra protection in their most vulnerable parts. But today, they would wear their crimson travel tunics paired with their slim black pants that were close to a second skin. With their faces covered with the thin black material known as the blood veil, no one but the leader of Mōsa would know who they were. This showed everyone that their loyalty only belonged to the leader of Mōsa and no one else. One thing was true no matter what the Misa warriors wore—they were always armed with their blades of amethyst.

Standing in the throne room, Sole remembered what the Darkness did to the warriors. On the day her hands glowed a fiery violet, she felt a mighty power burning at the palm of her hands. Masaine, her father's most trusted advisor and a survivor of the Darkness, told her of their losses while she was busy healing those still holding on to life and whoever the Holy Mother allowed her to save.

Nine hundred and eighty-four Misa guards met their demise. Right in this very room, she learned how she almost died several times while consumed by the Darkness.

"Nine hundred and eighty-four," she whispered.

The impact of that reality was not lost on her. By the time Sole was miraculously healed and awakened with magick, she could only recover the last sixteen living Misa Warriors. However, one thing was sure; as Sole traveled to Sundom, she would not leave Mōsa unprotected. Choosing to bring only five Misa warriors meant her people would be left protected as they continued to rebuild Mōsa in her absence. Besides, she would be gone for only a month or two. It wasn't a lifetime.

Shakily catching her breath, Sole looked at Nisa, dressed in Mōsa's royal blue travel tunic paired with her slim black pants. She looked beautiful with her long, coiled twists that were arranged in two large buns on either side of her head and adorned with golden clasps. Her brown skin dipped in gold, pierced nose, deep grey eyes, and full lips made it hard for most to look away. She was simply breathtaking. But sometimes, it was hard for Sole to look at her dearest friend without seeing the face of her late husband. They had been twins.

Sole still didn't know how Nisa navigated the loss of her twin brother, her parents, and most of the people of Mōsa. They would take this journey together, and there was no doubt Sole and Nisa would talk about the loss of everything. Just not today.

"You look like Gira," Sole said in a melancholy tone.

Nisa stopped in her tracks at the sound of her mother's name. She wasn't sure when the last time she heard anyone say her name was. Tears welling up in Nisa's deep grey eyes threatened to flow like the Matahira Falls, deep within their island.

"You think so?" Nisa grimaced at the plain tunic and pants combo she currently sported. "I am sure she is ecstatic to see me wearing the one tunic I hated to wear as a child," she said dryly.

"She would be very proud of you, Nisa," Sole said with a wistful smile.

Looking at Sole with her crooked smile, Nisa closed the gap between them and, facing Sole, said, "Stop distracting me. Now, let's go. They are waiting for us."

At those words, the two walked out of the throne room together. They both knew the cost of leaving

Mōsa. Generations ago, Sole's father had sailed away from Sundom to establish Mōsa, so no Mōsian would ever have to feel trapped into staying in a kingdom that didn't treat them right. Mōsians were supposed to sail away from Sundom, and yet, here they were, taking the opposite route.

But, they were Senior Advisor Nisa Asha and Queen Lia Soleidae Porte of Mōsa, and Mōsian women never backed down from an adventure.

Walking down the path hand in hand, Nisa and Sole could see the ship, aptly named the Radiant, at a distance. Surrounded by the deep pink and violet waters of the Serena Sea, the golden boat glistened like the sun.

Stopping Sole abruptly, Nisa grabbed her by the shoulders and turned her friend to face her. "There is one last thing I need to check off my list," Nisa said with her cherubic smile, "before the pink sands of Mōsa never kiss our feet again for a month or two or more, we must recite our prayer here and now."

Smiling, Sole knew what came next. And for a little while, the two women were transported back in time to when they were little girls, reciting the chant for Queen Lygia, who had taught it to them. Facing each other as they once did as young girls, Sole and Nisa held hands and began the prayer in solemn tones. "We were here before, when here was neither land nor sea. We are here now, in a land and sea we call our own. And here we will be, even when land and sea have ceased, 'til hereafter. Here before, here now, and here after."

One, two, then three repetitions of the Mōsian prayer that they had been taught.

Wiping Sole's tears away, Nisa gently hugged her and whispered, "I'll see you on the Radiant's starboard. Remember, the queen must walk alone, but you are not alone. You have me. You can do this."

Then she paused to make sure no one from the Radiant was close enough to hear them, and whispered, "They have no idea what your magick can do. Keep your secrets close to your chest."

And with that, Nisa walked ahead of Sole with her two maidens. Like Sole, Nisa and her maidens were of short stature with defined muscular arms and legs. Her mother, Queen Lygia, had always said, "We were built for war even if we don't look it and never asked for it." Seeing Nisa, her two maidens, and of course, the Misa warriors today, Sole finally understood why they were built for war.

But the question that nipped at the back of Sole's mind was, " Am I built for war?" There was only one way to answer that. Taking a deep breath, Sole ran her fingers through her hair, coiled to perfection and falling wildly past her waist. She reached up to adjust her father's old, faded crown on top of her head. She had refashioned the crown to hold her mother's tarnished mirror in the middle instead of a gemstone as a way to honor her parents who had ruled as equals. The crown was no great beauty, but it held the dignity of her parents' reign and that was enough for her. Her crown, Sole thought, trying on the words for the first time in her head. And then, Sole made her way to the Radiant and stepped into the world she had never wanted to enter.

CHAPTER 4

The Radiant

"Is her travel gear onboard?" asked Rivian, second-born son of King A'Dien Alacor II of Sundom, as he emerged from the captain's cabin from below deck. The Houses of Alacor and Avirel are the half-elf houses of Sundom, only identifiable by their pointy ears, bright eyes, and keen sense of smell. Although it seemed impossible for his large, six feet tall frame, he managed to navigate the tight quarters of his ship quite well. His ice-blue eyes swept over the Radiant as the wind swept through his white-blonde hair. His fair skin, weathered and kissed by the sun after years on his ship, was a warm golden contrast to his glacial features. His coloring's ability to be both warm and cold was characteristic of Sand Elves like the Alacors.

"Yes, they're here. Meanwhile, her queen, majesty, princess, whatever is taking her sweet time," Kia responded, rolling her green eyes. "Maybe she hopes we will take her awful dresses with us and leave her on this wet and sticky island these traitors call home."

Kia Ageala Etenaenon, a lean, graceful forest elf with blush-pink short hair and high cheekbones was second in command of the Sun Guard Army, and already a hardened warrior at the age of twenty and five.

Rivian knew about the betrayal of Mōsa that had resulted in the split of the Kingdom of Sundom, like any well-educated citizen of Sundom should. But he steered clear of politics, knowing that would never be the realm he moved in, given his birth status.

"But, seriously, look at them," Kia flicked her fingers towards the approaching Misa warriors, "Why do they have to wear such tiny, tight attire? A dress over thin, skintight pants? I will never understand how they fight in that."

Absentmindedly, Rivian corrected her, "It's a tunic, not a dress."

Kia only snorted in response.

"Yes, yes. Dress, tunic, whatever, I just need them to keep wearing those tight outfits!"

The interruption came from Luce Dragonmore, the most trusted of Prince Rivian's guards, current chief warrant officer of the Sun Guards, and the least trustworthy person when it came to women. He was a late addition, joining the Radiant crew a few days later by riding one of the Mako, Sundom's blue and silver ships designed for speed. He joined them under the guise of aiding their mission, but everyone knew he just needed a vacation after finishing the training of newly enlisted soldiers earlier than expected.

He bounded over to the pair who were watching the Mōsian women board the Radiant and slung an arm around Kia and Rivian.

"Those outfits may refuse to show anything and yet, they let me imagine everything," he said with an exaggerated waggle of his thick, dark eyebrows. "I mean, women have the right to wear what they want. Right?"

Kia dislodged Luce's arm with a sharp shift of her shoulder, her look of disgust telling Luce without words what she felt about his assessment of the women's outfits. Everyone knew Luce's desire went beyond supporting women. He was a lover of women and didn't discriminate. He chased after all women in equal measure, and clearly the Mōsian mahogany beauties would be a new conquest for him. Luce was up for the challenge. He followed their movements with his eyes.

"Shouldn't you be more concerned about their combat-readiness, given your job as a guard and all? Especially with their history of betrayal?"

Rivian could hear the note of frustration in Kia's voice and understood her position on this island and its people. But he wasn't here for power plays. He was on an errand.

"Dragonmore, keep it in your pants for at least the first day," the barked command came from the head of the Sun Guard army and Rivian's best friend, Zari. Rivian grinned. His friend's strict countenance, which had served him well as the commander of the army that was sworn to protect him, but at the same time, was a source of hilarity for him as his closest friend. They had grown up together as children and Zari had even refused to use the family name he had been born with, choosing instead to go by the name Zari of Alacor, after the reigning family of the only land he truly considered his home. Although Zari's parents were born in Mōsa, they left during the great exploration to Sundom, never to return.

Turning slyly to both Zari and Luce, Rivian said, "You know Zi, Luce, I just remembered something."

Zari simply raised an eyebrow with a silver stud piercing at him. Luce's attentions were solidly still placed on the women walking down the dock.

"Aren't they your kinsmen?"

Zari pressed his lips in consternation and said shortly, "I only know one kind of kin and they are from Sundom."

Luce was more chatty, a miracle given his attention span. "They may be my mother's kin, but Alacors are my family and Sundom is my home," he said. Then, shaking his head, Luce continued, "Only the Holy Mother knows why the first healer in four generations would come from this forsaken place."

Rising from the wooden chair leaning on the rail, Luce continued, "These are illiterate, weak people who have no strong moral beliefs. They live in their huts and call her a princess. A princess of what, exactly?"

As Luce and Kia shared a laugh over that, Zari turned to Rivian and asked, "Are you confident this is a good decision? Bringing this ruined princess and her tarnished crown to Sundom?" His sharp eyes, forest green on the right and indigo on the left, bore into the side of Rivian's face. When Rivian said nothing, he continued, "Yes, she could probably heal the king, but what good will it do for the whole of Sundom? Surely, your family does not mean to rekindle trading ties with them?"

Looking out at the purple waves crashing into the burnt pink sand, Rivian thought of his father. King A'Dien was the first son of King Esher, a mighty warrior who had raised a mighty warrior. Rivian thought how difficult his life had been being the son of a formidable father. Second sons were the ones not often nurtured. Their birth foretold war, loss, and death. The kings of Sundom kept their second sons away from the castle, never allowing them to get close to the court.

Rivian had spent most of his hidden years in the mountains of the Grimerg Rise near the Sanctum, where he had been sent to be trained in fighting and to read the numerous scrolls of Tresean history. All second born children were sent there for seven years or more, depending on how unnecessary their presences were in their own families. During these hidden years, Rivian had no connection with his family and often felt isolated. Although he was the second born son, the other pupils there knew he was the King's son. That put a target on his back, which made making friends difficult. That was until he met Luce, Kia, and Zari. Being second born children themselves, the four became each other's chosen family.

"And a queen at twenty and five years?" Zari scoffed, "She's barely a few years older than you. What does she know about running a kingdom, let alone wielding magick? I'm telling you brother, Mōsian women cannot be trusted."

Turning to face Zari, Rivian was surprised to see Nisa standing behind him, fuming silently as his friend continued to talk about Sole and the other Mōsian women. Rivian smiled and coughed loudly into his fist.

A quiet heartbeat later, Zari asked, "She is here, isn't she, brother?" still refusing to turn and face the offended woman.

"No, but she might as well be," Rivian said, swallowing a laugh.

Luce wormed his way between Nisa and Zari, a ready smile lighting up his handsome features. Being half Mōsian and half Sundom, his wavy dark brown hair and gray-blue eyes seemed to have the combined good looks of both peoples. Luce was also different from the others, as he had no tattoos of Sundom on his flesh.

"Please, dear lady Nisa Asha of Mōsa, excuse my brute of a superior. He has had a long journey," he said as he extended a hand towards her, meaning to help her into her cabin below. "However, I, Luce Dragonmore, vow to be more gentle and accommodating for you and all that you might need. And want."

Nisa simply huffed and refused any help from Luce, or anyone from the Radiant.

Zari was known to speak his mind, and it took many "lessons" in the silent bastion when they were younger to curb it. His mouth was a double-edged sword that often spoke the truth at the most inopportune times. This was one of those times. However, being the only full Mōsian descendant left him constantly feeling isolated from his friends, no matter how many names he dropped or changed. On the other hand, his dark skin and mismatched eyes made him a favorite with the ladies in Sundom.

"Looks like your charms won't work on this one," Rivian said as he placed his hands on Luce's shoulders and eased him out of his way.

"Welcome to the Radiant, Miss Nisa, your home for the next thirty moons. Will your mistress be along soon?" Rivian asked as he stepped between Nisa and Luce.

"You can refer to me as Lady Nisa Asha as only my friends call me Nisa," she said haughtily. "And last I checked, you were just my transportation, second son. Please also note that you are not allowed to refer to my mistress as anything but Queen Lia Soleidae Porte."

Nisa's steel eyes blazed under the sun, while its golden rays played over her raven locks and beautiful light brown skin. She was just as beautiful on the inside and people gravitated towards her. Usually. Today wasn't one of those times. Nisa knew Sole needed the people of Sundom to see the queen's adviser as approachable, but she couldn't let slights against Sole and her kingdom pass without addressing them.

She sidestepped Rivian and planted herself in front of Zari. It didn't matter that she had to look up, with him being almost a foot taller than her. With the authority of a goddess, Nisa said, "It is interesting how a son of Mōsa does not know the value of a Mōsian woman, especially the crown's second daughter."

She looked him up and down slowly before continuing, "It must be easy to pretend you are one of them walking around in your crimson sand tunics, carrying all their privilege while forgetting the blood of our ancestors."

As if on cue, the five Misa warriors boarded the vessel and stood behind Nisa in Khusela position, a five-point protective formation that covered her on all sides. They had boarded ahead of the queen, as was protocol to assure her safety, but they were also there to protect the royal adviser.

"I will remind you," Nisa went on heatedly, as if five of the most fearsome warriors of her kingdom hadn't just surrounded her, "that the last descendant of the house of Porte, the only healer in four generations, will board this vessel to try and save your king, while she puts the rebuilding of her own kingdom on hold. We are doing you a favor, and just in case you heathens don't know what happens after that, you need to look up the meaning of gratitude." In unison, the Misa warriors suddenly shouted, "Here before, here now, and here after," as Sole stepped onto the Radiant.

"There she is, queen of a tiny scrap of an island and bride to a dead prince," Kia had made no effort to tone down her whisper to Zari as Sole passed them by.

Those words ripped through Sole, causing her

lavender eyes to turn a deep, fiery, violet. Her right hand began to glow in the same shade of violet. Many were wary and maybe even fearful of her when her eyes changed, and today she spotted the same fear amongst Rivian and his people. Rivian, Kia, Luce, Zari, and all the rest of the crew of the Radiant cast their eyes down to the wooden floor, unable to hold her violet gaze.

Sole wanted to send a message, and that message was received. Closing her eyes, Sole silenced the rage growing inside her as her eyes settled back to the serene lavender hue.

Sole wasn't always on fire or brave enough to speak up. Being the king's second daughter often made her invisible in other people's eyes, and she liked it like that. Waking up with magick had changed everything. Now, people could see only her.

When Sole was younger, she was awkward and self-conscious about how she carried herself in social settings. She wasn't athletic like her sister Lola and didn't know how to talk to people like Nisa and Luna did. While all the children in the island were bathing in the Bay, Sole hid in her father's library. When she was briefly in the Sanctum, the other girls in Sanctum didn't notice Sole and rarely included her in anything. They probably didn't like how she looked too thin, too narrow, compared to the others who had been sent there to learn how to fight. But Nisa was different. She had taken Sole under her wing and protected her from day one, despite being two years younger.

This was why Nisa stood there looking like a battle ram, ready to smash every Sun Soldier that stood before her. Sometimes, the thought that Nisa would have made a better queen than her crossed her mind. But, such was her burden as her father's daughter and she wouldn't trade it for anything else.

Sole knew she needed to calm herself, or Nisa would do something impulsive to cause the first war in four generations. Besides, Sole thought, she really didn't have time for these Sundom pricks' posturing to bring her low. She had a job to do, and the sooner she got it done, the sooner she could go back to Mōsa.

Suddenly, a great longing came over her. What she wouldn't give to have Nasir there with her, to hear him say, "Smile more, Sole," one more time. She sorely needed him and his words as these Sundom guards discredited her value. Sole wondered why it was so easy it was for Sundom to make others feel small, as if that was all they knew how to do. Sighing, Sole moved forward.

The Misa warriors parted like the mountains of the Grimerg Rise, making way for Sole to join in standing before them. Looking at everyone, Sole's gracious smile was captivating as she slowly walked toward Nisa.

"Ni, what's going on?" Sole whispered through a guarded fake smile.

"It appears that the well-bred Sundom soldiers have all the privilege and none of the manners!" she seethed. Seeing Sole stand beside Nisa, Rivian stood up straighter, never taking his eyes off her. His smile revealed two small dimples that Sole thought would be charming if only they didn't belong to her enemy.

"Second Prince of Sundom, is this what I should expect from the citizens of Sundom?" Sole asked coldly. The threat in her tone was enough to make Zari stand in front of Rivian, ready to protect him.

Sole continued to address Rivian. "I understand that the King requested my presence to heal him, not for your people to ridicule what we've lost, how little we have, and our beliefs. I am here now because it is my duty as a wielder of magick and as a decent human being; you all must realize that."

"My apologies," Rivian said as he stepped from behind Zari and closed the distance between himself and Sole. "Sometimes my guards get carried away, Sole."

Looking at Rivian, bewildered, Sole asked, "Second-born Prince, I don't recall ever agreeing to be addressed so informally. Don't mistake my kindness for comfort, for you may not be happy with what you find."

Rivian smiled at that, revealing those damn dimples again. It made her furious.

He wasn't quite sure why he smiled at her utterly arrogant tone. Maybe it was because no one ever dared talk to him in that fashion, and perhaps he thought it was attractive.

"Control the rage, control the fire," Sole whispered to herself before insisting, "I demand that you refer to me as Queen Lia Soleidae Porte. Only my family and friends may refer to me as Sole."

Rivian's jaw tightened, and his brow furrowed at her command. Nevertheless, she was determined to teach this very spoiled, handsome prince how to treat her.

As he stared at Sole, she refused to look away even when his stare made her uncomfortable. It's like he is looking through me, she thought. But the days of looking away from bullies, princes, kings, and crowns were over. Sole often heard her mother talk about how the men of Transea had spread the falsehood that Mōsian women were like the sirens of the Serena Sea, desperate for a sailor. Now, all Sundom will know the women of Mōsa are not sirens.

"You might find, dear young prince, that these women," Sole said as she raised her hand to motion to her warriors, "have stories beyond what is between their legs. You will do well to remember that after your guard's unprovoked attack on my companions."

"You might also find it interesting, my young queen, that I am actually willing to listen," Rivian countered with a smirk. "Just as soon as you stop assuming the behavior of one is the behavior of all, or that things are always so easily black and white when in reality, the word protect can just as easily mean attack when taken from a different perspective."

Sole didn't know why his electric, deep blue gaze infuriated her, but she would not look away. Sole was determined to teach him how women of Mōsa should be treated. She cared not about his privilege. It was no match for what she brought with her, the will of her people and the magick burning in her soul. He may have all the privilege, but she had her people's choice, her Nasir's love, and the legacy of her dead king.

Who did this prince think he was? Without knowing it, her eyes had begun to turn a furious shade of violet once more.

Rivian saw the change in her and regretted provoking her. There was power behind her eyes, yes, but it spoke of so much rage and sadness that Rivian couldn't help but feel sorrow for this woman who had to assume responsibilities that he had luckily escaped, never mind the added burden of magick. And so, he changed his tune.

"Queen, my apologies," he began, his voice gentler now, more sincere, and less teasing. "I feel we have gotten off on the wrong foot. When you arrive at Sundom, you will meet my family. Today, allow me to introduce you to my second family."

Rivian gestured towards Luce and said, "I believe you've met Luce, a fierce member of my Sun Soldiers. He chases tail like it's a sport, but otherwise, he's harmless."

Luce had the audacity to give Sole and Nisa a wink. Rivian playfully hit him up the side of his head for that. Then he turned to his best friend.

"This is Zari, commander of my Sun Guard army and personal bodyguard."

"Pleasure to meet you, queen," Zari said as he bowed before Sole and reached for her hand. Quick as bird of prey, Nisa swatted his hand away. It was the custom of the women of Mōsa to have no one but their mate kiss their hands.

"I apologize for the earlier misstep, Queen of Mōsa, and I vow to make amends," he said smoothly and although he had addressed Sole, he kept his gaze on Nisa.

"I can vouch for him," Rivian said.

Just as he was about to formally introduce her, Kia

walked up to Sole with a sardonic smile spreading across her face. "Welcome aboard, queen. I am Kia," she said, without a single ounce of reverence in her voice.

Sole quietly assessed Kia and thought she was beautiful with her graceful, lean body that moved as though she was walking on air. Her eyes were a lush green, with brilliant pink hair that sat atop her head like cerise silk ribbons found in the markets of Mōsa. Her plum lips appeared to be as soft as suede. And yet, despite her beauty, there was something equally sad and cruel about the slight downturn of her lips. She couldn't quite put a name to it, but she knew she would have to ask Nisa or Rory to keep a close eye on her.

Making eye contact with Rivian's second family, holding a bright smile, Sole said, " It is a pleasure to meet all of you." Then, stepping back and gesturing to her entourage, she said, "This beauty is Nisa. She is not only my greatest protector but my dearest friend. Where she goes, I go."

Zari couldn't keep his eyes off Nisa. He noticed Nisa was as tall as Sole but a bit more curvy in all the right places. Her long, curly ombre locks were up in two buns. Her deep-set grey eyes were beautifully paired with her rosy, full lips. Her light brown skin would turn a golden hue once they arrived in Sundom, and he hoped he was there to see every new freckle that fell on that beautiful face.

Then, Sole looked towards her five warriors. Each of them stood stoic, staring straight ahead. Each beautiful war madien was about five feet in height, wearing varying shades of mahogany in their armor, with their dark coiled hair twisted up into various buns atop their heads. Known as the Sea Fairies of Mōsa Island, stronger and faster than the average human inhabitant of the island. Each warrior held the brightest brown eyes that become bioluminescent at night. But of course, no one except the queen would be able to know that. This all-female military regiment of the Kingdom of Mōsa is the most feared warrior unit in all of Transea.

"When protecting me," Sole began, "you will find they have very few words to say. But don't let them fool you; they will let you know when they are ready to have fun. If you don't want to lose an arm, don't ever try to reach for their masks. They never take those off."

Each warrior's plum armor had a pointed helm, a v-shaped tunic opening that exposed their eyes and mouths, and a rose gold pointed nose guard. Attached to the forehead was a crafted leather ornament piece shaped into three golden rings. The shoulders were oval, comprehensive, and small in size. They were decorated with a metal blade, starting at the front, curving towards the back, and ending in a sharp point. The breastplate was made from many horizontal layers of leather and fur with pointed edges and decoration pieces. It covered everything from the neck down and ended at the groin. The upper legs were covered by a skirt of horizontal layers of leather and fur that reached down to the knee. Leather boots protected their lower legs with a masterfully crafted dragon's upper jaw attached to the outer topsides. Thin pants made from leather and fur were worn beneath this all. These young warriors had existed for four generations. Daughters turned soldiers, from wives to weapons, they remain the only documented frontline female troops in all of Transea.

Turning back to Rivian, Sole said, "Now, if you wouldn't mind, please show us to our quarters, as we have a long journey ahead, and I must discuss important matters with my court."

Despite both their efforts to introduce their people, the air between himself and Sole remained frosty. Rivian wore his frustration on his face, and Sole realized this prince would be easy to read. She liked that.

Collecting himself, Rivian signaled two Sun Guards to escort Sole, Nisa, her maidens, and the Misa warriors to their quarters. But in a move that surprised both Rivian and himself, Zari maneuvered himself in front of his soldiers and said, "I've got this."

"Uh, no. I don't think you do," Nisa interjected.

"Lady Nisa Asha of Mōsa, I most certainly do," Zari said as he gave a small bow and motioned towards the large entryway at the end of the main deck. "I'm the one who had your living quarters prepared, and I most certainly know my way around her."

A boldfaced lie, Rivian thought, but kept it to himself.

"Her?" Nisa's face scrunched in confusion.

"The Radiant, my lady"

Nisa only huffed, but said nothing else.

Rivian also tried to keep his smirk away from his friend's painfully obvious ploy to get into the royal adviser's good graces. He only wished he could get away with teasing the queen as such, but things between them still seemed stilted. With an inward sigh, Rivian turned to the frosty queen and said in clipped, formal tones, "Queen Lia Soleidae of Porte house, these guards can escort you to your quarters. Please be at the bastion at sunset, where we will dine."

Sole tilted her head in his direction to indicate she had heard him.

Rivian couldn't help but feel affronted that she wouldn't grant him a verbal reply.

One by one, her entourage turned to follow the guards into the cabins below deck. When it was her turn to exit, Sole paused briefly, looked up at Rivian's ice blue eyes and said, "You mean, at moonrise."

Shocked that she was talking to him directly without a hint of scorn or haughtiness, Rivian could only stutter, "What?"

"In the west, we don't call it sunset," Sole said with a small smile, as if she was patiently teaching a child. "We call it moonrise. And if you don't mind, we prefer to take our meals in our rooms."

And then, quick as a blink of an eye, she turned to follow her people and headed down towards her cabin, leaving Rivian to stare at her retreating figure.

CHAPTER 5

Dreams and Portents

Clasping her hands in front of her, Nisa walked alongside Sole as they were led down a short stairwell that led into a long corridor with cabins on either side. Without bothering to hide her whisper from Zari, who was walking ahead of them, she said, "Sole, is this how the people of Sundom spend their time, feasting, fucking, and frolicking?

Sole's eyes widened at her friend's boldness and for a few shocked moments, she was torn between laughing out loud and admonishing her. Nisa just stared down at Zari's broad back as if her eyes were golden daggers ready to pierce his flesh.

Instead of bristling at her barb, Zari simply glanced behind him and said with a wicked smile, "I would say that those are the three things that make life worthwhile, but we've been on this ship for months and there have been no other women here, save for Kia and now yourselves. The opportunity for more amorous activities has not presented itself, so to answer your question, no, we do not spend all our time feasting, fucking, and frolicking."

That smile, more than his words, infuriated Nisa and she didn't know why.

"Nisa, stand down," Sole hissed through an awkward, forced smile as she placed a hand on her shoulder. Sole always knew how to talk her friend off the ledge.

Zari led them deep into the living quarters, making sure to put the Misa warriors and the maidens into cabins beside and across from the queen and her adviser. When Sole and Nisa finally entered their cabin, they couldn't help but marvel at what they saw. They had never seen such grandeur in all their lives. The velvet curtains the color of honey pooled on the floor in gentle waves. Scented candles made the room smell of cinder fruit, a fruit that only grew in Mōsa. Looking bewildered, Sole whispered, "It smells like home, Nis."

"As it should," Zari said from the doorway. "Our instructions are to make sure your journey to Sundom is as comfortable as can be."

Before Nisa could say anything to that, Sole thanked the Sun Guard commander. He then politely excused himself, but not before giving Nisa a pointed smile. Nisa ignored him.

When the door shut and they were sure he was out of earshot, Nisa looked at Sole and said, "Under whose instruction was it? That's the big question."

Sole herself had wondered the same thing as she enjoyed the smell of the cinder fruit in their room. "News must travel fast these days. Too fast, almost."

"One thing is for sure, the second prince did his homework," Nisa said as she looked at the stack of books on top of a white and grey marbled desk. Then she made her way through the quarters, inspecting their home for the next thirty days. Their cabin consisted of adjoining rooms, each with its private study. Sole's rooms were the largest, with vases filled with pink and lavender roses in almost every corner. Sole was overcome with joy when she found a note on top of the pile of books on her desk. It read, Princess, Sole, may these books make your first journey across the sea pleasant. -Prince Rivian

This pleased her for some reason.

But upon reading the note over Sole's shoulder, Nisa said, "Okay. It's official, I don't trust him at all. It's as if he studied you."

That snuffed out whatever pleasant feeling Sole had. Sitting down on the amber settee, Sole looked up at Nisa and said, "I fear you are right, Nisa."

Nisa and Sole's eyes met, each recognizing the

precarious situation they had found themselves in. Being the second daughter of a dead king was something Sole had to learn to live with. And now, here she was, journeying to a land her father had left behind, in order to save the life of the king who bore the same name as the one who had tried to have her grandfather killed. Well, almost the same name. But if the stories were true, then King A'Dien Alacor II was just as awful as his father, the first King A'Dien Alacor.

There were rumors that said that her father and A'Dien Alacor II hated each other because Rivian's father had met Lygia in her many journeys as a young woman and had been enamored by her. Coupled with their own fathers' rift, the romantic rivalry had only been another reason for Sundom and Mōsa to sever all ties.

Sole could see the possibility of it happening—her mother had been a very beautiful woman. She was the kind of woman who would always be larger than life, even in death. If Sole was being honest, she had always felt small. She found solace in hiding behind her books. She didn't make many friends; Nisa was her only friend aside from her sisters. Nisa was honest and loyal, just like her brother. Somehow, they saw her potential, her love for her people, and her ability to care for those who also felt small. Nasir had been the air in her sail. He saw her the way no one else ever had. Her eyes filled with tears as she remembered all the promises they had made to each other. They had vowed to claim every future as theirs, together, and here she was in the middle of enemy territory, alone.

Nasir always made Sole feel at ease. Except for that morning.

Waking up next to his cold dark lifeless body had been a nightmare. Sole could still see the gray eyes staring back at her. She could still hear the scream that came from the deepest part of her broken spirit. Her shriek had bellowed into a horrifying screech that wrestled with her anguish at the bottom of her gut. His loss had torn her to pieces and she knew she could never be put back together again.

Marrying Nasir and losing him the next morning was like stepping into the darkness after only seeing the sun for a moment. There was nothing more crippling than the morning after a tragic loss. The loss of him left her empty. She was a ship with no sail. She was a queen with no king. The longing for Nasir, the loss of her bonded, gripped Sole in a way nothing ever had. Her only saving grace, the only one who had survived the Darkness from her old life, was Nisa.

Tumbling down the rabbit hole of the tragedy that had been the last year and a half of her life, Sole's violet eyes filled with tears as she turned to Nisa and said,

"The Darkness took everything from us, our mothers, our fathers, sisters, brothers, friends, our future and our love. How can those Sundom soldiers laugh about it, Nisa? How can they laugh? Didn't they lose someone in the Darkness too?"

Nisa wrapped her chosen sister in her arms and responded, "It didn't take everything, Sole. We still have each other, and we still have Mōsa. We will get through this together."

This had been their ritual every night after the Darkness passed and Sole awakened. After a day of tending to their duties, of keeping it together so their kingdom could rebuild itself, Sole and Nisa would retreat to their quarters and grieve in private.

And now that they shared close quarters with each other, Sole and Nisa had to bear witness to each other's sorrow. While Nisa's sadness had morphed into a machine-like efficiency at work, Sole's would only take form at night. It was a terrible combination of sleeplessness and sad dreams. Fearing the recurring dream she had of her sisters, lost and unreachable, Sole refused to go to sleep. Then the fatigue would catch up to her, put her to sleep, force her to dream the same dream, and when she woke up, the whole cycle would start again.

On their third night in the Radiant, Sole had finally fallen asleep after evading it for days. As expected, she had the same dream she had been having every night since waking up with magick.

Sole was with her family by the Serena Sea. Her two sisters, Luna and Lola, played in the purple-hazed ocean as the moon rose, lighting up the sky in hues of pink and purple. Her sisters were so beautiful, especially when they had danced under the canopy of trees in the Iris Expanse, the last time she had seen them alive. No one could deny that the Porte girls got their beauty from their mother, Lygia. These dreams always ended the same way, with Sole moving toward the sea where her sisters played, but with every step she took to close the distance between them, her sisters seemed further and further away until they finally disappeared.

The sound of thunder woke her from the dream. Tonight was another stormy night and the lightning lit up her private chamber. The Radiant's rocking was a brutal reminder that her family was gone, that she was no longer in Mōsa and was on her way to the land of her enemies. Awake and unable to move or speak for a few seconds, sweat dripped from her forehead, and Sole couldn't shake the sense of pressure on her chest.

This wasn't the first time since waking from the Darkness that Sole woke similarly.

Rushing in, Nisa said, "Don't panic, love. You're safe now." Sole was relieved to see Nisa. Since the

Darkness, they had taken care of each other, and even now, Nisa came to her rescue.

"Was it the same dream?"

"Yes. My sisters looked as beautiful as ever, Nisa," Sole said in a groggy voice. "Luna's laugh chokes me up every time. I don't ever want to sleep again, and at the same time, I can't wait to sleep to see my family again."

"Luna's laugh always made the boys weak at the knees," Nisa said with a solemn look in her eyes.

"The dream is vivid, Nisa. I don't even know what a peaceful night's sleep is like anymore."

"Do you want to sleep, or shall I make you a tea?" Nisa asked with a gentle smile as she pulled Sole's hair off her face.

"I don't want to go back to sleep. I am sure the tea would help settle my nerves."

"I'll be right back," Nisa said as she stood to make her way to the the Radiant's galley.

And so it began, their nightly ritual—sleep, dream of dead people, wake up, and drink tea.

CHAPTER 6

Best Laid Plans

The wooden floors of the Radiant creaked under Nisa's bare feet as she walked towards the galley area. She went past the formal dining area and pushed the two white swing doors to reach the kitchen. Looking around for tea implements, she spotted a porcelain kettle that seemed as though it had never been used.

It figures, Nisa thought with a shake of her head as she filled it with water. Sundom citizens probably never knew what it meant to work hard to accomplish something, let alone boiling water for their own tea. Or buying something so ostentatious as a porcelain kettle.

Just as Nisa placed the kettle on the open flame, she heard someone stumble into the mess hall. Cracking one of the swing doors open, Nisa saw Rivian and Luce occupying one of the tables and opening a bottle of what appeared to be red berry vino. She had heard about this drink from her brother and she wished she could have a taste of it. But Nisa would never stroll up to these fools like she would the boys in Mōsa. Looking at them now like this, she felt this inebriation was another excellent example of why she had to protect Sole at all costs. Trying to listen to their conversation, Nisa leaned against the swinging door.

"Three nights at sea, only twenty-seven more sunsets to go before reaching the Dark Wilds, and then it's just a day's travel to reach Sundom," Rivian said as he poured himself some of the heady smelling wine.

"I just can't wait to be home to be welcomed by the ladies," Luce said, taking the bottle from Rivian and dumping it in his goblet.

"Ladies? Truly? I'd settle for one. Women take up too much of my energy."

"Bah, how boring."

Rivian shrugged and stretched out his long legs beneath the table, sinking into his chair. Women back home didn't really send his blood rushing south, so he couldn't quite share in Luce's enthusiasm.

"There is Selah," Luce pointed out, burping a little, "were you talking about her?"

Rivian frowned at that. He hadn't been thinking about her at all, which made him feel a little guilty. "I wasn't, actually. I just meant one woman in a general sense."

"So, you don't miss her, your intended?"

Rivian swirled the deep red liquid as he thought about his answer. "Maybe, just a little. It's not just her, though. I can't wait to be in my own house, my own room, my own bed, my own hot tub. The usual comforts of home."

"Does she not please you?"

"Besides her forest-green eyes, fair milky white skin, and bright white hair that cascades down her back? Those are pleasing to me, but I can't help but think there should be much more than that."

"Have you not had her? Say it isn't true, Riv" Luce asked earnestly.

"There was never a right time. But, I am sure there will be more than enough time when we get back home."

Selah grew up in the neighboring city of Avirel in Sundom and was promised to a son of Sundom, which was how Rivian had ended up with her. She had been promised to Rivian even before they were old enough to go to the Sanctum. Although they had met as children, it wasn't until they were older than Rivian began his arranged courtship. There is no doubt that Selah was smart, beautiful, and a force to be reckoned with. Originally, Rivian and Selah did not get along. Rivian felt like he couldn't completely trust her due to her father's political ties. It was only recently that Rivian's father encouraged him to spend time getting to know her. Being bonded to Selah could secure Sundom for generations. That was his duty, after all, as a second born son. He would find a way to make that work.

"Selah is a beauty, there is no doubt about that," Luce tipped his goblet to Rivian in approval. "But are you ready to be bonded to her for life?"

"If my brother needs me to marry her, then I have no choice. I will do what is suitable for Sundom."

From behind the door to the kitchen, Nisa stifled a gasp of surprise at the knowledge Rivian was betrothed. Men like that were always more dangerous and capable of deception, as opposed to unattached men. She will have to make sure Sole didn't fall for his charms.

"Well, then let's hope bringing her to Sundom will impact the prophecy." A new voice came into the picture and Nisa strained to see who it was. When Zari entered her line of vision, Nisa narrowed her eyes. Were they talking about Sole?

"Speaking of, how did you find that prophecy, Riv?" Luce asked as he poured himself another red drink, spilling some on the white linen.

"I spent many days and nights since returning from the Sanctum hiding from my father. His fists and disappointments became old very quickly. It's no secret we have never been close, but I am his son." Taking a gulp of his drink, Rivian continued, "I found my solace in the libraries of Sundom. I read every tome, scroll, book, and journal and a great many of them point to the eventual return of magick to our world. At the time, I thought it was the written babbling of an elder long ago. When my brother Rill sent me on this mission to retrieve the first magick healer in centuries and a dagger, I knew the prophecy would come to pass.

Staring off into the distance, Rivian recited the prophecy. "When the dark—"

Zari clucked his tongue and interrupted Rivian, "Brother, everyone in Sundom knows that prophecy."

Leaning in and whispering, Rivian said, "I know. But no one knows that it's incomplete. And I found the second part, thanks to the pile of old books and tomes my brother sent me through Luce."

At that, Luce thumped his chest and said, "That's me, express carrier of Sundom! But the books weren't for you, you know."

Rivian looked affronted, "They were half mine, I know. Half for the Radiant's library and half for the queen of Mōsa. Besides, I had a lot of time to kill on the journey. It's not a crime to read."

"Oh, my god!" Kia exclaimed, "Nobody cares who owns the books. What was the second part of the prophecy?"

Everyone laughed at Kia's impatience. Rivian said, "It went on to say that the Dark Wilds held the birth and death of magick through a dagger called the LifeDrinker, a dagger of broken bones. We all know my father has long been obsessed with regaining magick for our kingdom, and with him being sick, that plan must progress with haste."

"What part does Sole play in all of this?" Luce asked, suddenly impatient to get to the last part of the prophecy.

Both Rivian and Nisa, who was still eavesdropping, were startled at Luce's too familiar use of Sole's name.

"Queen Lia Soleidae Porte," Rivian said pointedly, "is the first of four generations to be given magick and the only one capable of handling the LifeDrinker. All we have to do is get the dagger, deliver her and the dagger to my brother, and have her heal my father. Once that's done, magick will return and we will be done with sailing all about Transea."

"So, that's all you need her for? Her magick?" Luce asked, slightly too clear for someone who had been gulping down wine.

Rivian frowned at that question. "Well, that's what this whole trip was for. So, yeah?" Soon after saying that, Rivian felt a strange twinge in his chest.

"Well, she is a beauty."

Rivian's head swivelled toward Zari, not quite believing what he just heard from his friend after all that flirting he had done with Sole's companion.

Zari shrugged. "I'm not blind. She is beautiful."

At his words, it was Nisa's turn to feel a strange twinge in her chest.

"I might make my move on the princess," Luce said with a devilish grin.

"You mean queen," Rivian corrected him, but no one seemed to have heard him. Zari was already laughing at the thought of Luce making a move on the haughty queen of Mōsa. He looked forward to seeing Luce be turned down.

"I am sure she would like some comfort since her prince can no longer keep her warm at night," said Zari slyly. "However, I have my eye on Nisa. My goodness, that short, brave, brown beauty speaks to my heart and cock. I'd love to grab those wild curls while I see if she is just as loud in bed."

Nisa's heart went up to her throat when she heard Zari talk about his interest in her. She felt like she should be offended by what she heard, but the heat on her cheeks said otherwise. It wasn't that he wasn't attractive, he was the enemy, and she had boundaries.

Laughing, and suddenly relieved for some reason, Rivian said, "Neither of you will do such a thing. These women are to be delivered unharmed to Sundom."

Luce guffawed and said, "We aren't going to harm them, oh dear holy Prince Rivian. We're just going to…

love them. Very deeply."

At hearing those words, Nisa was ready to storm in there and remind them women weren't objects to be possessed and spoken of like they were land that needed to be marked for territory, when suddenly a high-pitched whistle pierced through the dining hall.

"Shit, shit, shit," Nisa cried as she turned to the stove. The tea kettle boiling interrupted Rivian, Luce, and Zari's conversation, and she knew she had been found out. Without thinking, Nisa grabbed the whistling kettle with her bare hands. Then she let out a blood curdling scream, "Fuck! Fuck!"

Stumbling into the room, Rivian, Zari, and Luce sobered quickly. After assessing the damage, Zari grabbed a rag from the pantry, soaked it in cool water, and placed it on Nisa's burning hand. He held the cloth as he held her hand in place. Their eyes locked. Nisa noticed for the first time that he had two different colored eyes.

After turning off the stove, Rivian asked her how he could help.

Pulling back her hand, Nisa said, "How can three drunkards be of any help to me?"

"It looks like you need at least one of these drunks to help you make a simple cup of tea," Luce said with a sardonic smile.

Rolling her eyes, Nisa grumbled, "I can take care of making tea for my queen, thank you very much."

"I will accompany you back to your quarters," Zari said eagerly.

"That is not necessary. I will be fine," she said.

"No, I'll accompany you to your quarters and help make tea for the queen," Luce said, pushing Zari aside, not caring he was his commander.

"I said, I'm fine!" Nisa snapped, clutching her throbbing hand. "We're fine. We don't need anyone's help with either walking or making tea."

Looking at Zari and Luce, Rivian said, "You two go to your quarters. I will accompany Miss Nisa Asha to hers." It was given as a command, not a request from a drinking buddy.

Luce began to walk away, but Zari didn't move, refusing to take his blue and green gaze from Nisa.

"What's your problem?" she asked.

"Come on, brother. We need rest," Luce said as he grabbed the back of Zari's neck and walked him out of the room.

The last thing Nisa needed was for the Prince to discover that Sole had nightmares. But she didn't think she had an option. She begrudgingly agreed to have Rivian walk her to Sole's room. Before leaving the kitchen, she made sure to reach for the Dellurice and

Eliram lavender herbs, so she could steep them in the steaming water.

"Is she having trouble sleeping?" Rivian asked, looking at the herbs.

"I never said that," Nisa said sharply.

"You are using Eliram lavender and everyone knows it calms and restores rest. Is it the waves that keep her up?"

"What keeps my queen awake is not your concern, sir. "

"It is my concern if she's entrusted to my care and resides on my ship."

"Why do you care?"

"Didn't I just answer that?

"Here's the plan, I will care for her, and you continue to discuss her and me and our usefulness like we're chattel behind our backs," she said acidly. "You know, she is braver, stronger, and smarter than any of us."

"Of that, I have no doubt, Miss Nisa Asha," Rivian said with a gentle smile. "My apologies for my men. When we have a bit too much to drink, we become children. Please don't take us seriously."

"You know what? Our Mōsa men also became drunk with wine on occasion. However, never once did they disrespect Sole or any Mōsian woman. On the contrary, we were cherished, protected, and loved. I don't know how the women of Sundom are treated by their males, but I will say this. We will never tolerate disrespect. Never."

With that, Nisa turned and made her way back to their room without waiting for Rivian. Nonetheless, he followed her, walking with his hands clasped behind him. He caught up with her easily and fell into step beside her.

"You care for her very deeply?" Rivian asked, looking straight ahead as he walked alongside Nisa.

"Yes."

"Then you know it is better to let two people care for her than just one. We can do more for her together, yes?" Rivian rarely used the authoritative tone he assumed when in captain mode, but it seemed important to do so now. "Let me know what I can do to help her feel at ease, to feel safe."

"Safe? She will never feel completely safe unless you can bring Nasir back! Can you do that? Can you bring back her parents and sisters?" Nisa whispered as she let the rage come through with every crack in her voice. It was useless though, she knew that. The Darkness wasn't the prince's fault. He was just an easy target for her.

Stopping in front of Sole's door, Nisa warned him, "Prince, respect her pain if you want to help Sole. It has made her the healer she is today, and when she heals your father, the king, you will remember that everything that has been taken from her allowed her to heal your father, our enemy." Nisa refused to allow her tears to fall.

Their voices must have alerted Sole because her door opened, and there she was. "Nisa, is everything okay?"

Sole stood there in her purple silk chemise, and Rivian didn't know where to put his eyes. Holy Mother, she was a beauty indeed. One thing was sure, Sole was the most bodacious queen he had ever laid eyes on, which aroused him. The women of Sundom were not as brazen and bold as the women of Mōsa. Rivian had never seen anyone as alluring as her until he stood in front of her door this very night. Her tentative smile liquefied his insides. Maybe it's the liquor, he thought to himself.

"I accompanied Miss Asha to her quarters since she has been injured making tea," Rivian said as he winked at Nisa.

"What? Nisa, are you hurt?" Sole said as she reached out to Nisa, who was still holding her injured hand.

"It's nothing, just a minor burn. The prince exaggerates."

Turning to Rivian, Nisa said, "Good night, prince," and walked into the room, leaving Sole and Rivian alone in the hallway.

Suddenly, Sole felt as if she was naked. Sole hadn't felt this way since Nasir.

"My queen, I hope the tea helps you find rest. If you need anything, please let me know, and I will ensure you get it." Despite the smooth words, Rivian felt awkward standing there in the hallway, saying good night but not making a move to leave.

"Thank you, prince. It's very kind of you, but I assure you, I have everything I need."

Rivian stood there staring at her lips. He could stare at her face for hours, but he couldn't guarantee that he heard anything she was saying over his inappropriate thoughts of her. Nevertheless, he knew it was the drink and he had to make it to his quarters sooner than later.

"Prince?" Sole urged.

Holy Mother, Rivian realized he hadn't responded to her.

"Well, if you do need anything, please let me know."

A smile teased at Sole's lips as she chided him, "You said that already, Prince Rivian."

His eyes flashed for a moment, strayed to her lips, and followed the line of the silk chemise over her curves. Without thinking about customs or tradition, Rivian reached out and gently took her hand in his, luxuriating in the feel of her soft, slender fingers, her small, warm palm, and lifted her hand up to his lips.

"Please accept my apologies, you also seem to have the power to make me lose my mind. Have a good night, Queen Lia Soleidae Porte of Mōsa."

The moment his lips touched the back of her hand, an unthinkable, forbidden act in her world, she knew she wouldn't get any sleep tonight, for a very different reason than her dreams.

CHAPTER 7

In the Dark, the Stars Shine Brightest

"What took you so long to say goodnight to him? I've been worried sick."

Sole jumped in surprise when Nisa appeared behind her just as she closed the door. She fought to keep the blush blooming on her cheeks as she thought of how Rivian had kissed her hand goodnight.

"Nothing! He was just very insistent about being a good host or something."

Nisa's lips were drawn in a thin, tight line.

"Sole, I must tell you something. I fear we are in a nest of sand vipers."

Sole's eyebrows rose as Nisa took hold of both her hands and sat her down on the settee near her bed.

"They deceived you by telling you that they only need you to heal their king," Nisa stated gravely. "They will also use you to retrieve a dagger that holds the power of life and death! We must find a way to leave this ship before they can use your magick for their selfish reasons."

Sole's heart jumped to her throat and she put a hand on Nisa's mouth to keep her quiet. She listened for any sounds that indicated someone might be walking near their cabin door. When she was sure no one was outside eavesdropping, Sole dropped her hand from Nisa's mouth.

"I'm going to tell you something," Sole began, still debating with herself whether she was going to tell Nisa the biggest reason why she had come on this journey. She wasn't very proud of it, because it reeked of abuse of magick and selfishness—it was exactly what Nisa was accusing Rivian and his people of. She had known about the dagger and the vague rumors of it having the power of life and death of magick and she had been planning on using it to see if she could bring Nasir back to life.

"I—" Sole looked at Nisa, pure, honest, and loyal, and she realized she couldn't lose her. So, she decided to lie, for now. Maybe she would be forgiven for this deception once she had revived her twin brother. But for now, it was best to keep her in the dark.

"I've read about that dagger from a book in father's

library," she told Nisa. "There is a spell to neutralize it and only someone with magick can cast that spell. So fret not, I will not be used." She was relieved to see the tension draining from her friend's face.

But then Nisa's eyes clouded over as she remembered something else. "The prince also thinks he can charm you enough with his good looks to agree to their sordid plan," Nisa said, "and it is especially cruel because he isn't free to be charming anyone at all!"

"What do you mean?"

"He is betrothed!" Nisa exclaimed.

"And I am not interested in him," Sole reassured Nisa gently. "Most of all, I am still married to you brother in my heart."

Nisa looked at Sole and all at once, she realized how silly her worries were.

"Remember, we are here to heal a king because of my vow as a healer, and to open trade routes for Mōsa, because of my vow as a queen."

Nisa smiled at her friend and made her own vow to support Sole's actions as queen. Gently taking Nisa's burned hand Sole's magick rose to the surface healing her best friend once more.

On their fourth night on the Radiant, Sole managed to convince Nisa that it might be a good idea to actually socialize with the crew of the Radiant. This was, after all, first and foremost a diplomatic mission for the future of Mōsa.

Nisa only agreed to take their dinner at the dining hall under the condition that she would go and check if the people there were sober and civilized before she let Sole near them. So, when Nisa and the warriors entered the mess hall, they heard the Sundom Sun Guards laughing and caught the phrases "dead prince" and "queen of nothing," it wasn't hard to deduce that they were laughing at Sole's expense. Nisa had had enough and was about to let them all know.

"Oh, shit. Here she comes," whispered Kia with wide eyes, a bit more sober than the rest. Women typically approached Zari for a fuck behind-the-market store or to ask for payment. However, this tiny and mighty Nisa girl was intriguing. She was bold, brave, and spoke her mind with no fear. The women from Sundom would never be so brusque.

Intoxicated with berry wine, Zari thought he was whispering when he said, "And in conclusion, my theory is that the Darkness only takes those who are too weak to survive the kind of world where magick exists once more!"

When no one responded to him, Zari finally noticed

Kia and Luce's faces and how they were looking at something, or someone, over his shoulder.

"She's behind me, isn't she?" Without waiting for their reply, Zari looked back and saw Nisa standing there, practically breathing fire.

"Fuck."

Nisa stared at Zari like a serpent waiting to strike on the golden sands of Sundom. Turning to her, he said in the most joking manner he could muster, "Hey, little girl, isn't it past your bedtime?"

Zari had that damn grin on his face once more that Nisa couldn't help but be attracted to. Of course, she would never let him know that.

"What did you say?" Nisa's voice climbed an octave higher in direct relation to her climbing ire. Zari was taken aback when he saw her frozen eyes. "I'll only ask one more time. What did you say about the queen?" Nisa said with clenched fists.

Kia looked back and forth between Nisa and Zari. "Oh, Zari, be careful. I think this one bites."

"Shut the fuck up, fairy dust," Nisa spat at Kia. She knew this insult would rub Kia wrong as she was a descendant of the fairies of Sundom, with her pointy ears and pink hair. A long-lost people, fairies were considered extinct until about twenty years ago. When they emerged from the dark wilds, wanting to reacclimate, but many in Transea didn't welcome them. Fairies were evil creatures capable of serious harm to their enemies. Slowly, they began to reinstate themselves into society, but Nisa would never trust them. She knew they were evil.

"But Zi likes it even more when they bite!" howled Luce, almost falling over from too much drink.

Still sitting on his stool facing the small-statured annoyance, Zari said, "I said her kingdom could go into ruin if she continues to be a bride to a dead prince—"

Whap!

Nisa's palm smacked Zari's. In an instant, Rory and the other Misa warriors dropped to Khusela formation around her.

"You fucking bastard!" Nisa yelled.

"I heard women from Mōsa were angry, but this is a bit ridiculous, if you ask me," Zari said, standing as he rubbed his jaw.

Nisa drew her hand back once more but Zari grabbed it midair. His firm grip held her in place. In response, the Misa warriors pointed their short sharp blades at Rivian's second family as one mighty force. The room went silent. Zari looked back at Kia and Luce, who had their swords drawn. Zari knew their mission would be over before it began if he didn't squash this now. Staring back at Nisa, he saw her eyes were red as fire.

As her rage turned to tears that poured down her face, she bit out, "That prince you make fun of was my brother. He was my everything."

Not breaking their stare, Zari saw her pain and her ferocity. Raising one hand, he told his friends to stand down. Once Luce and Kia sheathed their weapons, Nisa motioned to the Misa warriors to do the same. And still, Zari held her arm.

"Let me go," she demanded.

Releasing her hand, Zari took a step back.

"Let's go where there is fresher air to breathe," Nisa said to the warriors. Together, the Mōsian women exited the lounge. Zari didn't know why he felt like an ass. But as Nisa walked away from him, something in him broke.

Later that evening, Nisa stood alone near the ship's stern, with only the light of the lantern that hung near the mizzen mast guarding her against the dark night. She let the breeze play with her black, sleeveless nightgown as it clung to her body. She didn't know what it was about the night sky that soothed her. As she contemplated this evening's altercation, she felt anger at herself for confirming a stereotype she knew wasn't true. For generations, the Mōsian women had been described as aggressive sirens by those in Transea. Her mother once explained, "If your people had been forced to leave their land in Sundom, the loss is felt by Mōsians even three generations later. We carry the loss of our people. We carry it deep within us everywhere we go. We must show the world that they can take our land, let us die of disease, and destroy our families, and we can still rebuild and love."

Nisa always found that frustrating whenever her Mama would say it to her and Nasir. But, tonight, she understood why she needed to cool her rage. Nisa missed her mother tonight more than ever. "But loss has a way of staying with you, and it shapes you," her mother would say.

The light breeze tickling her nose reminded her of the late nights at the bay with her new sweetheart of the month. Nisa loved boys, and they loved her. What she wouldn't give to be back there under the purple palms with pink sand between her toes.

Her peaceful moment was ruined when she heard voices coming her way. Recognizing them to be Zari's and Luce's, Nisa began to walk to her room, irked that she even had their voices memorized now.

However, she wasn't fast enough. Zari caught her on her way back to her room and when he asked her, sober this time, "May we speak, little Mōsa?" Nisa melted a little. She forced herself to ignore him and continued to walk away.

Reaching for her arm, he spun her around and raised

his hands in defense. Then, lowering his voice, he said, "I owe you an apology, little Mōsa."

That got her attention and she stilled her anger.

Feeling out of place, Luce excused himself, saying, "I think Kia is calling me." She wasn't, but it was the only excuse he could pull out of thin air to make his escape.

Nisa allowed Zari to lead her across the main deck towards the bow of the ship.

"It's darker there," Zari said.

Nisa's blood spiked and she asked nervously, "Why do you need it to be dark? What are you planning? I swear to the Holy Mother—"

Zari placed his large hands over her delicate shoulders and turned her around to face the vast expanse of the sea. Without the light of the lantern, they could see the millions of stars populating the night sky and below, the bioluminescent ocean glowed bright. If one squinted, one could hardly tell where the sky began and the sea ended.

Nisa could only gasp at the sight. She had never seen the sea like this and she fell quiet, admiring the view.

Zari stood beside her, silent as a statue. After what seemed like an eternity, he said, "My family was poor and couldn't make a living in Mōsa that was enough to support three young sons. When my family left for Sundom, my youngest brother died on the journey. He was buried at sea, which is why I don't really mind being on the ship for months at a time."

"It makes you feel closer to your brother," Nisa whispered with a tremor in her voice.

Zari nodded.

"That's how I feel about Sole," she shared with a sad smile. "Being with her makes me feel closer to my brother. I suppose she feels the same way. We were twins, did you know that?"

Zari shook his head. Then he touched her soft cheek, and said, "Then you only have to look in a mirror and you won't have to miss him."

Nisa snorted and cracked a smile despite the tears in her eyes, "Pfft. I'm so much prettier than he was."

"I'm not too sure about that, I'd have to see his picture to confirm," Zari said.

Nisa caught the sarcasm and allowed a slight grin to twist her lips into a crooked smile. Zari could tell she was letting her guard down, so he said, "I am truly sorry for saying what I said about your brother. His loss must have been tough. I know how it feels."

Nisa nodded, and said, "It was difficult for me, and especially for Sole. In one night, we both lost our future and our past. Of course, that's not something one gets over quickly, but we have no choice because Sole has a kingdom to run."

Leaning on the banister facing the sea, he said, "It is extraordinary that you and Queen Lia Soleidae Porte still have each other. She is lucky to have you."

Nisa appreciated his effort to start doing and saying the right thing.

"We are lucky to have each other."

"I get it. It's how I feel about Rivian and the crew. They are the only family I have too," he said as he took in the night air. Zari looked into Nisa's eyes and continued, "It must be a great comfort to have each other to talk to about such hardships."

"Sole has never spoken about that night," said Nisa. "But I was there. I heard her piercing scream of agony. If I'm honest, sometimes I hear it in my dreams. It's something I hope never to hear again. You may see her as frail, but she is the bravest person I know."

Nisa's mind went to that night. That night Sole and Nasir danced along with their family. Lola and Luna danced, giggling as they often did when together. King Axel toasted his daughter calling her his "Moonbeam," and Nasir was the most beautiful man in the room.

It took Nisa a moment to remember she was not in Mōsa, having gone deep into the memory as she did. She reminded herself she was on a ship to Sundom. These losses that cut sharper than a Sun Sword were her reality.

"I saw what was left of my brother," Nisa shared, holding back her tears. "Black sunken eyes, pale cold grey skin. To me, his hands were the most terrifying. I'll never forget that they were once so strong. He used to climb trees with just one hand or lift me up when I was a little girl so I could see the festival lights. The last time I saw his hands, they were frail with black fingertips. How could this have happened to us? No. How could this have happened to them?"

"I am sorry this happened to you, to all of us," Zari offered kindly.

Shrugging, Nisa looked out to the sea. "The world turns, and we with it," she said with uncharacteristic sageness. She turned sharply to him and said, "But the next time you joke about the losses of my family, friends, or people, I'll cut you right where you stand."

Something in her eyes told him she meant it. With that, Nisa sauntered down the main deck to head back to her quarters. Halfway through, she stopped and turned back to him.

"Good night, Zari, and keep your foot out of your mouth," she said, a teasing lilt in her voice. She tossed her hair over her shoulder and left him there, smiling like an idiot as he watched the sway of her hips as she walked away.

CHAPTER 8

A Place for Us

Sole awoke to the memory of the words Luce said to her yesterday. Don't trust anyone, not even us.

Luce Dragonmore hadn't been quite who she expected him to be, often knocking on her cabin door just to spend time with her, making sure she was all right. For someone who presented himself as a mindless, heartless, womanizer, he could be quite caring. His warning had sounded so strange, that she now found herself thinking about what could have driven him to say that.

Sole must have woken up six or seven times that night. Not for long each time, but enough to break her sleep. There was a new nightmare, a new dark memory of what she had lost, with every interruption. Seeing her sisters, hearing them laugh, and yet being unable to touch them weighed heavily on her soul every time. Yet, she also knew sleep was the only thing that could save her from the demons she would face the next day.

When Nisa had told her everything she had overheard about Rivian's plan to make her fall in love with him so that she will agree to retrieve the LifeDrinker for him to bring back magic to Sundom, she had found it hilarious. It was a dumb plan, but she doubted if Prince Rivian cared much about it beyond trying to gain the love of a father who only cared for his first born. She didn't really need to fall for Rivian to claim the dagger, because that had been her intention all along—retrieve the dagger and use it to revive Nasir. She just had to get away with keeping the dagger for herself.

Now, it was a waiting game. She either had to wait for Rivian to bring up the Dark Wilds, or find a way to bring it up herself without raising any suspicion.

She also wasn't sure how she was going to revive Nasir, if there was any spell or ritual involved. But she was going to try. Everything that she had read about the prophecy always led to the Dark Wilds. But then, it went back to the question of whether she was ready for the unknown.

Books weren't infallible. They were written by people, and people were flawed. But prophecies were a different matter. The prophets who wrote them weren't just flawed, they were more often than not plagued by madness. And here she was, sticking out her neck for a prophecy.

No, not prophecy. Love. It was for love. She loved Nasir, still. Didn't she?

Unable to stand the sound of her own thoughts, she tiptoed out of her room to get some fresh air.

Right across the hallway, in the captain's quarters, Rivian was restless. He never had trouble sleeping when at sea. The rocking of the waves steadied him. But unfortunately, tonight was not one of those nights. Instead, Rivian found himself tossing and turning.

"Who does she think she is?" whispered Rivian as he sat on his bed and slid on his crimson slim-fit trousers, his thoughts on Sole. He needed some fresh air and the sweet scent of the Serena Sea. Stepping out of his quarters and into the dark hall, he took the stairs that would take him to the main deck. Barefoot, he stepped onto the landing and took a deep breath, letting the sweetness of the sea air carry him to thoughts of home. As a second son, Sundom had never been a safe place for Rivian, but it was where his brother was, and that was home to Rivian.

There was nothing like the sound and smell of the sea to calm him, and no one in Sundom understood that. As he neared the forecastle deck towards the Radiant's bow, he saw the true beauty of the Serena Sea emitting its bioluminescent blue glow against the moonlit stars in the night sky. Sometimes Rivian wished he could escape the politics, betrayal, and responsibilities and live on the Radiant with his chosen family. Sighing, Rivian whispered to himself, "Duty comes before dreams."

Standing there alone, he thought of how long this journey would be to get home. If he was being honest, he dreaded the return to Sundom. He truly didn't have any life there. He was only as good as he was useful, and right now he was useful because he was transporting the first magick healer in centuries.

What would become of him after he accomplished that and delivered her to his father and brother?

To his right, he heard someone coughing. He looked over and found the exact object of his thoughts—the ill-fated, beautiful, dark Princess of Mōsa, now crowned queen.

"I guess I'm not the only one who can't find sleep tonight, huh?" he asked her.

Sole nodded, and then after a moment, she asked him, "Does the sea keep you up as well?" Slowly, she walked closer to him. Only so a conversation between them wouldn't feel like two people shouting at each other over mountains, she reasoned. If she was going to talk to him, then she might as well hold a conversation at a reasonable distance.

What is she wearing? Rivian thought to himself. Her emerald-green, fluffy robe was undone, hanging off one shoulder, revealing a delicate white silk chemise that popped against the deep bronze of her skin. Her skin reminded him of the sard ring he wore on his finger, a gleaming stone of deep brown, mellow facade. Although the robe covered most of her body, it also clung in all the right places revealing her curvaceous waist. Her copper-toned hair swooped in coils over her elegant neck. Her cheeks were a deep shade of mahogany, and her lavender eyes held his gaze. But it was her lips of honey that looked syrup-sweet that captivated him.

"Thoughts of the journey keep me up, not the waves," said Rivian finally, hoping Sole hadn't noticed him ogling her. He suddenly regretted putting on these damn silk crimson pants. He hoped he would not become aroused, seeing her in that flimsy silk gown. That would be the last thing he needed. But one glance at Sole told him she didn't seem to be paying him any mind. Her gaze lay solely on the distant sea.

She must think me a child, Rivian thought bitterly. "What keeps you awake at night, princess Sole of Mōsa?" he asked her, further closing the distance between them.

"Unfortunately, young prince, the past keeps me up at night. I wouldn't expect you to understand," she said dismissively, still facing the glowing sea. "But honestly, the ocean does make me uneasy, especially when no land is visible for miles and miles."

From this angle, with her long coils freely running down her back, she looked like a young girl, given a gift she never asked for. Her eyes could make any man standstill in the daylight, but in the darkness, that was when her eyes captivated Rivian most of all. The most enchanting golden-lavender eyes peered at him through light lashes. He couldn't help but stare at Sole, who preferred always to have her nose in a book.

He wanted to tell her how beautiful she was, and he wanted to touch that mahogany skin. Instead, he said, "I would say we all have nightmares, my queen."

"Mine are often of the future. Being the second-born daughter of a dead king, and all. Isn't that what you and Kia often laugh about?" Her light tone belied the anger behind her question. When Rivian looked shamed, and rightfully so, she continued, "Is it so easy to mock the losses of others? Does your privilege protect you from the tragedies of life, Sir?"

That stung him. Rivian noticed how referring to him as Sir hurt more than anything she ever said. Well, this ship is sinking fast, he thought to himself, almost laughing mirthlessly at the unexpected pun in his own thoughts. Frustrated, he wondered why he always said the wrong thing around her. He was known as one of the best flirts in Sundom, second only to Luce Dragonmore, but there is something to be said of this Mōsian woman. She was nothing like the other women in his life. Sole intrigued him, and he didn't know what to do with that.

Taking a step back and crossing her arms, she said, "Unlike what you're taught at Sundom, being the second-born daughter or son is an honor. My father and mother raised me and my sisters to be who we are supposed to be and not who the crown says we are supposed to be."

His status had always been a sore spot for him and Rivian couldn't help but be angry as he said, "This idea is motivated by emotion rather than purpose. I have a purpose in being a second son. I remind my brother of that every day. I inherit nothing but my father's ire. We are the second-born our fate, our worth is never given it must be made and the cost is blood. So I have made way for myself. Bringing you to Sundom is part of that purpose."

Bristling at being called emotional and purposeless, she countered angrily with more accusations "Don't you live in a world where people secretly flee from your father's reign at night? Your privilege of sailing across the seas with your golden guards doesn't look like suffering."

"You don't know of what you speak of, princess. I'd ask you to take heed of your words," he said, but in truth he knew he should stop speaking. Rivian could not understand why this woman frustrated him so.

"I'm a queen, not a princess," she snapped. "Take heed, says the fair-haired prince with the big smile, who has never seen struggle. You don't know what actual suffering looks like. You spend your time dreaming about a future, while there are those of us whose realities haunt us day and night."

"You have no idea who I am or how I see the world," Rivian spat out.

"That's right. I also know that where I come from, we don't overcome hurdles with mindless violence, warmongering, and weapon smithing. We are led by our love of our people and our reality."

His knuckles turned white as Rivian balled his fists, "Unlike you, queen, many of us aren't proud of our history, but we can change the future. That is what I plan to do. Change everything. My brother and I are building a place for us."

Surprised at his statement, Sole looked at his beautiful, tanned face wondering what he meant by that.

He held his breath, waiting for her to speak.

"A place for us?" she asked with brows furrowed.

"I am building a world where second-borns can live

in peace, thrive, and have a purpose beyond their birth status," he said, as if revealing his deepest, darkest secret. "My brother, Rill, believes it can happen."

"And how do you plan to accomplish that, second son? From your ship?" she asked him, amused.

Rivian fixed his ice blue gaze at her and said, "Now, who mocks? I suppose that is only fair. I mock your tragedy, and you mock my dreams."

Sole fell quiet, taken aback by his honesty and the realization that she was capable of the same cruelty she had accused him of.

"Here is some free advice, princess," Rivian said, speaking in a low, lethal tone. "You will soon learn that you are no longer in Mōsa. People will stare at you because of the dark skin you carry, and no one in Sundom will acknowledge you as a princess, let alone a legitimate queen. Instead, they will see you as the second daughter who only got her throne because everyone else more worthy of it had died, with nothing to offer but—"

Sole interrupted with a raw, shaking voice, saying, "My magick! You forget, young prince, that I am the only being in Transea with the power to heal your beloved father. That is a gift I can take away at any time."

Rivian's jaw twitched.

When Sole realized what she had just said, she

sucked in a breath. She had just threatened to withhold the use of her power for selfish, vengeful reasons. It went against everything she had promised the Holy Mother on the day she had exhausted herself trying to save everyone in Mōsa, choosing her duty to her kingdom over her desire to save only her family and husband.

Closing her eyes to calm herself, she decided to take a few moments before saying, "Please, forgive me. I have said things I did not mean out of anger. However, I promise you this, Prince of Alacor, there is indeed a place for second-borns like us. My parents believed it, and I do too."

When she opened her eyes to look at him, she looked a little lost. "I don't know why you make me so angry. I don't think it's your fault, though. I think I'm just angry and you're—"

"I'm here," he finished for her, "and all the people you love aren't."

Sole didn't know what to make of that, so she opted for silence. She didn't like that he could wound her so easily, and hated it even more that she was capable of wounding him right back. She did not need this sort of complication. Not when she had so much on her plate, a kingdom to rebuild, a legacy to uphold, and magick to conquer. She needed to put some distance between herself and Rivian, before things got even more complicated.

After a while, Rivian said quietly, "I must ask you for forgiveness as well, my lady."

Sole pretended the generic title did not sting a little.

Rivian looked at her with tired eyes, "Forgive me. I sometimes say too much without thinking things through, and end up saying absolutely nothing at all. For some reason, I keep forgetting myself around you."

The last part felt too much like a confession, but Rivian was too wound up to notice.

Steeling herself for what she was about to do, Sole said, "There is nothing to forgive. If you meant anything to me other than a ride to my destination, maybe it would have warranted an apology. But you see, second prince, for me to forgive you would mean that you matter to me, and frankly, you do not."

She was cold, confident, and unforgiving, but her eyes told a different story; they were young, vibrant, but full of pain. He had no idea why he kept pushing her buttons when he wanted to gain her trust. She would never agree to help him change the world if he couldn't earn her faith.

When Sole ended her diatribe with a curt, "Good night then, sir," Rivian fought the urge to say something, anything that would make her stay. But instead, he said nothing as she walked away from him and disappeared into the deck below.

CHAPTER 9

Dangerous Encounters

"She's unbearable," Rivian told his crew after yet another unsuccessful attempt at getting Sole to come take their meals with the rest of them at the mess hall. "She still refuses to join us for meals. She refuses to speak to anyone other than her escorts. For someone who wants to heal the world, she is reluctant to be part of the world."

"It sounds like she has gotten under your skin, brother," Luce said with a grin.

"I haven't seen a female get under your skin since you and Kia—"

"No need to rehash the past," Kia interrupted Zari with a bored eye roll. Zari was infamous for pointing out the obvious, no matter how inappropriate.

Rivian and Kia had known each other since their seventh year. She was the first friend he made while at the Sanctum. Back then, her pink locks toppled down her back, unlike the short pixie cut she wore now. At first, Rivian found her frustrating and captivating simultaneously. Although the two eventually decided they were better off as friends, their blood bond as a group of second-borns, along with Luce and Zari, connected them to each other for a lifetime.

"It is not the same," Rivian insisted, oblivious to the fact that Kia did not want their past to be brought up. "Sole is more frustrating than Kia ever was!"

Kia didn't like being compared to the queen. She fumed silently as Rivian continued, "How am I ever to achieve my goal if I can't get her to trust me? If I can't get her to have a meal with me, what chance do I have in hell of convincing her to get a dagger in the Dark Wilds?"

"Give her a break," stated Luce. "The girl is new to the ocean and our ways. It will take time."

Kia looked at Luce with questioning eyes, saying, "I think Luce has a crush on our princess."

Chiming in, Zari said, "I don't blame him. Have you seen her ass? I know we were told that Mōsian women were evil sirens who destroyed every man they encountered, but not in the way we originally thought. They didn't tell us their stunning looks and quick wit would weaken any man. I mean, have you looked at all the Misa warriors? They are hot. I wouldn't mind one of them taking me over their knee," Zari said, gazing off into the distance.

Smacking Zari on the back of the head, Rivian said, "I thought you were hot for the little feisty one? Nisa?"

Zari grinned at him, "I am. But she's not, or doesn't seem to be. Maybe I can find out by making her jealous?"

Kia rolled her forest green eyes at him, "You're a child, Zi, if you think that still works."

Rivian thought about it and said, "Well, if nothing seems to work on the Mōsian women, maybe changing tactics would work. It is especially hard to earn their trust. I need more time."

"Time is exactly what we don't have," insisted Kia. "She must learn—"

"Good evening, Prince Rivian Alacor," Nisa's voice interrupted them. The room went silent as they wondered how much this little beauty had heard. "Queen Lia Soleidae Porte of Mōsa wishes an audience."

"Tell your queen that if she seeks an audience, she may come join us for the evening meal. This is the only place where I will grant her an audience this night," Rivian stated.

"Careful, brother, let's not upset the queen before you have had a chance to learn her," whispered Zari.

Rolling her eyes, Nisa stated, "I will inform our queen of your offer. One last thing, Prince. She is not as frail as you think. Push her far enough and she will push right back, and I pray for all of you if your intentions with Sole are not true."

An hour later, Sole entered the dining hall. Only Rivian remained, as the others had gone down to the cargo hold to drink. A long table could be seen from the doorway. He sat at the ornate table decorated in deep crimson and gold, the Sundom banner colors. Somehow in this space the table seemed more formal than the rest of the room. Rivian looked at her and he was struck once more by how breathtaking she was. And yet, her violet eyes only reflected a deep, cold sadness.

Walking alongside the wall closest to the large dining table, Sole studied the frames that held pictures of Rivian's family lineage. "I remember when my father used to travel all of Transea. We were braver during those years," she said as she continued to trace Rivian's family tree. "My father would return darker than I'd ever seen him. He always said that the golden suns burn our skin, but not our soul. He dared to live amongst the monsters, who considered themselves lucky to have their families at their sides."

When she reached the portrait of the first King A'Dien Alacor, she stopped, but continued talking. "Then, in the night, I would hear him tell Mami that he had been amongst the monsters of Sundom. Shortly after that, we stopped traveling outside of Mōsa and ceased all of our trading with Sundom."

"Those monsters are long gone, queen," Rivian said.

"Are people not monsters too, Prince Rivian of Alacor?"

"I have seen my fair share of monsters, queen."

"I see you still aren't referring to me as I have requested," Sole said, piercing his icy blue gaze. Continuing to walk the room with her hands clasped in front of her, Sole said, "My mother once told me that we were never meant to be Mōsians, insisting that our true home was in Sundom and that we would see our home again one day. I never wanted to see Sundom. And yet here I am sailing there without my family."

Speaking gently, Rivian said, "Then, if that's the case, I fear you will find that Sundom has more monsters than we can count. This trip will treacherously require us to be at sea for thirty moons. It will need much of you. I hope you are up for the task."

"Am I ready? I have seen the Darkness take my family, friends, and love. I have survived being consumed by the Darkness and have healed my people, and you ask me if I am ready?" Sole scoffed at that. "Prince Rivian, Mōsians have experienced more loss than most Transeans and definitely more than those of Sundom. We carry our grief with us everywhere we go. Not out of choice but out of duty."

"My apologies. I did not mean to insinuate that you aren't ready," Rivian was getting tired of constantly apologizing whenever he was around Sole. "We have only just begun to see the losses in Sundom. This is why I feel that this loss is still new. I am sure that it's hard to keep up with the days and months that have transpired since you were first hit with the Darkness." His soft honesty surprised her. She could deal with a spoiled wicked prince. But, somehow hearing him now, here she knew this version of Prince Rivian could be her undoing. As difficult as this arrangement had become, Rivian was still the prince of the most powerful realm in Transea.

"It's been a year, seven months, and thirteen days since I last saw his face," she said as her eyes looked far away with her voice cracking.

"What was he like?" Rivian asked, although it pained him to do so.

Looking at Rivian with a sad smile, Sole began, "He was everything. Compassionate, funny, intelligent, and had the most fantastic smile. He dreamt of more. He always said, 'Sole, I'm going to take you to the sea to learn the world. The world deserves to see your smile.'"

"And here you are, at sea."

"I never wanted to leave Mōsa, but I would have gone

anywhere with him. I just wanted to be where he was. 'Smile more, Sole,' he would say, 'The world needs to see you smile.'"

Rivian didn't know what to say other than, "I am sorry this happened to you." Sole's answer was a noncommittal shrug of her shoulders. Rivian wasn't sure what was happening to him. Still, he somehow didn't like the idea of Sole loving another. With his jaw tightening, he forced himself to think of something else. Finally, he decided to focus on her face. She is stunning, he thought to himself. Those full lips and her sultry alto voice were alluring.

Sighing, Sole looked out to the sea. "If there is one thing the Darkness has taught me, it's that the world turns, and we with it. Nisa and I say that all the time. It's comforting. I thank the Holy Mother every day for her grace during this horrifying time."

Looking at Sole, a bit perplexed, Rivian asked, "How can you still believe in the Holy Mother, knowing what happened to those you love?" Rivian was raised to praise the Holy Mother publicly but it was very different behind the castle walls. The Holy Mother was not the topic of conversation at their dinner table. He admired Sole's dedication even if he couldn't understand it.

"I believe in the Her despite what I have endured. Since I woke from the Darkness with this." She lifted her hands to show him the constant violet glow. "Magick, I couldn't quite understand what it meant. Why would I be the first healer born in four generations? Those in Transea only see Mōsa as a place where nothing good can come from it. So every day, I prayed. I asked the Holy Mother for her wisdom and for her to lead me on the path I should take."

"So, did she answer you?" Rivian asked.

"She did." Standing and securing her pink blanket around her shoulders, she attempted to cover her flimsy silk nightdress. Continuing, Sole said, "But that is a story for another time." Turning to return to her room, Sole said, "I have shared too much. It must be my lack of sleep."

"Please, Sole, don't go," Rivian surprised himself with the hint of desperation in his voice and the very bold use of her name. Where had that come from? Sole noticed it too.

Looking at him, bewildered, she said, "Very well. Enough about me. Tell me something, Rivian, what has the Darkness taught you?"

For the first time, Rivian realized she had said his first name without any title, without any scorn. He wasn't sure why this pleased him, but he would have to think that through later when he was alone. Maybe she was finally letting her guard down enough for him to get to know her and earn her trust.

Reflecting for a moment, he said, "The Darkness taught me that if I want to save my people, I must do something about it. So here I am in an empty dining hall with a beautiful princess, now queen, learning about the world beyond Sundom. But I must know, how did the Holy Mother answer your question?" He held his breath as he waited for her response.

Although she wondered why the prince wanted to know, she explained. "In all honesty, it took me many months before the Holy Mother led me to the information I needed. Have you ever heard of the Signant Requiem?"

Rivian's heart skipped a beat. He knew that tome. It contained the prophecies of Mōsa. This was it, this was his chance to steer her towards the Dark Wilds. "No," he lied.

"As a child, my father taught us that this was the first book of prophecy written by the original Mossian settlers. You may think me foolish, but in that Requiem, I discovered something. Finally, I found the answer I was looking for."

She caught herself before she could say any more. Swerving, she suddenly stammered, "I'm… I'm getting tired, so I think I'll go get some sleep now."

Rivian was suddenly there, in front of her. How he

had quickly gotten up from his chair to her, she would never know. But his large warm hands on her arms were very distracting.

"Queen, don't run away from this. How will we ever learn from each other if we don't talk?" Rivian said. "What did the prophecy say?"

Sole huffed, but eventually relented. "Fine, what I share with you next must stay between us, second prince," she said as threateningly as she could while trying to dislodge her arms from his hands.

"There goes that title again. I'll keep our little secret only if you call me Rivian."

"What? I am being serious." Sole said, crossing her arms, her brows furrowed.

"So am I," Rivian said, crossing his own arms with his devilish smile highlighting those damn dimples that Sole wanted to resist but knew she couldn't. "I caught you doing it once. I liked the sound of my name from your lips, no titles, no nothing."

Locking eyes with Rivian, Sole said, "Prin... Rivian, the prophecy said that once the three are reborn, the bond shall bring forth an age of magick and an era of sorrow."

"You say this was a prophesy written by original Mōsian settlers?"

Sole nodded solemnly, then she noticed a strange

expression on his face as he digested her answer. "What is it? Why do you ask me that?"

Rivian's ice blue eyes were fixed on her in such an intense gaze that Sole found it impossible to look away. "Every child in Sundom knows one prophesy by heart," he began, "and it's only a slight variation from yours."

Sole's eyes widened at that. Was he truly sharing a guarded prophecy from Sundom with her while she was trying to figure out a way to get him to help her revive her dead husband?

"When the dark throne rises," Rivian recited, "the three shall bring forth an era of magick and sorrow."

He very conveniently left out the most important part of the prophecy—when the dark throne rises, and a betrayer lies in the sands of Sundom. Rivian hated lying to Sole, but he couldn't very well tell her that a great evil threat to the world would rise in his own kingdom and that the dagger they sought could also be used against her. He desperately needed her on their side.

Sole's mind worked, trying to figure out why the prophecy was different. "It kind of makes sense, if you think about it. The first settlers in Mōsa were from Sundom, so it's logical for them to bring over their beliefs from Sundom. But why delete the first part for Mōsa?"

"I'd like to know the answer to that too. Among other things."

Sole raised an elegant eyebrow at him, "Among other things?"

Rivian bent his head close to her, his nose almost brushing her forehead. "Both prophecies speak of three beings bringing back magick. Tell me, princess, what do you think about that?"

Sole stepped back, trying to put some distance between them. "Don't be coy, Rivian," she said, "We both know we're thinking the same thing. I believe I am one of the three."

Rivian gave her an infuriating wink, and said, "I know, princess"

"Queen."

"Queen, you say you're one of the three, if so, where are the other two?"

"That's another great question for which I have no answer. I came here tonight hoping you or your library here on the Radiant would have the answers I seek. I have looked everywhere, but to no avail."

Rivian's hand snuck around hers as he whispered, "Let me help you find the answers you are looking for, Sole. I am sure if we put our heads together, we can find the answers we seek."

His hand against hers burned. He didn't know if it was because of his desire for her and how his hand itched to touch more of her than just her hand, or if it burned because a plan was beginning to form in his head, all thanks to her. One of these nights, he was going to conveniently leave all the scrolls about the LifeDrinker and the Dark Wilds in the library, and neglect to include the one scroll that accurately described the real power of the LifeDrinker.

Sole, meanwhile had gotten excited over his use of the word, "we." Did he just express interest in working with her? That brought her closer to her goal, closer to Nasir. Sole wasn't sure why that made her uneasy, but with Rivian, everything made her uncomfortable. Finally, pulling her hand back, she said, "This is not your problem. Why should I trust you to help me with this, Rivian?"

"Because I was the one who asked you when you were going to stand up and change the world. How could I deprive you of my brilliant mind?"

Sole couldn't help but grin at that. Her bright eyes could make a man forget his name.

"We are on this journey to change the world; why not do it together?" he said as he looked into her eyes.

Feeling herself flush at his glaze, Sole refused to look away. "We can work together as long as no one else knows about it. I don't trust your soldiers, and I am pretty sure you don't trust mine, or why else would you have Luce constantly dropping by for a visit? We know he is there to watch us. But we entertain him, and my ladies like to look at his grey-blue eyes. "

Rivian tensed at the knowledge that Luce was visiting her. He'd had no idea.

"Queen Sole, I was unaware that Luce has been visiting you daily. I will ensure that those visits stop immediately. The last thing I want is for you or your consort to feel uncomfortable."

Waving her hands to indicate it was all right, she said, "Please don't, my ladies would be bored to tears without his visits. It keeps them entertained. Besides, he has been teaching us much about the women of Sundom. And may I say, it is quite sad that your women do not know how to fight."

"I will allow his visits to continue under the condition that you allow me to help you on this journey. We can meet at the library between our cabins every night to go over the texts and see what else we may find. If Luce ever makes you uncomfortable, you will come directly to me." Sole noted a possessive tone in his voice, but agrees to his terms.

And so, for many nights Sole and Rivian met at Alexandria, the Radiant's massive library. Rivian would watch Sole intently as she became consumed with every book, prophetic tome, scroll, and requiem she got her hands on. Rivian met every night with anticipation as he looked forward to seeing her in the library. The two began to bond over books, hopes, and laughter as the nights went by. Sole had no idea Rivian could be so funny and a little charming, but she would never say that out loud.

One night, Rivian didn't arrive at their usual meeting time and Sole saw it as an opportunity to look for anything that would point her towards the Dark Wilds and give her the ability to bring it up in conversation to avoid any suspicion. After a few minutes of digging through a box of scrolls under the desk that Rivian had been rummaging around the night before, she finally found it. It was an ancient scroll that detailed a source of power that had the power over the life and death of magick. Sole was thrilled when she saw the picture of the location for this weapon. There it was, the Dark Wilds, a system of caves inside a forest right before the Sundom border. All the books inside her library at Mōsa spoke about the power that lay hidden in this forest, and she knew without a doubt that her destiny would be tied to it.

When Rivian finally entered the library, she showed him what she had discovered. Turning to her, Rivian said, "I will take you there. "

"What? No. I can go with my warriors to explore the cave myself. Maybe you can send Luce with us."

"Absolutely not." There was that possessive tone again. "I will take you, Sole. I promised to help you through this, so please let me do that. We will explain to my people that I wish to show you the island before we make it to Sundom. So they will not disobey my orders."

For all her hesitation, she couldn't seem to see the fault in his plan. And so, she agreed with him. Rivian breathed a sigh of relief when she did not protest.

"You can tell your warriors and Nisa the truth, as it will be easier for them to trust that this is real and that I would never do anything to betray you," he added.

Sole noticed how he said that last part. Gentle and determined. Convinced this would be her best option to find the weapon, Sole agreed to carry out this plan and go to the Dark Wilds with Rivian.

In the meantime, she decided to do so more research while waiting to reach the lands of Sundom.

CHAPTER 10

The Price of Privilege

He wasn't sure why it bothered him that Luce was always visiting with Sole, but that would have to wait until later, because something else bothered him more. Rivian hadn't seen Sole at all today, and that was unusual. After coming to a truce and actually finding a way to work together, spending most of their nights at the library, and with her walking about and sometimes taking her dinner at the dining hall, he had gotten used to seeing her.

But Rivian hadn't seen her at the Bastion dining hall, the bow, or the promenade. He tried to find sleep, but the bed felt wrong. Restless, Rivian made his way to the library, the place he was sure Sole was. Upon arriving, he noticed the door to the library was cracked open, and a low glow came from the rose gold lamp on his desk.

Gently pushing the door back, he saw her reading in the champagne-colored setee with a rose-colored blanket covering her tiny feet. Looking at her sitting there, he thought, The air changes every time I see her. His informants had told him that Sole was known as a shy bookworm who spent most of her time working at the local library and reading the classics before the Darkness came. This was why Rivian chose The Radiant as his ship of choice for this voyage, as it was the only one with a library.

Startled, Sole sat up, shouting, "What the fuck?!" Her breath left her for a quick moment. Sole knew it was a slight overreaction, but this had been the first time in a long time someone had snuck up on her. She had been immersed in the story she was reading, The Great Sundom Armies.

He took a step back as she stood and looked at her whole body with slow deliberation. Rivian felt as if he stared at her for an eternity, though it was only a second. The air in the room shifted, and he wanted to close the gap between them. But, staying rooted in his spot, Rivian leaned on the door frame with his arms crossed. He thought this way, she wouldn't see his hands shaking.

"My apologies for scaring you, princess," Rivian said with that perfect slight smile.

"You know, where I come from, people get handled roughly for sneaking up on someone like that," she said, rising from the settee.

"Sneaking? Is it called sneaking when you are on your own ship?" he said with one eyebrow twitched up. Changing the subject, Rivian stood tall, slid his hands into his pockets, and entered the library, saying, "I hope your accommodations are to your liking."

Tilting her head to the side, Sole tucked her coiled cinnamon hair behind her right ear and then looked away.

"Do you not like your accommodations?" Rivian asked curiously.

"The accommodations are perfect. Perfect for the King of Sundom," she whispered to herself.

"What was that?" Rivian said, looking affronted. Were they going to start fighting again so soon after they had just found some level ground?

"I am just curious. Do you ever think all this is too much for one family to consume?" Sole asked, gesturing to the ornate library.

"Being that you are a royal, you would understand. But maybe it was different in Mōsa." Stepping closer to Sole, he said, "My family worked hard for all of this."

Ignoring his comment about Mōsa, Sole asked, "Help me understand how your family worked hard for all of this? Tell me about their sufferings, their toiling. Because as I sit here and read the history of the The

Great Sundom Wars, all I see is rape, pillaging, enslavement, and death. What exactly is excellent about that?"

Sole crossed her arms across her chest, pushing her breasts up atop her gown, and asked icily, "Does privilege come so easy to you?"

Rivian shifted his gaze from her plump, perfect brown breasts and pretended to look at the books at the desk. But, if he was honest, he had no idea what books he was looking at. What is happening to me? he wondered as Sole looked at him with those deep violet eyes, waiting for an answer. Speak fool, Rivian thought as he struggled to remember what she was talking about before he got distracted. Ah, their history.

"Well, princess, maybe you can tell me how your people fled their homeland of Sundom because it got too hard? Did you read the part in the book where your people betrayed our trust? Is this the reason why you are a princess in title alone? Where is your army? Where is your gold? Where is your right to rule?" Rivian surprised himself with the harsh tone and questions he posed to Sole. He started to apologize when suddenly, something very unexpected happened. Sole burst into tears, frustration burning in her eyes. Rivian looked away. He couldn't bear to see her cry.

"Prin...Queen Sole, forgive me, the night is late, and lack of sleep keeps me saying all the wrong things to you."

Wiping her tears with the back of her hand, she said, "Prince, have a fair night," and began to walk out of the room, grabbing her smooth, pink blanket on the way out.

"Damnit, Sole!" Rivian yelled before she could leave the room. The way he said her name stopped Sole from taking another step. She might even let it slide that he didn't add princess or queen before her name.

"I am sorry," he said, taking long strides so he could stand in front of her. "I can't imagine how the Darkness has changed your life, but I would like to learn. You are right. My people have caused unspeakable tragedies, and we have benefited from them. That doesn't mean I agree with them. It also doesn't mean I hate my people. But I believe a new day is coming to Sundom, and I hope you are there to see the new world my brother will create when he is king. You talk of changing the world for Mōsa. Do you plan to do that hiding in your cabin or in the library?"

Facing each other, nothing was said for what seemed to be an eternity. Rivian couldn't look away as she stood before him in her pink silk nightgown, her coiled hair flowing over her shoulders and down her back. He imagined smelling her lavender-scented hair.

Breaking the silence, Sole sniffled and asked, "When is breakfast served in the Bastion?"

"Nine and twenty," Rivian replied, stunned. Sole had always taken breakfast alone, in her room.

With every air of a queen she could muster, Sole wiped her tears and said airily, "I will make sure to be there early so that we can continue to discuss the history of our people. Are you up for the challenge?"

Rivian grinned at her. "Absolutely," he said, "I will see you in the morning, princess." Then, taking two steps toward Sole, Rivian added, "Before you go, there's one thing you have to know. You were wrong about one thing."

"About what?" Sole asked, curious.

"Privilege does come easy to those who have always had it, but it always comes with a price so steep, we end up paying for it all our lives."

She absorbed what he said and filed it away for debate later. Then she said, "Have a fair night, Prince of Sundom."

Watching her make her way to the door, something tightened his chest. He couldn't let her leave. He wouldn't let her go. Grabbing her by the arm, she turned, facing him. His gaze flickered from her lips to her eyes and back. He could feel her magick crackling in the space between them. While maybe it's nonsensical at this moment, all he wanted was her. It's everything he can to drown out his frustration and desire for the

Queen of Mōsa. He leans in and kisses her.

Her full lips are surprisingly soft when they meet his. Startled, Sole stiffened in his grasp, suddenly giving in and leaning father into his hold. His arms wrapped around her waist, pulling her tighter as his hands cupped her cheeks. She hadn't been touched like this since Nasir, and her body wanted it...now. Sole's heart soared with his gentle caress, yet disturbed by how her treacherous body was responding to the Prince of Sundom. Her enemy. Her magick's fire ran through her body as Rivian deepened the kiss. His tongue pried her mouth open. Sole moaned at his delicious taste. Heat shot through her middle, and that same heat was throbbing between her thighs. He could smell her arousal. This was a dangerous game they were playing. Walking them back to the settee, Rivian sat as he pulled in her waist, drawing her closer. To his surprise, Sole straddled him. He groaned as she settled on his lap. Sole sucked in a gasp as she felt him hard and thick beneath her. His hand coaxed her face back to his.

"Sole, you taste so much better than I imagined," he groaned into her ear. Her head fell back, allowing her long braids to touch his knees, granting him more access to the length of her throat.

"I never want anyone else to touch you again. Since I saw you, I wanted you for myself."

She sucked in the air, her center contracting as she clawed at him. A burn consumed her chest as she whispered, "Oh, Nasir."

His hands soften, turning into soothing strokes, and then they are gone. Then, with chest heaving, Sole asks, "What's wrong?"

His cold stare confirmed something had just shifted. Lifting her off his lap, he stood as he desperately tried to regain control. What the fuck was he thinking. She called out her dead mate's name, not his. He didn't understand why that pissed him off so much, but it did. She didn't matter to him, right? Then why did that pang of jealousy consume every part of his soul, extinguishing his arousal?

"This was a mistake," he spat out. "When you are out at sea for too long, your mates begin to look appealing."

As if awakening from a drunken spell, Sole was bemused by Rivian's abrupt pause.

"Did you just call me your fucking mate? I assure you my 'mates' don't get to stick their tongues down my throat. Only my husband has ever…."

"That must be why you called me by his name," he spat.

Staring at her, he saw her magick pulse in her lavender eyes. She was about to explode.

She closed her eyes and found some semblance of

peace when she uttered, "I am sorry, Rivian. I fear that my past still haunts my present. Truly I am sorry." She exited the library wrapping her silk robe tightly around her as if it were armor.

Rivian had no idea when he stopped breathing but managed to catch his breath. He reminded himself that he was here to save his father and his people and couldn't care about anyone, especially not Sole. He needed her to get the weapon, and that was that. Tomorrow, he would begin his mission to gain her trust before they made it to the caverns of the Dark Wilds.

CHAPTER 11

A Most Royal Debate

Sole entered the Bastion dining hall in a royal blue tunic and black leggings. Her black ankle boots finished her polished look. She was determined not to make a big deal of last night's riveting kiss. She would stick to the plan and find the weapon to raise her prince. Her Naṣir. Rivian noticed her hair was held up in a high ponytail. Her hair was exotic, vibrant, and stunning. He had never met a woman in Sundom quite like her.

"I must say, prince, I am surprised to see that you made it to the Bastion earlier than I," Sole said without making eye contact with Rivian.

With that incredible smile, Rivian said, "I am sure if my mother were alive, she'd never let me live it down if I left a lady, let alone a princess, or a queen, waiting." He got up, as was required of a gentleman, when a lady approached a table and pulled out a chair for her.

I am sure your mother would be proud of her son.

I mean, at least you have one redeemable trait." She wondered how it was that they had not bonded about their common loss. Here sat the motherless second-born children. What a sad pair indeed, Sole thought to herself.

Grabbing his chest, Rivian said jokingly, "Ouch, princess! Listing down all my shortcomings so early in the morning? I think you and my mother would have gotten along just fine." Then, he added a wink for good measure. He only got an eyeroll as a response.

This was it. He was sitting down in front of Sole at the dining hall at breakfast. Just the two of them. They were having breakfast. Together. He could hardly believe it.

The clink of silverware on teacups brought him out of his reverie, and he shifted his attention to the pile of books he had beside him. Grabbing several of them and placing them in front of Sole, he said, "I stopped by the Alexandria library this morning and grabbed several books about Sundom that will help you better understand our history."

Sole looked at him askance, and said, "Prince, I will remind you that your history is my history. I assure you, I have read them all."

Deciding to humor him, she picked up one of the books and looked it over. A spark of recognition lit up her face as she said, "Like this one." She tapped it with one elegant finger. "Here, your people rewrote our history to make themselves the heroes of the story."

Winning her over would be harder than he had originally thought. Quickly, he tried to apologize for imposing, but Sole interrupted him.

"No apologies needed," she said, "You can't help where you were born or who raised you. I thought it would be best to learn about your people from you," she said with a smirk.

Meeting her challenge, Rivian said, "I would love to answer your questions, but first, let's order our food. Then we will get right to it." Waiving to a server wearing a long white tunic and white gloves, Rivian ordered his usual eggs, toast, and Margolin juice. Sole ordered a small fruit bowl with porridge and a warm tea with honey.

As the server left their table, Rivian noticed Zari and Kia entered the Bastion. Seeing Rivian with Sole, their shock was evident. Rivian raised his glass of Mangolin juice as he greeted his friends.

As Sole turned to see whom Rivian was looking at, he was captivated by her profile. He found Kia staring right back at him with a razor-sharp green stare. Worst of all, Sole noticed.

"So, how long has it been?" Sole asked as she dipped her spoon into the steaming porridge the white-haired server had just delivered.

"How long has what been?" he asked Sole.

"How long has it been since you were with Kia? That is her name, right?"

Coughing up his juice, Rivian asked, "What?"

"I am no fool, prince. I see how she looks at you. Please tell me you aren't one of those men who can't tell when their best friend is in love with them," she said as she stirred more honey into her tea.

"I am not sure I should be having conversations like these with you, Queen Sole."

"Do you mean because I am a queen or a woman? Either way, I know what love and sex are. I was married, after all. My people are open about all things, including our sexual exploits. Are the people of Sundom this reserved with matters of love or sex?" Sole asked before sipping her tea.

"The women of Sundom do not discuss things of such nature, but I welcome your honesty and can't wait to see how Sundom women respond to you and your escorts. To answer your first question, it has been three seasons since Kia and I have engaged in any, as you call them, exploits. We both agreed we were better as friends and brothers at arms."

"Really?" Sole said, raising an eyebrow, "Three seasons is a significant amount of time. She still looks at you like that?"

To hide his blushing cheeks, Rivian began to eat his breakfast with gusto. No woman had ever dared ask him about his sexual relationships, and if he was being honest, it unnerved him.

Rivian thought it was only fair if he asked her the same question. "I would imagine you had quite the list of lovers before you mated," he said, grabbing a piece of toast.

"If I am being honest, not many boys were interested in the girl with glasses who spent her days in the library reading books. They wanted to date the girls who knew how to swim, run, and climb. That girl was not me, but Nasir was different. He saw me, the real me. And he loved me for it. That's why I think our love grew quickly. He never tried to change me," Sole shared, her gaze going distant.

"I didn't mean to have you relive your past. My apologies," Rivian whispered.

Laughing, Sole said, "I bet you are not used to apologizing this much, are you, Prince of Sundom?"

Caught off guard by the teasing manner in which she spoke to him, Rivian could only stare at her, wondering if this was a different woman. Sole met his gaze, broke into a smile, and the smile grew into laughter. It was infectious, and before he knew it, Rivian found himself laughing along with her. Together, they laughed so hard it earned them stares from the others sitting in the Bastion.

When they finally quieted, Sole asked him, "Did you go to the Sanctum as a child?"

"I did," he responded as he resumed eating his breakfast.

"How long did you stay there?"

"I had the pleasure of staying there for seven long years, give or take a few months."

"That must have been hard for you," she said, in a sympathetic tone.

Her question shook Rivian as no one had ever said that. Not his friends, not his family, no one. No one ever questioned the Sanctum, or its purpose, or looked closely at its effect on the children who were sent there. No one in Sundom, that was.

Looking at her, he said, "I was scared at first. I missed my brother and never wanted to see my father again. But, I also know that if it hadn't been for them," he pointed to the table where Zari, Kia and Luce sat, "I would have never survived those seven seasons. They became my family, and we have been together ever since."

The silence between them became an awkward reminder of their very different worlds. Finally, breaking the silence, Rivian asked, "How about you? What was your time like in the Sanctum?"

"It's funny you would ask me, because that is where we first met," she said with a sly smile. She had been holding onto that information for a while, wondering when he would catch up.

"I beg your pardon?" Rivian nearly choked on his toast. How did they miss this in the research he had his team do?

"I met you during my first and only season at the Sanctum. I was seven and sitting along near the Pillars of Truth during recess. When you walked up, three Sundom boys were torturing me. One of them had taken my book, the other was about to break my glasses when you grabbed him by the hand and threatened to kick his ass."

Trying not to get consumed by her bright smile, he replied, "There were many cruel boys at the Sanctum, and I couldn't bear to see them bully anyone. I had no idea you were one of those they had tortured."

"Well, I never got to say thank you then because my parents pulled me out after only a few weeks," she quipped with a fond smile, "And now that you're here and I'm here, I can. So, thank you."

All too soon, she had finished her breakfast and she was standing up and saying, "Thank you for keeping me company at breakfast, Rivian. I'll see you in the evening at the library. I have much to do."

Reaching out and touching her hand before she could leave the table, Rivian asked, "Queen, would you meet me here for midday supper? You owe me for saving your glasses and your book."

He held his breath as he waited for her to respond.

"Yes. I suppose I can do that, prince."

"Rivian. Please call me Rivian," he said with a charming smile as he rose to his feet.

"I will meet you here at midday, Rivian." she affirmed with a small, regal nod, and left the dining hall to go straight to the library.

Rivian watched her, thinking he liked the sound of his name on her pink lips. Her deep voice gave an air of solid confidence that was easy on his ears.

Once Sole left the Bastion, Rivian found his friends staring at him. They made their way to his table.

"So, anything you want to tell us, Riv?" Luce asked as he took hold of a chair and spun it around so he could sit on with his arms folded over the backrest.

"Leave him alone," said Kia as she crossed her arms over her chest. "You all know why he's doing this and why we're helping him. It's for Sundom."

"Exactly, this isn't serious," Zari said. "Right, Riv?"

"Of course not. Sole is the key to getting us what we

want," he said as evenly as he could. Turning to Luce, he asked, "How many more days before we arrive at the Dark Wild caverns?"

"We should arrive during the sixth night," Luce replied easily.

"Great. I have much to do to earn Sole's trust in six nights," he said with a tinge of regret.

"Kia and Zari, make sure that my brother is informed of our progress and that we're almost done with our mission."

Zari looked at Kia and said, "We will make the necessary arrangements." Kia nodded at him in confirmation.

Luce hesitated a moment before mustering up the courage to say to Rivian, "Brother, we may have made a mistake. The queen and her escorts are strong, brave women, unlike any we have ever known. Maybe we need to rethink our next move."

Zari frowned at him while Kia threw confused looks between Luce and Rivian. Whatever complicated web they were weaving wasn't good for their plan.

"I don't know Luce," Kia said tartly, "maybe you need to rethink where your loyalties are?"

The easygoing demeanor gone from him, Luce turned sharply to Kia and said, "I am loyal to our cause. I do want our plan to work, and if there's some gross miscalculation on our part regarding how well the Mōsian queen can be manipulated then—"

"No," Rivian said firmly, his eyes trained on Luce. "We have prayed for this moment since our time in the Sanctum, for magick to return to Sundom, for Sundom to be a safe place for everyone. She is the key to that dagger. I will not let Sundom suffer because I feel sorry about hurting the Mōsa princess turned queen," Rivian said as his stomach flipped and his brow began to sweat. He suddenly wished he had his brother's skill for subterfuge and lying.

"Riv, this will destroy her," Luce said. "Are you sure?"

Kia snorted. "And we're supposed to care because? Dragonmore, you're useless if you've gone soft."

Rivian held up a hand to get all of them to stop talking. "At this point, we have no other way out of this."

Staring off into space, Rivian ran a frustrated hand over his face. He wasn't sure how he would be able to betray Sole, but he knew there was no other option. Once she found out about his betrayal regarding the true nature of the LifeDrinker, he knew she would never forgive him.

"Well, whether the little Mōsian queen will be hurt or not is not our real concern here with this plan of yours," Zari said as he tried to steer the conversation to a more important matter. "I don't like the idea of you going to the Dark Wilds alone with her. As your army general, my prime responsibility during this mission is to keep you alive while you deliver the girl and dagger to your brother. I wish you would change your mind about this, Riv."

"My decision is final," Rivian said, and slammed his fist down on the table, hammering in the idea that this was not open for debate. "Sole and I will journey to the Dark Wilds alone. The journey will not be easy, as it will take us half a day to reach the caves from the shore when we land, and another half to go into the caves and retrieve the dagger. I expect Luce to be waiting for us with the dinghy by the shore the next morning, ready to bring the queen and me back to the Radiant to prepare for our journey to Sundom. I hope we will acquire the weapon by the time we come out of the caves."

Luce continued to protest. "Riv, I don't like this. You and the queen will need protection, and it makes the most sense that I accompany her and you to make sure you are both safe." He tried appealing to Rivian's sense in seafaring and pointed out, "The sky looks like it's about to open up and you know how dangerous that is for a large ship. Given the sharp rocks that guard the Dark Wilds, the Radiant can only take you so far, and you will have to take the dinghy. What if something happens to her or to you?"

Rivian's jaw tightened at hearing Luce suggest that

somehow he wasn't enough of a soldier to keep Sole safe. Turning to face him, Rivian felt a fury rise within him. Was Luce seriously trying to make the princess his most recent love interest? Over his dead fucking body, would Luce get one more fucking second alone with Sole. He knew she was not his to possess, but she was under his protection. He didn't know what game Luce was playing, but somehow during this journey, he had forgotten Rivian was the captain of this ship, and Rivian would remind him of that right fucking now.

Luce continued, "Riv, it makes perfect sense that I join—"

"Let me be clear," Rivian cut him off, addressing no specific person, "Queen Sole is under my protection. She also possesses magick and can fend for herself." Then his eyes lasered in on Luce as he said, "So, this idea that you have, Luce, of spending an exorbitant amount of time with her, ends today. I have never issued such an order. Let's not get the roles confused here, brother. She is not to be approached again. Do I make myself clear?"

Nose flaring, but chastised, Luce simply said, "Yes, my prince. I understand."

"That is all, Luce. You may leave us."

Linking eyes with Zari, Luce made his way to the door and closed it behind him. There was a silence in the room as Zari and Kia took in what had just transpired between Luce and Rivian.

Zari stepped closer to Rivian, who stood as if frozen like a statue. Cold eyes stared back at him. Zari had never seen Rivian like this, not since that one time he was defending Kia from some boys in the Sanctum who wanted to have their way with her.

Unfortunately, many young girls sent to the Sanctum experienced their fair share of abuse. In this instance, Rivian and Kia had been courting for a couple of months when a group of boys surrounded her in between classes. Rivian had been running late to walk her to her next class when he approached the group of boys closing in on her. Rivian had had enough when he witnessed one of the boys touch Kia's long pink hair without her permission. Charging the group, Rivian had grabbed that boy by the hand and broke it in three places. By the end, Rivian had beat them senseless and it was worth the six nights he had earned in the detention box. Before entering the box, he made sure Zari walked Kia to and from class until he returned. It dawned on Zari that Rivian felt something for Sole. This could ruin every plan they put into place.

With a low tone, Zari asked, "Riv, is there something you would like to tell me?"

Looking up at Zari, who was almost an inch taller

than Rivian, he said, "What are you talking about?"

Kia's forest green eyes blazed in fury at the direction of the conversation. "This point has gotten stale. I'm leaving you boys to howl and grunt like animals," she said in short, clipped tones. She turned on her heel and left the room as Rivian and Zari battled it out.

"Come on, Riv, are you making me point out the obvious?"

Rivian didn't like being interrogated by the commander of his army guard, so he moved away from the dining area and started walking back to his quarters.

Zari caught up to him easily and followed him into his cabin, just as Rivian was about to slam the door shut.

"Riv! What the hell is going on between you and the queen of Mōsa?" Zari asked as he squeezed through the door to face an irate Rivian.

Rivian whirled around and snapped, "Nothing! I don't know what you're talking about."

"Very well, I will spell it out for you. That shit that just went down between you and Luce isn't all right. It's as if you are claiming your territory."

"I'm not some dog. I'm not claiming any territory. All I said was that she's under my protection."

"Riv, there's protection, and then there's possession," Zari bit out through clenched teeth. "Is there more going on between you and Sole that I should know about?"

Rivian narrowed his eyes at Zari. "The last time I checked, you weren't the one in charge of this mission, nor the captain of this ship."

"No, I'm not," Zari acknowledged, his tone gentling, "But I am your brother, and we have never hidden anything from each other. I know what you look like when you are falling for someone. Is there something I should know?"

Sighing, Rivian made his way to his marbled desk, and planted his face in his hands. "I don't know when it happened, but at some point over these last twenty days, we have grown closer."

"And by closer, you mean?"

Rivian wanted to tell him how she captivated him the first night he met her in Mōsa or about their many nights in the library where he sometimes pretended to be reading beside her when he was actually taking in her scent and beauty. Tell him how she consumed his every dream and how her laugh brought him a peace he had never known. Instead, he said, "I feel as if I am going mad, brother."

After a long silence, Zari said, "I can sit here and tell you all the reasons this is wrong. You have a plan. We have a plan. Part of the plan is deceiving her. How do you plan to go through with this when you also want to fuck her?"

Rivian was out of his chair in seconds and slammed Zari against the wall, pushing his forearm against his friend's throat. "Don't you ever speak about her that way again!"

Zari, shocked at the ferocity of Rivian's anger, couldn't say anything as he caught his breath.

When Rivian realized what he had done, he let go of his dearest friend, full of disbelief at his own actions. "Zari, forgive me. I forgot myself. Something has changed. I have changed, and I don't know what to do. All I know is that our attraction is a well-balanced kind of madness, and I do not regret it."

Zari straightened his clothes after their mild scuffle and said coldly, "Duty before desire, remember that, prince."

CHAPTER 12

Into the Dark Wilds

This world was never meant to survive the Darkness, so who was she to toy with who survived and who didn't? That was what Sole thought as the Radiant dropped anchor near the edge of the Dark Wilds. Coming from Mōsa's vividly beautiful landscape of greens, blues, and purples to the contrast of the scraggly greys, blacks, and browns of the Dark Wilds was disconcerting. Rock formations that looked like onyx spears stood guard in front of the unwelcoming island, making it impossible for the Radiant to come any closer. As the crew prepared itself for the four-day standstill near the Dark Wilds, Sole took the time to observe the island. It was a chaotic ecosystem of huge, sharp boulders that rose from a mush of black sand and mud that met the sea. Roots of overgrown trees sprawled across the shore. Grains of poison soiled their barks and gleamed like the enchanted sand of Sundom. Beyond the shadows between the trees lay the system of dark caves the island was known for. The decaying air and smothering ambiance provided the perfect home for those who worshipped darkness.

"Are you sure about going through the Dark Wilds with me?" Sole asked Rivian once again. Her question was out of concern for his safety. She was giving him an out. But what she really wanted was an excuse to back out.

He paused from untangling the rope that held the dinghy they were going to use to address her. "It's a little too late for second thoughts now, princess, you think?"

Sole gave him a withering look. "I'm just making sure you know what you're getting into."

Rivian chuckled and began lowering the dinghy from the side of the ship into the water. "Yes. Rest easy," he told her. "You and I will cross the forest and reach the caves by nightfall, get the dagger, and then in the morning, the Radiant will be waiting for us. After that, we journey by land to Sundom's capital. I've been in the forest a couple of times, I know where danger lies, and I know where to find shelter."

Sole gulped and put on a brave face. "And what about the caves?"

Reaching for her hand, Rivian said, "Don't worry, I won't let anything happen to you."

Nisa rushed to Sole's side. Her look was filled with fear as she gazed upon the Dark Wilds for the first time. Nisa took Sole aside to speak with her away from Rivian's ears. "Sole, I still don't trust any of these soldiers. Are you sure I can't come with you?"

Sole nodded gravely. "There are very few people in my life who I trust, Nisa, and you are the only one left alive. I promise I will summon the Misa warriors with the light whistle if I am in danger."

"Does he know about it?"

"Of course, not. No one but you and the Misa's know of the whistle."

Glancing at Rivian, who was busy preparing the Radiant for docking, Nisa said, "I can see how he looks at you. I've only seen one person look at you with those eyes."

"What eyes? " Sole asked with her eyebrows raised.

"He looks at you like Nasir did. And it scares me."

Sole brushed off her friend's concerns and said, "There will be none like Nasir. I have lost much in this life and I'm still reeling from it. I have no plans to open that part of my life again."

Sole wondered where the lies started and where truth began in what she had just told Nisa.

"Have you told the prince that? Because it seems like he's trying his hardest to squeeze himself into your life."

As if on cue, Rivian approached them and asked, "Are you ready?"

Sole was more than grateful for the distraction, and quickly nodded at him.

Luce stood behind Rivian and met Sole's purple gaze. He walked closer to her and said, "Queen, I can't make Rivian see reason. However, I will happily accompany you if you prefer we join you on this retrieval mission."

Rivian's jaw tightened at Luce's words, "We will be fine but thank you for the offer, brother."

Sole could almost cut the tension between Rivian and Luce with a knife. She made a mental note to ask Rivian what was happening with the pair. But that would have to wait until they were alone.

Alone with Rivian. She didn't know why being alone with him unnerved her, but it did. Of course, she would never admit this to anyone, but the idea of being alone with Rivian made her stomach flip.

There was no time to question it as she and Rivian boarded the dinghy and they were lowered into the rising tide. Rivian made quick work of rowing them to the shore, magnificently maneuvering the small boat between the dangerous spikes of stone and mineral with his muscled arms. Pretty soon, they were stepping onto the murky mix of sand and mud, taking care to move quickly so as not to sink. Then, they were in the forest that guarded the caves of the Dark Wilds.

"Will you give me the silent treatment the entire time we are here?"

Rivian's voice broke through Sole's thoughts as they went deeper into the forest.

"Have I not spoken at all?" Sole asked nervously.

Rivian gave her an incredulous look. "The last time you spoke to me, we were still back at the Radiant."

Sole blinked. "Well, it wasn't that long ago."

"It's been an hour and a half."

Sole couldn't help the small smile that broke out. "You're counting?"

Rivian laughed. "Yes. It's very lonely trudging through a forest with a beautiful woman who won't say anything to me or even look at me," he griped. "Talk to me, Sole. What is going through that head of yours?"

Sole sighed. That's exactly what she wanted to avoid, but seeing as they were currently on their way to the cave, she had to make a decision fast.

"I know about your plan, you know," she said quietly. "There's no need to pretend you want to know me, or my thoughts."

That stopped Rivian in his tracks. "What plan?"

Sole continued to walk ahead, carefully looking at where her foot went, anything to avoid looking at Rivian as she talked. "Nisa heard you talk about it with your crew and told me everything. We're not at the Radiant anymore. We're at the Dark Wilds to get the LifeDrinker, and in a day or two, we'll be at the capital of Sundom. You're almost done with your mission."

"Sole..." He reached out for her hand. He pulled her back to him and held her shoulders tightly. "Look at me, Sole."

"It's all right," she murmured, refusing to look up at him and focused instead on his chest and the smattering of dark blond hair peeking from the vee of his shirt. Then she felt Rivian tip her face up and she had no choice but to meet his ice blue eyes. They really were beautiful.

"You don't know everything."

Neither do you, she wanted to say. But instead, she said, "Don't worry, I'll still get your dagger for you, if that's what you want."

"I do want it, Sole—"

"Then that's what we'll do." Sole pulled away from him as she said, "I'll still help you. I only ask that you drop the charming act. It is incredibly unfair to me, and your intended back at Sundom."

Rivian followed her in silence, at war with himself. Then, after a long stretch of silence, he said, "Before I left for Sundom, my father informed me that I was to be married to Selah Grado, a powerful minister's second daughter. It is the age-old story of second sons and daughters being married off to strengthen alliances. So, we have been in the process of getting to know each other."

"Courting, as lovers do."

"No," he said sharply, "negotiating terms. There is no room for love in marriages like this. And as a second son, I shouldn't even dream of love. I figured, as a second son, I didn't need it anyway."

But Sole waved him off and said, "I do not need to know all of this Rivian. I said we're still getting the dagger. Didn't you hear me?"

"But then, I met you," he continued as if he hadn't heard her.

Sole wasn't ready for this. She didn't need this right now. She was in the middle of making one of the most important decisions in her life and it should only involve her and Nasir. No one else.

She sped up her steps across the forest floor. But of course, with Rivian being taller than her, he caught up to her easily. So Sole did the only thing she could do at the moment—run.

She ran and ran even as she saw the spiderwebs shimmering just as she pierced through them. The forest was ancient. Centuries-old trees with sprawling limbs guarded the darkness, blotting out any sunlight.

Clumpy combs of wet moss dangled from their rotten boughs. Underneath the moss, lethal vines sprinkled the mulchy floor. A pungent tang oozed from every sentient being in the forest. It was indeed a place to make her veins freeze over. Everything considered edible in another forest was nauseating here. It left Sole with the same sickening taste of the Darkness and she felt as if she was going to keel over any minute.

Unfortunately, her foot caught on a large tree root that she didn't see which sent her sprawling into a hidden ditch. Down she went, rolling on the wet forest floor as she screamed and caught twigs, dead leaves, and all manner of forest critters in her hair and clothes. It felt like she had been falling forever until she hit the freezing waters of a deep river that flowed back out to the sea.

Panic took over her limbs. She had never learned how to swim back in Mōsa. She thrashed underwater as she sank deeper and deeper.

This is my punishment, she thought as the struggle died out of her. I shouldn't have come here to claim a dagger that can defeat death and use it to revive Nasir.

And with that final thought, she gave up and let the water take her. In her mind, she whispered, Holy Mother, has this always been your answer?

The last thing she saw before falling unconscious was Rivian's face.

When she woke up, she was warm and toasty, and the sweet smell of pine permeated the air. She wondered if she had finally died and gone to heaven. So she opened her eyes a crack to check if her fate was as she thought it to be.

What she found instead was a naked Rivian beside her in front of a fire. Groggily, she thought that it might actually be her version of heaven.

"Good, you're awake. Now I can get your permission."

His gruff voice alerted her to the fact she was not dead, this wasn't heaven, and the most glaring of all was the fact that she was also naked under the pile of dry leaves as large as a window that he must have gathered while she was unconscious.

"What? What permission?" Her voice sounded rough to ears.

"Here's the short version, princess." Rivian said, half mad, half amused. "You drowned. I saved you. We're both wet and in danger of hypothermia. I stripped you. You have an amazing body. So do I. Don't deny it. Out of respect for you, I decided to let you have all the makeshift blankets instead of cozying up next to you while you were unconscious and sharing body heat—which is the most effective way to ward off hypothermia."

Sole's head spun, trying to catch up to what Rivian was saying.

"But now you're awake. And seeing as I saved your life, you owe me. That means you'll scoot over, share that pile of leaves and your body heat with me."

"What?"

"You can't let me die."

"I don't see why not!"

Rivian narrowed his eyes at her. "I didn't let you die."

Sole closed her eyes, knowing she was defeated. She rolled over to the other side so she wouldn't have to look at his naked body.

"Fine," she said in a small voice. She heard him give out a triumphant whoop before she felt him settling in behind her. The moment his skin touched her, Sole's body turned into an inferno.

Rivian moaned behind her, likely finding comfort in the waves of heat coming off of her.

"You know, I just realized I have magick," Sole said.

"Shhh," Rivian whispered as his arms snaked around her, the smattering of golden hair on his forearms tickling the underside of her breasts.

"I can just heal us."

"Try it."

When she put out her hand, the only thing she did was make a purple fireball that healed nothing.

She felt Rivian chuckle behind her as he bent close to her ear and said, "We're not sick with hypothermia yet, magick healer. We're just cold. There's nothing for you to heal."

She huffed at him in response and all he did was tighten his arms around her further.

"Now, settle down, Sole."

"You've been a little too free with my name lately."

Rivian's legs shifted beneath the blanket of dried leaves and she sucked in a breath as she felt the strong column of his cock at the small of her back.

"It's fitting for the moment," Rivian murmured as he nuzzled the hair on top of her head, "Right now, it's just you, and me, and this forest. No titles, no kingdoms, no daggers, no magick. Just a man and a woman and heat."

Sole bit her lip as she fought the urge to squeeze her thighs together, an ache beginning to bloom inside of her.

"You're safe with me princess," Rivian assured her. "The cock at your back isn't a threat."

Sole knew, even if he hadn't told her that, that he was never going to force himself on her. It unsettled her that she knew so little of him, but she felt like she had known him her entire life.

Her gaze drifted around her surroundings to distract her from their warming bodies. The floor of the woods was full of shadows and rocks, and that was as far as she got. As hard as she tried, she couldn't ignore the feeling of his arms around her, the way her nipples were hard points of yearning while his hands and fingers were only millimeters away from them, how her entire back was cushioned by his muscular chest and firm abs.

"Holy Mother," she whispered to herself.

His entire form felt like it was sculpted to perfection, from broad shoulders to sharp masculine facial features. But it was his blue gaze that had always captivated Sole, and she was grateful that with her back to him, he didn't have that advantage of setting her on fire with his ice blue eyes.

But then, one of his strong legs wormed itself between her thighs and she was terrified he would feel her dripping all over him if he moved more. What she wouldn't give to widen her thighs over his large, muscular leg, and move her hips just so…

"Be careful, princess. I can smell your arousal."

Sole swallowed. "The Alacors are half elf and half wolven. I forgot," she said, willing her hips to still and her thoughts to stop straying.

"We can rest here for the night," Rivian said, his voice a low rumble behind her. It wasn't helping to calm her inflamed senses. "Can I ask you something?" he said, figuring it was easier to talk to her like this, with her back to him.

"What would you like to know, Prince Rivian?"

"Do you think you could ever love another?"

Startled by this question, she readily answered, "I don't think I am destined for love again."

"I am sorry if I brought up hard memories with my question."

Several long moments passed before she said, "After surviving the Darkness and gaining magick, I didn't think I deserved more."

"More?"

Rivian felt her nod and he tightened his hold on her. His fingers brushed against a hard nipple, and he heard a tiny mewl escape her. He hadn't meant to do it and quickly apologized.

"It's all right," was her breathless reply.

"Do you regret your love for him?"

"Never."

"Then honor his love not by closing yourself off to the world but letting the world know how amazing you truly are," Rivian said sincerely. "And you are an amazing woman."

Sole's heart melted a little bit more after hearing him say that. Not knowing how to respond, she changed the subject and said, "Do you think they'll wait for us if we take too long in retrieving the dagger?"

"When dawn rises, Luce and Zari will be there at the

shore and stay there until we appear, no matter how long it takes. I am sure nothing will keep Luce from finding you," said Rivian as his jaw tightened.

Sole shook her head and admonished him, "Is he not your brother in arms? Why should it distress you that he has become a friend to me?"

"I am not distressed. Just curious how the Queen of Mōsa has found a kindred spirit in a Sundom soldier."

"Why should it surprise you when I found a kindred spirit in a Sundom prince?"

The words were out of her mouth before she could stop them. Bewildered by what she had just said, she sped ahead and kept on talking, "What is the matter with you? You asked me to try to be pleasant and try to make friends. I did that. You asked me to read the books in the library, and I did that too. But, then, you insist I come with you on this journey which, I might add, is already a disaster, and I did that too."

"Sole…"

"Holy Mother! If there is anything I have learned on this journey with you, Prince Rivian, it is that nothing and no one can please you!"

Without warning, Rivian twisted her around to face him, his arms like steel bands, caging her in his heat. But nothing could prepare her for the blaze in his blue eyes.

"You please me, Sole! Dear Holy Mother, you infuriate me to no end, you frustrate me endlessly, you make me lose my damn mind, but above it all, Lia Soleidae Porte of Mōsa, you please me."

Sole couldn't breathe. All she could do was stare at him, his words ringing in her ears.

"Just being in the same room with you pleases me, Sole. It doesn't matter if it's the library, in the mess hall having breakfast, in the luxurious cabins of the Radiant or on dirty forest floor. It is enough for me to be with you. In case it's not obvious, I'm fucking in love with you."

Sole closed her eyes as his words washed over her. She was so afraid to believe they were true. even though she knew Rivian wouldn't lie about something like this. But it was frightening to have someone hand you something she had wanted forever. Someone to call her own. Something she thought she'd never have again because she knew how much it would cost to have it ripped away.

"Look at me, Sole."

Oh Holy Mother, that soft tone did her in every time. She opened her lavender eyes, and his hand cupped her face.

"Why do you look so scared? "

Licking her lips, she whispered, "I'm less than thirty moons older than you. You told me you didn't remember me at all in the Sanctum, and now love? How do I know you won't change your mind? You are insane."

"I've been in love with you for some time. I just had to see it for myself. And now I can't let go of you. Not ever." Staring straight into her eyes, he said, "You can see I'm being honest with you, now, can't you?"

Sole swallowed, then nodded. "I may regret this tomorrow, but yes. I feel you are telling me the truth." But the fear continued to cripple her.

"I'd be lying if I told you we had an easy road ahead. But one thing is certain. No more lies."

Sole's heart skipped a beat at that, knowing one half-truth she still kept hidden. But Rivian didn't notice it as he went on, "I've never been in a real relationship before. I'm going to mess up regularly. There will be moments you will wonder why you gave me this chance. But Sole, I will give this everything I have. I swear it to the Holy Mother. All I ask in return is that you do the same for me… for us."

Holy Mother, as foolish as this felt, she really wanted it. But how could she dream of this?

There were things she still needed to tell him. "Rivian, there is something I—."

"You're wrong, you know," Rivian interrupted her as his hand caressed her shoulder and slid down the curve of her back, leaving goosebumps in its wake. "I do remember the first time I saw you through my window at the Sanctum. I saw you stand up to those boys who bullied you every day. When you turned around, I thought, Holy Mother, what a beauty. Something clicked in me, and two things became clear, I had to protect you, and my girlfriend at the time no longer existed the moment I saw you."

"What? You told me that you didn't remember me?" She said, confused.

"At first, I didn't, but when you mentioned me stepping in to defend you, it all came rushing back. That was when I ran down the stairs as fast as possible and fucked up those boys. When you stood up and said thank you, I realized you were a Mōsian. I didn't care. I told Zari about the encounter, and he told me I was insane. But I didn't care. I planned to find you the next day and ask if I could walk you to class."

Then Sole remembered why that didn't happen. "But the next day, I was gone," she said.

He nodded and said, "Your parents had come to take you home. After that, I focused on my studies and getting out of there. As the years went by, you faded like a sweet dream. That was until the day you stepped on the Radiant. After your reminder, it all flooded back. I knew I needed to get to know you, and I couldn't screw it up this time."

"Well, you're doing a bang-up job! Do you always treat your ladies this way? You said it, I'm from Mōsa, and you are from Sundom. We are enemies."

"That is not what we are, and you know it."

"What I am is forbidden fruit. You must know that now."

"What you are is you. Smart, brave, witty, steady, loyal, and fucking beautiful. I fell hard, Sole, and there is nothing I can do about it."

Her throat thickening, Sole bit her lip again as he curved his hand across her nape, pulling her so close to him that her nipples were crushed against his hard, warm chest.

"You taught me that you are my equal," Rivian said roughly, his control slipping as her legs shifted restlessly against his own. "Shit, you are probably way beyond me. But I want you to be as attached to me as I have become attached to you. I was undone the moment I saw you board the Radiant. When you smile, my heart feels like it is crashing into a million pieces. When I cause you pain, I can't resist thinking of what an ass I am."

He bent his head, their foreheads touching, and said softly, "It's not easy to see you now like this, so soft." His hand started travelling down her arm, the dip of her waist, the swell of her hips. "So warm, so sweet."

Then his hand spread around a generous globe of her buttocks and squeezed just as he pressed a muscular thigh between the valley of her legs.

"And so fucking wet for me."

Sole let out a moan that could have been heard all over the Dark Wilds.

His mouth took her mouth, and his hand was suddenly at her breast, molding their shape to his large palm. "You are a force like I have never known Sole," he whispered into her lips. He drew back from her, waiting for a response.

Sole looked up at him with her electric violet eyes, and said, "Kiss me again, Prince Rivian. Drown me in your kisses and make me forget everything."

Her muscles tightened as he kissed her neck and slid his hands down her body. His tongue collided with hers. This kiss was uncharted. Nasir had been a fantastic kisser, but she had never been kissed like this before. Never.

He moved over her as his teeth gently nipped her lower lip. Lifting his head, his chest rose and fell raggedly. He closed his eyes and moaned when he felt her small hands begin to explore his chest and down his stomach. When he reopened his eyes, they were like molten lava staring back at her.

"I love the feel of your skin against mine," Rivian

rasped as he leaned down to ravage her lips once more, making sure to let her feel all of him, but taking care not to put all of his weight on her. His voice was low, hoarse, and desperate. His hand gently traced the sides of her breast, and he sat up as if he wanted to study her deep mahogany skin that glowed in the firelight. Removing her golden hair twist, Sole's coiled locks cascaded over her shoulders like a sea of cinnamon-brown consuming the grass around her. Staring at her puffy, pouting pink lips, he couldn't help but run his thumb over her bottom lip and feel how soft they were.

Sliding his hands down her flat stomach and thighs, he curled his finger against that heated part of her. She was so wet that his fingers had no trouble finding all her exposed nerve endings. She jerked with pleasure. She was no virgin, but lovemaking never felt like this.

Then, staring at her with a deep hunger in his eyes, he inserted another finger into her heat and began to slowly, deeply, thrust them into her aching center. He wanted to see her come apart for him.

When he looked down at her sex, wetly swallowing his large, thick digits, his mouth watered. So he lifted her hips and the next thing she knew, his mouth was on her. His tongue delved into her heat as he gripped her cinnamon-colored breast. His head twisted as he released a cry of deep please out of her. The strokes on his tongue were fierce and possessive. He sucked, licked, and kissed her sex until she reminded herself to breathe again. He feasted, and she was lost. Her passion caused her to move under him, but his hands held her in place. The heat growing in Sole was fierce, almost too intense. Her toes curled, and she yelled, "Please, don't stop!"

Choking on a scream, she was undone. Tight spasms took over as his mouth moved up to her neck.

Rivian whispered, "Sole, you taste delicious." He groaned. "I need more, more of you."

She was still trembling when the head of his cock nudged her core. He didn't go in yet but gave her a swirl of anticipation. His fingers trembled as he gripped her hips, and with a thick and needy voice, he said, "Sole, I am losing control."

"I want you too," was Sole's needy reply, followed by a swivel of her hips, letting him know in no uncertain terms what she wanted.

Smiling, he thrust deeply into her hot core. The feel of him filling, stretching her, dominated her, made her lose her mind. He held her there, and there was no hesitation. He moved fast and hard. Sole felt his throbbing length go in and out of the entire length of her body. He had her head spinning with pleasure.

"Rivian," she whispered, catching her breath. "Don't

stop."

Suddenly he slid out and shifted her body to face away from him. He drew her hips flush against his. His hand on her back arched her over as he shoved himself into her again and again.

"Hold onto me," he commanded and Sole's arms reached back and held firmly onto his thighs. When he was sure that Sole was fastened around him, he began pounding in and out of her mercilessly. The sounds he made as he took her were scandalous.

Sole loved it.

Then Rivian's hands tightened on her hips and he rose up without warning.

Sole moaned in surprise as her knees and feet left the floor and she was suspended in midair, anchored to the world only by the strength of his arms and his cock inside her.

Looking at Sole with his passionate blue gaze, he said, "Brace yourself, sweet princess."

He lunged in and out of her body and she loved how she could do nothing but moan and take his fucking for what seemed like forever.

Then she heard Rivian mutter, "I need to see your face when I fill you up." She felt herself being lowered to the forest floor once more. Rivian spun her around to face him. Then he sat down on the ground and spread his legs. His long, hard cock stood proudly, wet with her juices.

He took her hands and guided her down onto his lap. Her breasts rubbed against the warmth of his chest as she felt him slide her back down onto his waiting cock. He was so deep in her this way, and yet she wanted more.

He changed the angle of his thrusts, and her sensitive clit was hit full force by his rocking pelvis. Here was no control, no restraint, and Sole didn't want to run. His slick feel and dominance consumed her. His hips rolled, and his head kicked back as she gasped for air. She saw him watching her breasts move with every thrust and that made her push them out further.

Deep stunning thrusts consumed both Sole and Rivian as they found their bodies wrapped tightly around each other. And suddenly, something happened. All she could feel was his lust and love for her. This had never happened to her.

He watched her, obsessed, as they both crashed into each other. The waves of lust crashed into both of them like a tsunami. Together, they came undone.

Minutes later, Rivian watched her sleep and thought she was the most beautiful being he had ever seen. But how could he go through with his plan and risk losing her?

"Your thoughts are so loud," Sole groaned as she woke and reached out for him, almost on instinct.

She opened her eyes enough to see his staring at her and her body flushed hot. When he felt her reach down to grasp his hardening cock, his mind went blank.

He said nothing, simply watching her intently as she slid down his lean hips. His body jerked as he felt her hot mouth close around him.

They were in the Dark Wilds and this moment belonged to them and them only, both of them wanting to make the moment last longer, to have more to remember, before things would eventually come crashing down and they would be forced to let go of each other. But not tonight. Not just yet.

CHAPTER 13

Out of the Dark Wilds

They moved in the dark of the night, just a few hours shy of the dawn. Wordlessly, they had extinguished the fire that had warmed them up through the night and left the forest floor that had been witness to their whispered confessions. Their bodies that had moved so in tune with each other were now stilted and awkward, as if the growing space was preparing for the lies they were now both rehearsing in their heads.

They had a job to do, a love to betray, and a dagger to claim. There was no more time for anything else, or any other emotion.

By the time they reached the mouth of the cave, Sole had come to a decision. She followed him into the dark, lighting his way with a brilliant purple flame in the palm of her hand.

It wasn't challenging to locate the LifeDrinker. It almost called out to Sole's magick. Glowing in harmony with her flame while luring them in. In the deepest, darkest corner of the cave, betwixt ferocious rock formations arranged like deadly ancient sea monster teeth lie the glowing blade. It was a dagger unlike any other. The hilt was fashioned from the bones of those long past. Twisting and writhing around a core of what looked like a living red rose only to extend, become narrow and yawn with a slicing smile for a bevel.

Neither of them moved for a few quiet moments. Then, Sole reached out to Rivian and curled her hand around his bicep. It was the first time that she had touched him since last night.

Her hand was icy cold.

Rivian looked at her and said, "Having second thoughts? Just tell me, Sole."

Sole shook her head. "No, my mind has never been clearer. We're going to get the dagger. But I need to tell you something first."

Rivian felt like screaming at her. Don't be brave. Be afraid. Tell me you don't want to get the dagger. Tell me you want to run away with me, and I'll keep you safe. He wanted to yell all those things at her, but he kept his mouth shut.

It wasn't just his kingdom that was at stake here, but the rest of the world. If the prophesied betrayer rose in Sundom, and the dark throne along with him, the world wouldn't have a chance. He had to get that dagger.

"I haven't been honest with you."

For a moment, Rivian wondered if it was he who had said it. But when Sole said, "I knew about the LifeDrinker and Dark Wilds before I ever saw them in your library, even before I saw you and set foot on the Radiant. You thought you were taking me here, but I was the one who wanted to go here. You see, before I met you, all I ever asked the Holy Mother for, in exchange for healing all those who asked to be healed, friend or enemy, was the chance to revive Nasir."

Rivian's heart stuttered with her confession.

"You were going raise him from the dead? Are you insane?" His yell reverberated throughout the cave as if asking the question again and again. Was she the betrayer? Even thinking about her that way felt like a betrayal for Rivian.

"Shut up," Sole hissed, "Don't collapse the cave on us. I said that was what I had planned before I met you. Calm down."

"How? How do I calm down, Sole?"

"By shutting up and letting me finish."

"Fine."

"If you're going to be this way, we might as well just get the dagger and get this shit over with."

"I said, fine! Finish this story."

Sole drew on every last shred of patience she had as she continued speaking. "I said, that was all I wanted before you. And then you happened!"

Rivian snarled, "I'm sorry I ruined your dance with the dead."

"Oh, shut up!"

"Yes, Lia Soleidae Porte of Mōsa, tell me more of your evil plans!" Rivians blue eyes flashed angrily at her. Sole's pulse quickened when she saw the blue of his eyes turn to an amber glow and her skin prickled at the electricity in the air. Then as quickly as it appeared, it was gone.

Sole thought she had dreamed it up, and so she continued. Shaking her head to clear the cobwebs in her brain, she said, "Seriously, I never thought you would be this dramatic. Well, my evil plan, as you call it, was to take the dagger, revive Nasir, and give you the dagger if you still wanted it. I know you think it holds some sort of power and I really don't care for it. All I wanted in the world was—"

"Nasir! Nasir! Yes, I get it! The forest gets it. The cave gets it! Tell me something I don't know, Sole."

Sole simply looked at him, out of patience. "I love you."

That shut Rivian up.

"When I met you, all thoughts of reviving Nasir

disappeared. Why would I cling to the past when you were here, present, and most of all, alive? Loving you didn't feel like I was committing a crime against nature, against magick. Loving you felt right." Sole, smirked at him. "Did I do it right?"

Rivian could only whisper, "Do what right?"

"Tell you something you don't know?"

Rivian nodded. He moved swiftly and crushed her lips with his in a bruising kiss that promised wicked things later, much later. Sole let him ravage her mouth, and the pushed him when she began to need air.

"Now let's get this damn dagger and get out of here," she said with a grin. Her fleeting grin dropped when the amber glow in his eyes came back. She wasn't afraid of him, never. But she did want the truth after she had told him her truth.

Gently, she cupped his smiling face and asked, "Now, is there anything you would like to tell me? A secret you want to share?"

Rivian's heart dropped to his stomach, "Like what?"

"When were you going to tell me that you also have magick?"

Of all the things Sole could say, Rivian hadn't expected this. He burst out laughing, hunched over and slapped his thighs as he laughed and laughed.

"Sole! I'm the unwanted second son. If there's anyone

going to be blessed with magick in my family, it would be Rill!"

Sole frowned at him. Could it be that he was not aware of what he was doing? Slowly, she eased her hand behind her and willed the purple glow in her hand to die down.

Instantly, the cave turned to amber.

"You have no idea, do you?" Sole said, as Rivian's laughter died down.

"Holy Mother, Sole! Stop changing the subject. Are you just shy because you confessed that you love me?"

"Rivian, you have magick."

"A magick cock, maybe," he gave her a salacious grin.

Sole rolled her eyes at him. "Look around you, Rivian!" she snapped.

Still clueless, Rivian made a show of looking around. "Okay? Now what?"

"What color is the cave right now?"

"Dark yellow, like amber."

"What color signature is my magick?"

"Is this a trick question to know if I really know you and therefore will measure how much I love you?"

"Just answer the fucking question!"

"Fine! Purple!"

Sole waited for him to put the pieces of the puzzle together.

"Your magick is... purple," he said as he looked around, truly looked around. "Why is the cave..."

"You're lighting up the cave with your magick, Rivian," she said as she showed him her hand, empty of the purple flame.

"I know one more way to confirm this," she said with a determined look on her face. Then, quick as lightning, she ran towards the LifeDrinker.

Horror gripped Rivian as he screamed at her, "No! Sole, stop!"

Both he and Sole stumbled back as a blast of amber wave came out of his outstretched hand the dagger flew up in the air, vibrated in the middle of the cave, and then landed cleanly on Rivian's palm.

Sole grinned as she whispered, "Rivian, you have magick."

He smiled at her as his hand closed over the hilt of the LifeDrinker. "I have magick," he said with wonder in his voice. Then, he slipped the dagger into the satchel he had carried just for it. Grinning wickedly at Sole, he stretched out his hand once more, testing a theory that had formed in his head.

"Now, my love, let's get out of this damn cave," he said as he flexed his fingers. A wave of amber light came once more and Sole found herself sailing across the cave to land inside Rivian's outstretched arms. "I can't wait to test out this magick while we're in bed," he said as he pressed his face into her neck. "Oh, Sole, all the things I can do to your sweet little body."

Sole swatted his chest as she giggled, "You get magick after entering a mysterious cave and all you can think about is how to use it while we're having sex?"

Rivian inhaled her sweet scent once more before releasing her so they could make the trek back to the beach and back into the Radiant. The relief he felt when Sole's hand never touched the dagger was incomparable to any feeling, even learning that he had magick. He didn't know how the dagger worked just yet, or how dangerous it was for her. But he wasn't going to risk her hand touching it, not while he was alive.

"Let's get out of here," he said as he pressed a kiss to her temple.

A voice inside her head pinched Sole, and she stopped walking. Turning to look at him, she said, "Before we go, what will we tell the others about the dagger, your magick, and us?"

Smiling that crooked smile, he pulled her close to him as he whispered, "I am not about to give you up."

"Neither am I," she concluded.

"I sense a but coming."

"I think we should wait for all of it. You still need to figure out your magick, the blade and this," motioning her hands between the two of them.

Gently brushing her long locks behind her small ear he spoke in quiet tones "So now we are the ones keeping secrets? I like that," he whispered with voice low and gravelly.

"I'm serious!" as her voice echoed in the cavern.

He could detect some fear in her voice, but mostly he felt her protection, or was it, love? Either way, he would do anything she asked.

"I know, and I agree. We will keep what we have found and what has transpired between us for now."

Eyes locking in passion and agreement, they stepped out of the cave system into the wild expanse of the dark forest, hand in hand.

CHAPTER 14

Heart's Betrayal

Back at the Radiant, Sole and Rivian tried their hardest to keep their hands off each other in front of his crew. She also stayed within earshot of him to make sure he didn't accidentally reveal that he had magick.

On the trek back, they had agreed on three things. One, that they would keep Rivian's magick a secret from everyone until they figured out what triggered it and if the dagger had anything to do with it. Two, that they would keep even the existence of the dagger a secret, until after Sole had healed Rivian's father and figured out what Rill's plan for the dagger was. And three, that Rivian should hold on to the dagger. Should anyone question them when expressing they didn't find it, Sole's things would be the obvious first place to search.

In truth, those were all Sole's conditions and Rivian just found himself agreeing to them because they served him perfectly. That placed her out of danger of the dagger, and he had an excuse to be near her all the time. And since he was sure that Rill's intentions with the dagger were pure, he would be able to hand the dagger to his brother after Sole was satisfied with the outcome.

It truly was perfect, except for the fact that he was betraying his whole crew. It was a price Rivian was willing to pay, if only for a few days.

They were about to dock at Akariar, the port city of Sundom, and from there, it was a few days journey to the capital, where the palace was. Once his responsibilities to his family and to Sundom had been fulfilled, he would make it up to his chosen family, the second sons and daughters of the Radiant, and tell them the whole truth.

He just had to keep himself from strangling Zari, who kept giving him dark, disapproving looks. He knew Zari had been trying to corner him since he and Sole got back from the Dark Wilds, but there was never any chance for a private chat.

But now that they were about to disembark, Rivian considered allowing his dearest friend a chance to yell at him. So, instead of stopping by Sole's cabin to let her know they were about to dock, he went straight to his own cabin, knowing Zari had been following him. At least in his room, their argument would be private.

Sure enough, only a few minutes after he had shut his cabin door, he heard Zari's distinctive knock.

Steeling himself for the fight that would ensue, Rivian called out, "I know it's you Zari. Come on in."

A few doors away, Sole had been impatiently waiting for Rivian to collect her in time for the Radiant to dock at the port city. She had been excited to be on land after being at sea for so long, and to see civilization after the harrowing experience at the Dark Wilds. She knew the sound of his footsteps and was perplexed when it didn't stop by her door, and instead, she heard him head straight to his cabin. She sagged in disappointment.

However, she perked up a few moments later when someone knocked on the door.

"Come in!" Sole said.

When Luce stepped into the doorway, she couldn't help the feeling of disappointment that came over her. If Sole was honest, his lambent, meltwater-blue eyes made him appealing. Coupled with his dark hair, his eyes captivated. However, they weren't the same as Rivian's. His eyes bewitched her.

"Stop thinking about him all the time," she whispered to herself. "You aren't an eight-year old girl with a crush!"

Would she ever stop thinking about his eyes, those golden, firm hands that caressed her body?

"Sole, are you with us?" Nisa asked. Sole hadn't

even seen Nisa as she entered her room through their adjoining door. "Luce asked you if you were excited to see Sundom."

Apparently, aside from being blind, she was also deaf.

"Oh! My apologies, Luce. The waves kept me awake the whole time we were at sea. So, I am eager to be on land again, whether it's Sundom or anywhere else."

"And so you will," he said as he smiled. "Come up to the deck with me and let me show you our port city. It's visible now."

Sole looked at Nisa, whose bright eyes had begun to shine in interest. Having nothing to do, Sole shrugged her shoulders and said, "It wouldn't hurt to watch Sundom from afar and familiarize myself with its silhouette against the sky."

So they made their way up to the viewing deck which was right above the captain's quarters. Luce wasn't lying about Akariar, it was highly visible from where they were. And as the Radiant crept closer, the bustling city came to life.

"This is the first time in four generations that anyone from Mōsa has stepped on Sundom sand," Luce said as he stood beside her. "What do you think so far?"

Sole looked ahead of her and was taken aback by the rippling blanket of the blue jeweled sea. Squabbling gulls flew overhead, harassing the merchant sailors.

The horizon was edged with rich ginger and pinkish tint as the gulls flew into that place where sun and water meet.

"It's captivating."

The briny air carried a different smell from the sweet smell of the Serena Sea. What captivated Sole and Nisa most were the waves of golden dunes that lay before them. As Sole looked at the dock, she saw what appeared to be a sea of red and orange tents sitting upon the glistening white sand.

Sole pointed at them and asked Luce, "What are all those tents for?"

Smiling, Luce said, "Ahh, yes, that is the market at Akariar, where you can find just about anything and everything." Then, he leaned into Sole's ear with a sly smile and whispered, "Take care of your pockets and gems–this market is renowned for being busy and crowded."

"What is that delicious smell?" asked Nisa.

"Ah, you can get the best roast around right here in our market but don't tell my mum I said that," Luce said with a devilish grin.

Sole and Nisa laughed. Then, Luce looked over at Sole and said, "You look different today, queen."

Nisa beamed beside Sole. "She looks stunning in her mother's Sundom clothes, doesn't she?" she said.

Luce nodded his head and winked appreciatively at Sole, "Yes she does."

Sole felt as if this journey into the Sundom capital was like going into battle. That was why wearing her mother's golden armor felt appropriate. The suit was made from the finest woven threads of gold Mōsa had to offer. Her silk sleeveless bodice housed a plunging neckline forming a V from her neck to her navel with golden embroidery covering her chest. Her form-fitting cream leggings had a sheer glaze accentuating her muscular, lean legs. She coupled that with her cream-colored linen cape embroidered with the golden waves of Mōsa.

Freed from her braids, her chocolate coils hung low, resting on her lower back. In traditional Mōsian war gear, Sole marked her mahogany skin with golden ascar paints. Her face held the dark bronze glow of the Mōsian markings, while her breast bone was adorned with outlines of their moons. Her serene face had two vertical lines of gold that settled on her high cheekbones. Her full crimson lips had one golden vertical line that settled on the center and glistened in the setting sun. The crown that she had fashioned from her father's old crown and mother's mirror sat atop her head.

Nisa suddenly sighed and said, "Well, as much as I enjoy looking at the city, I have to go and make sure Sole's travel trunks are ready to offload when we disembark."

She turned to Luce and said, "May I leave her in your care?"

Luce nodded his assent.

Just as Nisa turned, a great commotion rumbled from below. Startled, Luce, Nisa, and Sole looked down and wondered what was happening. When rising voices reached their ears and the sound of breaking furniture reached them, all three spun into action and ran towards the captain's cabin.

Below them, Zari's voice had reached a fever pitch as he yelled at at Rivian.

"Do you not understand the consequences of your actions?"

Rivian could only shake his head as he tried to ward off the dizziness that came after Zari had punched him square in the jaw. He had to let Zari get his licks in. His entire room was a mess of wrecked furniture and various broken things. His books were on the floor, his window had a hole in it, and his cabin door hung precariously on one hinge.

"Zari, you don't understand—"

"Of course I don't! I am not a spoiled prince like you are! I will never trade in the fate of Sundom for a little romp in the forest with a woman!"

"Fate of Sundom? Holy Mother, that's a little too

much, Zi."

"Do you just think with your cock all the time, Rivian? Couldn't wait to get into the sack and didn't spend another hour looking for the dagger when it became too much, huh?"

"We did look very hard for it, Zari. I don't know what else to tell you!"

"Not as hard as you fucked her, I presume?"

This time, Rivian didn't hold back and launched himself at Zari.

"I told you never to speak about her like that!" he yelled as his fist connected with Zari's nose, tossing him to the deck. "You know nothing about her!"

"I know enough to know that she isn't worth sacrificing the whole of Sundom."

Rivian's heart ached and desperately wanted his dearest friend to understand. "Zi, the dagger can't bring back magic to Sundom. That's not what it does."

Zari froze, "What the fuck are you talking about? Isn't that what Rill told you when he sent you on this mission?"

Rivian shook his head. "He also sent me books, scrolls, and tomes that taught me about the dagger. I think that was his roundabout way of telling me something important without broadcasting it to everyone."

"You're talking about the prophecy?"

Rivian nodded, "Zi, the prophecy speaks of a betrayer rising from the sands of Sundom and the dagger, LifeDrinker, the only thing that can defeat this betrayer's dark throne, is also the only thing that can kill someone with magick. It can kill Sole."

"And yet, you took me to the Dark Wilds, anyway, knowing that?"

Rivian's blood froze as he heard Sole's small voice behind him. He whirled around, horrified to see Sole standing there with Nisa and Luce.

"How much did you hear?"

"Enough to break my heart," was Sole's wooden response.

Then they all felt the unmistakable thud of a ship dropping anchor as it reached the dock. Silence came over the group. The Radiant's journey had finally come to an end, but none of them felt the triumph of a sailor's homecoming.

Then they heard the sound of small, graceful feet running across the deck and taking the stairs two at a time. When it reached them, they saw it was Kia, breathless from her effort to tell them, "Rivian, it's Rill. He's coming aboard to see how well you did on your mission."

Then, upon noticing the state of the captain's quarters, Kia asked, "Holy Mother, what the fuck happened here?"

Suddenly, Luce approached Sole, and said, "Sole, you are the strongest woman I know. Your life has been filled with great joys and losses, but you have survived it all. You will survive this too."

Sole looked sadly at Rivian, unable to find comfort in Luce's words. And then suddenly, she felt a terrible pinch in her neck. Reaching up to her neck, she pulled a red-feathered dart.

Slurring, she called out Nisa's name. Then she turned clumsily and caught a glimpse of Rory and her Misa warriors at the far end of the corridor, slumped on the ground, including Nisa. Each one with a similar, red-feathered dart embedded in a similar fashion.

Before she could fall to the ground, Rivian caught her as he cried out her name.

"Ri…" His name was a faint whisper on her lips. With rage burning behind his eyes, he knew that his eyes had turned amber. And so he buried his face in her neck to hide his eyes from his friends.

"What have you done, Luce?" he bellowed as Sole fell unconscious.

"Give her to me, Rivian," Luce said gently, as if he was talking to a rabid animal. "You will understand in time. Just please, give her to me."

"Rivian."

He knew that voice.

Schooling his features as best as he could, Rivian looked up to find his brother standing in the wreckage of his cabin in the Radiant.

"Give her to me."

He felt a prick on the side of his neck, as darkness overcame him.

CHAPTER 15

Gilded Cage

When Sole awakened from the dart's deep sleep, a terrifying familiar feeling held her captive; she was alone with the one thing she never wanted. Magick.

It took Sole a moment for her eyes to adjust to the bright light. The sun never shined this bright in Mōsa. She heard voices around her, telling her to take it easy. Her entire body throbbed with pain for some reason. Opening her eyes, the faces staring back at her were not familiar.

"Queen, you were given a dose of medicine to keep your journey into Sundom private," said the tall, lean man with sun kissed brown skin. He wore a white linen tunic that was see through, showing his lean abs.

Sitting up, Sole struggled to catch her breath. There were two or three Sundom citizens surrounding her bed. Grabbing her hands and legs, they forced her back onto the soft pillows. The room spun and her blurry eyes became heavy once more. As she fell back to her deep sleep, she only had one question. "Where is he? Where is Rivian?" before the deep sleep consumed her once more.

As her eyes closed, Sole had the same dream again. She was back in Mōsa, sitting on the pink sands of the Serena Sea as the orange-pink sky danced across the bioluminescent ocean. The pink moons rising. Standing, she walked towards the waves. The laughter of her sisters Luna and Lola drew her in. Lola's wet wavy hair laid flat against her deep brown skin. Luna's laugh seemed so natural. She never thought she would hear that laugh again. The more they splashed water on each other, the faster Sole ran to her sisters.

Suddenly Luna's hazel eyes, her mother's eyes, stared back at Sole. Standing next to Luna, Lola reached out her hands toward Sole, saying, "Where have you been, Sole? We have been waiting for you." Overcome with grief and joy, Sole's eyes filled with tears. Putting her hands in Luna's, the girls cried, hugged, and Sole couldn't help but believe this was real. Maybe she had finally died. Perhaps she could finally find peace. Lola looked at Sole with eyes full of love saying, "I can't wait to see you again."

Luna grabbed Sole's hands, whispering, "Once the three rise, the bond shall bring forth an age of magick and an era of sorrow. The sorrow is coming, and we must prepare. Wake, Sole, wake."

As quickly as those words were spoken, Sole awoke to a pool of dripping sweat on an unfamiliar bed. Looking around, Sole saw a strange, beautiful golden room with flowing burnt orange silk curtains.

Sitting on the bed, Sole sat facing the geodesic dome room that perfectly combined comfort and luxury like she had never seen before. Rising from the bed, her bare feet made the warm wooden floor creak. Making her way to the domed-shaped windows, it was clear she had made it to Sundom.

Pushing the vibrant orange curtains to the side opened the view of mountainous golden sand dunes surrounding the city. From her large windows, Sole could see the desert palace of King A'dien. Queen Lygia once told Sole that the desert palace was spectacularly located on beautiful, irrigated estates, including a sanctum, seasonal baths, and an official hall with an ornate golden throne room.

Turning from the window to face her room, Sole knew two things. First, Sundom was exquisite; second, it was her magnificent prison.

Sole thought back to her dream, No, it wasn't a dream. It was a vision. Her sisters were waiting for her. Could they be alive? It was impossible. Thinking back to the words Aurora had told her when she asked about her sisters, she said, "They were gone." Not dead.

"Not dead," she whispered. "I need a plan. Someone has to do something, and that someone has to be me."

As she waited for Rivian, her jailer, to come for her, she would find a way to gain his trust. Then, she would escape this place with her guards and Nisa, and together, they would go in search of Luna and Lola. But first, she needed a plan. As a young child she was known for her strategic planning which is why her sister Lola always picked her brain when it came to getting revenge on the cute boys that often tortured her.

Sole opened the door to her gilded cage and saw two maids in white linen tunics waiting to bathe and dress her. When asked what this was about, Sole was informed that she, her maids, and the Misa warriors had been summoned by the king. They were all expected to show up at the evening feast.

And so, she allowed herself to be bathed and dressed by the servants, who probably doubled as her jailers. She would be patient until she could get some answers.

There was a knock at the door, and her tall blonde maid went to open it. She saw Zari and Luce walk in. Sole took a step back. She had no idea who her friends and foes were. She raised her glowing hand and said, "Don't come any closer."

At seeing her rage, Zari said, "Sole, Queen Sole, you have every right to be upset. Our apologies for the harsh tactics of Luce. He wanted to make sure you were not seen upon entering the castle. The…" Zari cleared his throat and continued. "The king wanted to ensure he introduced you at the feast this evening. This way, we could ensure you were safe."

"Where is Nisa? If you have harmed anyone in my court, I will—"

"Sole, I would never allow any harm to come to Nisa. I assure you she is safe and you will see her this eve. For now, we only ask that you allow us to explain everything to you this evening," Zari said with concerned eyes.

"Where is he? Is he afraid to face me?" She asked Luce.

Cautiously closing the distance between them, Luce approached, saying, "Rivian is probably avoiding you, but he will be at the feast this evening. You can talk to him then."

"I will go see your so-called king, but I will not sit quietly after I was tranquilized and separated from my entourage. If they are not brought to this room by this eve, I will bring these walls down in search of them. Do you understand?"

Zari and Luce looked warily at her hands, wondering if she was just as capable of damage as she was with healing.

"Now, leave me!"

With stone faces, Zari and Luce made their way to the door.

"Oh, and Luce?" she called out and waited until the tall handsome man who had once made her laugh on the Radiant turned to her.

"Yes, my queen?"

"Never come to my room again or directly address me by my name or title. You, sir, are no friend of mine."

When the door shut behind them, Sole returned to her preparations for the feast. After hours spent prepping, bathing, and being groomed, Sole glanced in the mirror. She could barely recognize herself.

No longer wearing her tattered travel garments, she entered the hall in the most elegant rose gold gown to ever grace the palace. A pattern of roses and vines on lace circled her delicate neck. The same lace hugged the curve of her breasts in a V pattern that ended just below her navel. They were held together by a sheer chiffon that was so close to her skin, she almost looked naked, save for the lace. Her gown clung to her generous hips, down to her thighs and flared out from her knees in a beautiful mermaid tail bottom, with a slit up her right leg that ended mid-thigh.

No one could take their eyes off her. Standing at the

entrance, they announced her arrival.

"All rise as we welcome Queen Lia Soleidae of Porte house, the second daughter of Mōsa, risen healer of the Serena Sea, the blessing of Sundom, the unbreakable wielder of magick, and the last of her name."

The intricate rose gold beading pattern atop the lace on her gown gave her the illusion of being dipped in shimmering pink rhinestones when they shone the spotlight on her. As she walked, the delicate fabric clung to her body, falling to the floor and splashing like a cascade of rose gold. Her long diamond earrings dangled down to her shoulders, emphasizing her long delicate neck, made even more provocative with her cinnamon-colored hair gathered in soft, elegant swirls on top of her head.

The music in the banquet hall was vibrant, and the guest were all chatting and rustling about in their fancy golden rags. Adorned with varying shades of gold, Sole was taken aback by how this vibrant city feasted while the rest of the world died from the Darkness. The long table at the center of the room was lavishly decorated with gorgeous white roses. The smell of delicious meats covered the room like a sweet perfume.

"Sole!" a powerful voice called from the crowd. Turning, she saw Nisa running to her. Sole almost didn't recognize Nisa in her solid gold two-piece dress. The golden fabric band stretches across her chest, exposing her shoulders and firm stomach. Her fitted long golden skirt with a cutout that extends to her hips highlighted her amazing legs. Paired with her clear glass heels, it made her a goddess. The men of Sundom were not ready for Nisa.

Embracing, the two women almost cried, but they knew this was not the time for tears. They had to devise a plan. While they hugged, Sole whispered, "Are you all right?"

"Yes!" Nisa laughed off Sole's apparent concern. "They didn't harm us at all. In fact, we were treated like royalty with servants attending to all our needs. Now, tell me, how are you, my queen?"

"I am a good, sister. But we have much to discuss," Sole said, hoping no one was listening. "Tell me, Nisa, where are the girls? Have you seen Rory?"

"They are well," Nisa said, placing a gentle hand on her friend's arm, trying to calm her. "Zari has assured me they will be here tonight."

"Zari? You're still speaking to him?" she asked Nisa incredulously.

Nisa looked confused by her reaction. "Um, yes, why wouldn't I?"

"They drugged us and snuck is into the palace!"

Nisa waved her hand and said, "That was Luce. Zari

is innocent."

"But—"

"Lady Nisa Asha and her royal highness, Queen Lia Soleidae Port of Mōsa," a tall, bearded servant who appeared beside them startled the two women. "Your presence is requested at the table of honor."

Nisa and Sole had no other choice but to follow him as he escorted them to the high table where the king and his family would be seated. Sole held a royal expression, but beneath the table, her damp fists crushed the delicate silk of her evening gown. At the same time, her glistening heels tapped a rapid rhythm. Suddenly everyone rose as the royal family waited to be introduced.

"Showtime," Nisa said as they rose from their seats.

CHAPTER 16

Oaths

"This is bullshit." Rivian paced the ornate crimson rug in his father's study. "You know this is utter fucking bullshit, Rill."

Lounging in the crimson leather armchair Rill said nothing.

"What's the matter, Rivian? Did you forget your oath?" Luce added to taunt him as he leaned against the mantel right across the huge antique table.

Rivian's eyes heated like hot coals and he looked away in case they were amber. "I will deal with you later, brother," he said acidly, his tongue souring on the last word.

Pushing off the marbled mantel, Luce strode towards the doors.

"You know, Rivian, while you were out cavorting with the queen, we were ensuring Sundom still stood. So, if you want to blame anyone for how things went down, you only have yourself to blame." And with that, he was gone.

Turning back to face Rill, Rivian continued, "Brother, I brought her here thinking Father needed to be healed. Why did you not write to explain that Father, our king, had already died?"

His brother, the fucking bastard, seemed bored. Standing, Rill said, "Riv, my apologies for not reaching you sooner. Please, forgive Luce's judgment in darting the princess and her entourage. He did so on my order."

"He darted me, too."

With jaw tightening, Rill spoke, "He did, but only after I asked where you were. Luce explained that you had become compromised, and darting you was the only way we could get her into the castle, as I had requested."

Dumbfounded, Rivian answered, "Compromised? That is bullshit."

"I grew close to her to gain her trust, and in the Dark Wilds, we searched for the LifeDrinker, Dagger of Broken Bones. It's the only weapon known to kill the betrayer. And make no mistake, with magick rising, the betrayer will come."

Locking eyes with Rivian, Rill gave him a slow clap and said, "You have done well, little brother. After the feast, you will bring Sole to me, and she will bring the dagger, and I will keep it safe."

Through gritted teeth, he said, "For the hundredth time, Rill, she does not have it." He wasn't lying, that was for sure.

In a fury, Rill left the table and began to pace. Then he suddenly stopped and faced Rivian. And with with eyes of ice, eyes Rivian had only ever glimpsed in his father's face, Rill asked, "Who else knows about the dagger's true power?"

"Only Sole, myself, Luce, and Zari. We agreed not to tell anyone until we reached Sundom. Until we reached you."

"I knew I could trust you, Riv. Luce said you were too far gone, but I knew different."

"Brother?" Rivian said, reaching for Rill's arm. "I have one more thing I must tell you about the queen and what has transpired."

With a sardonic smile, Rill interrupted Rivian, "Are you about to tell me that you bedded her? Do not fret. Luce tells me she is a great beauty and was hard for you to resist. Although, if you ask me, I think Luce has it bad for the queen. Also, Kia reported that you may be under some sort of mage spell. I must admit that one made me laugh out loud."

Clenching his jaw, Rivian's heart rate increased. Then, as if seeing his brother for the first time, Rivian leaned away from Rill.

Closing the distance between them, Rill lovingly cupped Rivian's face and whispered, "Riv, this is what we always dreamt of. Our father is gone. You and I are here. Let's create a new Sundom together."

Stunned, Rivian asked, "Rill, was this what you wanted all along? Power? This isn't you. This isn't what you promised me when you sent me off to Mōsa."

"Enough!" Rill roared. Realizing the protrusions of his tongue were becoming visible, Rill composed himself. With a low, firm tone, he said, "I am not only your brother. I am your king. The days of doing whatever you want are over. I will warn you about this once, because you are my brother and I love you. Never contest me again."

Dusting off Rivian's lapel, Rill said, "Now, make haste. Your fiance, Selah, is waiting for you to escort her to the feast."

With that, Rill left the study.

Standing in his father's study alone, Rivian realized three things.

His brother has changed, which made Rivian fearful; Luce could no longer be trusted; and Sole was in grave danger.

At that moment, Rivian knew he would have to find a way to get Sole out of Sundom, no matter the cost.

But first, the hard part, gaining her trust again. And maybe one day, her love. That would take time, which was something they did not have.

First, Rivian would have to face Sole for the first time since his betrayal and their arrival at Sundom. To make matters worse, he would do it with Selah on his arm.

Staring in the golden mirror behind his father's brash desk, Rivian whispered, "Fuck." His neck and face were hot with rage. "How in the world will I ever sort this out?" Then, with a resentful heart, he made his way to Selah.

CHAPTER 17

The Great Feast

The great hall was usually full of its curia when his father was king. But standing here now with Selah on his arm, the room felt unusually crowded.

Upon reaching Selah, he couldn't help but be taken aback by her beauty. Her long hair was white as the snow on mountains, draped in flowing waves down her back. But her crooked smile, the one she reflected now as her eyes met Rivian's for the first time, intrigued him the most. Selah has the greyest eyes Rivian had ever seen. When she smiled, her eyes seemed to light up, and many Sundom men lost their train of thought. Her lips were thin and small, and the top one came together to make a perfect M. As he drew closer, her slender hands reached out to embrace him. If he was honest, they had grown closer before... well before everything. But, seeing her here, his stomach clenched because he knew she could never give him what Sole did, as beautiful as she was. With Sole, he was safe, at peace, and in many ways, home. For now, Rivian would play the part of groom-to-be until he could find a way to devise a plan. But, first, he'd have to find a way to save her.

Approaching Selah, Rivian's smile appeared crooked. It was the best he could muster at the moment. They embraced and exchanged other empty pleasantries. "You look lovely."

It wasn't like it was a lie. She was a lovely woman. Selah's bare collarbone was exposed for all to see as she glided across the room in her strapless crimson gown. She was beautiful, but he felt empty when he was with her.

"Thanks, Riv. You don't look too bad yourself," she said as she touched his arm, beaming up at him. Then, biting her lip, Selah looked down and said, "I heard about your father, and I'm sorry. For what it's worth."

Unfortunately, Selah knew all too well the relationship Rivian had with his father; that was the one thing they both had in common. Both were second born children to fathers who never loved them. That was what had bonded them before he left for Mōsa.

"Thank you, Selah. I still don't know quite how to feel about it. To be the second son of a dead king should mean something, but I have many things I must address that keep me from dealing with that loss."

Although they had never kissed or been intimate, it was expected that they would begin to plan their bonding ceremony upon his return. So how would he tell Selah that this would not be taking place? That he loved another? He could barely admit it to anyone other than himself and Sole. It seemed like no one would be happy about their union, except for them. But just because they hadn't told anyone yet, didn't make it any less accurate. It also didn't matter that right now, she hated his guts. He was still very much hers, and she was still very much his. He just needed to remind her of that.

When Rivian realized Selah's grey gaze was upon him, he snapped out of his thoughts of Sole.

Breaking the silence, Selah said.

"I heard the Mōsian Princess is quite lovely. Kia tells me the princess has grown quite fond of you."

He knew he would tell Selah but not now, not here, and damn it, not before they entered the great hall where Sole was.

As beautiful as Selah was, she was equally fierce and conniving. The last thing he needed was Selah being set ablaze in an electric lavender fire. Shit, he didn't know if that was what Sole would do when he laid eyes on him tonight.

"We can discuss my Mōsian adventures at a later

date. But, for now, let us feast." Placing her arm in the crux of his elbow, they entered the great hall and waited to be introduced.

"All rise!" the tall Sundom guard with the grey beard called out.

"Let us welcome the second born son of Sundom, Captain of the Royal Sun Guards, Master of the Radiant, protector of magick, and brother to King Rill, Prince Rivian Alacor of Sundom. Accompanied by his fiancé, the lovely Selah Grado, second born daughter of Sundom, a scholar of the Aviran, and soon to be the Second Princess of Sundom."

Making his way to the King's table, Rivian's heart stopped to see Sole and Nisa. His hands were sweating and he hadn't realized that he had stopped walking. He had stopped breathing. Coming to his aid, Zari stepped in front of Rivian and Selah. Bowing to the prince, Zari's eyes held concern. Wary eyes of green and blue hues locked on Rivian. Blocking Rivian's view of Sole, with a frozen smile and gritted teeth, Zari explained what Rivian had just now realized. "It seems that your brother, the king, believes that having you sitting next to the Mōsian Princess will ease tensions."

"What the actual fuck is going on, Zari?" Rivian said through gritted teeth facing Zari.

Luckily, Selah couldn't tell how tense Rivian actually

was. He could feel his heart beating so hard he thought everyone could hear the thumping through his chest.

Closing the distance between herself, Rivian, and Zari, Selah asked, "Is something wrong?"

Noticing the men were as if in a trance, Selah turned to see what captivated them when her ice-blue gaze landed on Nisa and Sole. "My goodness, Kia wasn't kidding when she said the women of Mōsa were rare beauties." Pointing to Sole, she continued, "Is that the one with magick? She seems harmless enough. I mean, look at her. She is tiny."

While Selah was distracted, Zari put his hands on Rivian's shoulders and locked his gaze onto Rivian's, whispering, "You can manage one feast, brother."

No matter what their disagreements were, Zari always had his back. And tonight was just another example of his steadfast loyalty.

"You have been in tight situations before. This will be a piece of cake." Then, with a crooked smile, he said, "Be princely and shit. We can sort all this out later tonight."

Taking a deep, shaky breath, Rivian touched Selah's lower back, guiding her to the Kings table. He gently pulled Selah's chair placing her directly in front of Nisa. Reaching his seat, he sat in front of Sole.

Making eye contact with Sole for the first time, Rivian

realized Zari was wrong. This would be the hardest thing he would have to do all his life.

As she sat there in front of him, she pulled her glance away. Unable to look away from her, Rivian said, "You look beautiful."

Remembering the last time he said that to Sole, he smiled, a genuine smile. He remembered her face by the firelight in the Dark Wilds, and how she had met his gaze, bold and unflinching, unafraid of the thing blooming between them.

Tonight, she just looked away from him. There was sadness there. He tried to catch her eyes, at the very least. Any sign, any contact to ease the tension.

"Darling, are you not going to introduce me to your new friends?"

Selah's voice had never grated at Rivian until tonight. Through gritted teeth, he said, "Lady Nisa and Queen Lia Soleidae of Porte, I'd like you to meet Princess Selah Grado, Second Daughter of Sundom."

Putting her right hand out for Sole and Nisa to kiss it as is customary, Selah added, "Also, his fiancé."

The Mōsian women looked at the thin, cream-like beauty as if she was insane. Rivian thought he saw Sole's nose flare, her dead giveaway when she was irate.

Nisa's voice cut through the awkward stalemate

between Selah and Sole when she explained, "Only our partners kiss our hands in Mōsa."

Selah dropped her hand, miffed.

From the corner of his eye, Rivian noticed Zari making his way to the king's table. Sure he was on his way to Nisa, he was startled when Zari actually approached Sole. Rivian's jaw tightened as Zari asked Sole for a dance. Although Sole looked bewildered as to why Zari would ask her and not Nisa, she relented and took Zari's hand as he escorted her to the dance floor.

Rivian let himself just for one second take her in with his eyes. He admired her steady feet in those golden heels as she danced across the floor with Zari. Her toned muscular legs gleamed in the glowing lights cast by the sconces and dangling crystal chandeliers, her stunning rose gold gown offsetting her smooth moonstone skin. There she was, his fierce, decisive, beautiful Sole.

He tried hard not to stare at her ass in that dress or linger on how her beautiful updo revealed her long neck, making her look like a golden goddess. It was official... he was a fucking animal around her. He could barely hear the music playing or what Selah was saying because Sole looked so damn good. She was delicious in the rose gold gown, and he wanted to burn Zari's hands for being that close to her.

***

Sole refrained from rolling her eyes at Rivian for the hundredth time. His mere presence infuriated her. He was the man she thought she would have a second chance with. But he didn't choose her. Instead, he decided to lie; he chose to break her heart. And yet even now, looking at him, all Sole could think was, "Holy Mother.. he is alluring." Rivian wore a black suit and white shirt, both cut to his powerful arms and muscled body, and the effect was devastatingly beautiful. Add in his golden hair slicked back, and Sole was lost. Distracted, Sole could barely hear when Zari came to their table to ask Sole to dance.

As if taken out of a trance, Sole stood and gave her hand to Zari. As mad as she was with Zari, she appreciated him asking her to dance so Sole didn't have to sit there one minute longer than she had to with Rivian and his fucking finance. Within days of arriving in Sundom, she has been drugged, threatened, and imprisoned, all while having her heart broken into a million pieces. Tonight she missed her family most of all. She missed being surrounded by people she could trust. She sincerely wished she could be at ease, but this was not the place to put down her armor.

The back of Sole's neck prickled as she and Zari

made their way to the dance floor. The men stared as if they wanted to eat her for dinner. It was apparent from their frowns that the elven women didn't like her. The dance floor was consumed with a cluster of beautiful Sundom elvens. Sole didn't think she would ever get used to the lustrous gilded attire of the people of Sundom. Everywhere she looked, they glittered across the room like the embers of the fires in Mōsa. Their cream tanned skin brushed with golden dust made the passersby regal, polished like the gold they adorned themselves with.

In contrast, Sole's long, coiled hair was a statement. Her dark skin against the pinkish hue of her very tight gown made her uneasy. At the same time, she looked forward to dancing. Dancing in Mōsa had always soothed her. She was comfortable on the dance floor, a lover of music and dances.

"Don't think I don't know," Zari interrupted, jolting Sole from her trance.

"Know what?" She asked with questioning eyes.

"That you love each other." Sole couldn't think how to reply to that, so she looked away, continuing the steps of this Sundom dance she picked up very quickly.

With a nervous laugh, Sole finally replied in a low voice with gritted teeth, "Fuck you. I have known love in my lifetime, and this is not it. Love does not betray, lie, or imprison you. On the contrary, love sets you free."

"Queen Sole, with all due respect, you don't know anything. But I can assure you if Riv had his way, you would be safe and away from this place."

"You mean, if Riv had his way, I would be dead by now."

Zari shook his head at her and said, "I have known Riv since we were boys. We have fought over toys, politics, and yes, even girls, but he's like a brother to me, and when he tells me he is in love, I believe him."

Sole raised an eyebrow at him, skeptical. "Weren't you against the idea of us right from the very start? Why are you changing your tune now, so very late in the game?"

"You aren't the only one who feels betrayed," Zari said cryptically.

Sole scoffed at that, but didn't say anything. She really wasn't interested in whatever sob story they had cooked up. She was the one they had offered for slaughter. She was pretty sure she was allowed to wallow and be selfish for a few days. Or months, if she felt like it.

"Queen, look at him," Zari said subtly, gesturing to Rivian as he spun Sole around. "The way he looks at you now is how he looked at you when you first stepped on the Radiant. And I am pretty sure he plans to break my hands this evening for having them on you on this dance floor."

After two sharp turns, Sole glided to the next step, bringing her back closer to Zari.

"I would ask that we change the subject. Your prince is of no importance to me."

"Really?" Zari said with a sardonic smile. "Well, then, queen, you have a strange way of showing your disdain for Prince Rivian."

Shifting her focus to Zari, she locked eyes with him as the dance steps began to speed up. "You know you didn't only lie to me. Nisa is a casualty of you and your plan. She will never admit it, but you broke something in her that I don't know I will ever get back."

"I know what the ramifications of our action and inaction have done. I will forever suffer the losses that come with that. As I fear, Riv will have to experience it as well. Both of us have been raised with the idea that duty must come before desire," Zari said. "But there's a difference between Rivian and I. He's a prince, and that comes with certain freedoms, ones I don't have. I'm a mere soldier, and most of the time, our happiness will evade us for the rest of our lives."

"And you're all right with that?"

"I have to be. There should be no greater happiness or love in my life than that of serving my country. Such is the way of the soldier."

Sole was silent after that.

She, too, feared the weight of the loss she will have to endure. Maybe one day, she would come to cherish that month at sea with Rivian, a precious time where she found herself again. But, unfortunately, today was not that day. That infuriated her and left her feeling terribly alone. But she would never admit that to Zari and definitely not to Rivian. During that month, Rivian shared many things with Sole about his past. Together they talked about everything and nothing. Sometimes, sitting in that library's silence and watching him read in the moonrise brought her such peace. He had shared so much, and the more she learned, the more she found herself sharing, and the more she wanted to know him. Until she had fallen in love with the second prince of Sundom.

When Zari finally led her back to the table, Sole tried hard to relax on the elegant high backed golden chair. But when her gaze landed on Selah's hand and how easily it rested in Rivian's, her throat constricted. Then she shifted her gaze up to Selah's extraordinarily beautiful face. Wondrously fair, her skin had a glow that seemed to capture the attention of every lord in attendance. Her silver-grey eyes, paired with her long, bright silver hair, made her look like an elven goddess. But it was her quiet confidence that drew Sole in. She had never possessed that. Confidence like that was what Sole needed now, here in this space.

Feeling Sole's gaze on her, Selah turned her angelic face to Sole and said, "Queen Sole, I hope the last thirty days weren't terrible with these Sundom men for entertainment."

Nisa quickly placed her hand on Sole's lap to calm her burning rage. "The journey was pleasant," Sole said through a tight smile, "I spent most of my time reading in the library."

"Oh, dear Holy Mother!" Selah exclaimed, hand on her chest, "I hope Rivian didn't bore you with all his talks of prophecy, history, and changing the world. Seriously, I don't know where he gets it." Uncomfortable, Rivian's jaw tightened as he shifted in his seat. Sole didn't know why her words pierced her, but they did.

"Actually, I found my time in the library to be quite pleasant and informative. Rivian is actually very well read himself."

Rivian, grateful to Sole for her unexpected defense, suddenly smiled at her. It was that smile that Sole hated, the one which revealed those damn adorable dimples that turned the knots in her stomach. But she wasn't watching him. Her eyes were on Selah.

"Oh my, your eyes are glowing," Selah said louder than Sole would have liked.

To that, Nisa responded, "Yes. Her eyes glow when she hears bullshit."

Avoiding laughing at Nisa's stab at Selah, Rivian spit his drink all over the table. Sole couldn't help but smile at his reaction. Quickly composing herself, she remembered that he promised her the world and delivered heartache.

Then, Sole watched as a group of beautiful fae made their way to Rivian and Selah. Persuaded to walk in the garden with her friends, Selah kissed Rivian on the lips and said, "I'll be back soon, love."

Rivian's eyes lit up and he sat up straighter. No sooner had Selah left, when Rivian turned to Nisa and said, "Lady Nisa, would you give me a few moments with Queen Sole?"

"Over my fucking dead body," Nisa said through a saccharine smile.

"Nis, please get me one of those delicious cakes as I fear I will need something sweet to help swallow the bullshit the Second Prince is about to present," Sole said coolly.

Making one last attempt to have Sole reconsider being alone with Rivian, Nisa said, "I don't want to leave you."

Tilting her head, Sole held Nisa's gaze and said, "I assure you there is no more harm that he can cause me than he has already provided."

Her words were a slap to his face, but he knew he deserved it, and more.

Whispering meaningless gibberish, Nisa walked over to the desserts with Zari following closely behind.

Sole waited for Rivian to speak. Then, with a voice thick with conviction and guilt, he asked, "How are you? Has anyone hurt you?" Realizing that the last question was probably the wrong thing to ask, he immediately followed it with, "Sole, are you well?"

"Second Prince, I assure you, I am well," she said, her voice detached and weary.

"I know I have much to explain about my mission, the king, and—"

"Your betrothed," she said with glowing violet eyes and breathy explosive words. "She is quite lovely. Your perfect match."

"Yes, that too. I need you to know that I cannot stop thinking about you. When I woke up after being darted to find that you were not there, it was as if I couldn't breathe. Controlling my magick took much effort. Sole, you are all I want. I know I have much to atone for, but if you give me that chance..."

"You don't get to do that anymore," she said in a voice that could cut glass. Rivian could detect fear in her voice, anger, and curiosity. Which was what he wanted.

"I was a fool," she said with tears in her eyes. "And tonight, this fool, dressed in this ridiculous ensemble, has to sit here and watch you step right back into your gilded cage as if nothing happened. Well fuck that, and fuck you."

"First, you look gorgeous in that gown, and every guy in this court knows it, which is seriously pissing me off. Second, I have not forgotten your touch, your bright smile, and how those eyes look when I am on top of you. But most of all, I need you to know I love you."

"To be clear, Second Prince. I regret everything you and I did. I regret meeting you, and I regret ever thinking that I could ever love you. I don't think I ever did." Her words stung, clearly flung out to hurt him and end the conversation. It worked for now.

With a flat and steady voice, Sole gestured behind Rivian, saying, "Now, why don't you be a good fiancé and pull that seat for your bride? She comes quickly."

His tone could have frozen entire countries as he said, "This conversation is not over, queen. I will find you, and we will make this right." Then, turning to greet Selah, Rivian assumed the role of a dutiful prince. Sole wanted to go back to her chambers and cry her eyes out before she lit this room up with her magick.

Just then, the royal herald ushered everyone to stand. The King was about to enter the room.

When Rill Alacor walked in with his golden, ruby-encrusted crown, Sole's head spun. She realized that the king, the old king, the one she had been summoned to heal, was dead. Rivian's brother was as beautiful as a white panther and just as deadly. A terrible feeling bloomed in the pit of her stomach.

Making his way to Sole, Rill raised one eyebrow and said, "Bow before your king."

CHAPTER 18

King of Sundom

Refusing to bow, Sole smiled, never taking her eyes off the tall giant of a man. She clenched her fists to hold back her magick as it surged through her veins. In one deft motion, the king crossed the space between them and stared deep into her eyes. Pulling back, he simply said, "Amazing. Your violet eyes are simply amazing. Such power."

White-blonde, well-groomed hair hung over a refined, charming face. Dead gray eyes set narrowly within their sockets watched intensely over Sole's face, body, and maybe even her soul. His smooth skin beautifully complimented his eyes and mouth. If Sole hadn't known he was Rivian's older brother, she would consider them twins. This was the face of Rill Alacor, the newly crowned king of the Sundom elves. He stood high among others in stature and alluring in personality. There was something inexplicable about him, perhaps it's a feeling of coldness, or maybe it was simply his comfort. Nonetheless, Sole was curious about him and what he had in store for her.

"Hello, your highness," Sole said, knowing the High Kings never liked to be addressed as your highness. She was starting off on the wrong foot, but she didn't care. She'd had enough of the Sundom assholes her mother had warned her about. She knew who she was, a daughter of a king, and even if her knees quivered, she would never let anyone in this room know it.

Licking his lips, the king said, "My brother informs me that you are a rebel of sorts. Intriguing."

Sole glanced around. "I believe congratulations and condolences are to be made. Which do you prefer, your highness?"

Rill's lips thinned and his gaze locked on her. So grey. So menacing. So focused.

Sole chose that moment to introduce Nisa. "King Rill," she began, "May I introduce you to Lady Nisa Asha of Mōsa, my primary adviser."

For a fraction of a second, Nisa went unnaturally still. Rill's eyes widened at the sound of her name. Turning slowly to face Nisa, his gaze hardened as he said, "I hope your stay in Sundom has been pleasant, Lady Nisa."

Nisa gave a little sniff. An actual sniff. What the hell

is wrong with her, Sole thought.

Collecting herself, Nisa licked her lips. "Sundom is quite a lovely land; I would find it more to my liking if Queen Sole and I were not in separate quarters."

Not taking his gray gaze off of Nisa, he said, "Rivian, make sure the queen and her entourage are moved to joint quarters this eve."

Zari's jaw went rock hard as he realized that the king may be enamored with Nisa. He didn't blame the king or any man for desiring her, but he knew he could do nothing but wait to get a moment alone with Nisa and hope she didn't slit his throat. Sole was right. He would have to quickly make things right with her or lose her forever.

A muscle in Rill's cheek tightened as he turned to the court and said, "Dance and be merry, for the princess, forgive me, queen of Mōsa has made it safely to Sundom." With that, the music, dining, and dancing resumed as if they had been frozen for a brief moment in time. There was no doubt to Zari that Nisa was his. His girl was brass and fucking bold. She went after what she wanted and it made him proud.

Taking her seat once more, Sole passed by Rivian as he subtly drew in a breath, pulling Sole's gentle lavender scent into his lungs, letting it settle him as he composed himself once more. The first night he met with her, her scent haunted him. Every morning on the Radiant, he waited for that scent to settle him. Thinking back, it was why he becomes so upset at her refusal to spend time with him. The absence of her scent was making him irritable and intense.

She had a face so beautiful it made his chest tighten. Her large violet eyes, delicate full lips, cute dimple, and long coiled hair looked like the mermaids of old tales his mother told him as a boy. But even when she was calm, she held a steely and unnerving stare that said, "I am the Queen of Mōsa, and you will never control me."

She drank everything in with that gaze, like a jaguar taking in their surroundings from the mountain top. And when she opened her beautiful mouth, her deep, sexy voice came out, unaware of what she was about to say. She was much shorter than him. Though slender, her toned body, full breasts, and gently curved hips captivated him every time she walked into a room. Especially now, in that pink silk gown. Before Sole, his mind had been a very dark and lonely place. A place of bitter rain, black clouds, and mental chaos. Even surrounded by people, he'd been lonely, never sad or happy... he just was. She changed everything. She changed him. He would not lose that. Not now, not ever.

Settling onto his highbacked golden throne adorned with the two suns of Sundom in hues of rose gold, and gold, King Rill feasted, laughed with his advisors, and often held his steely gray gaze on Sole as if he knew something she didn't.

King Rill held himself in confidence and power, emanating an aura of complete control. Sole could tell it was rare for Rill's control to fracture, just as it was for him to hold joy so closely. Rivian had told her he was duty driven, committed to overthrowing his father at all costs.

"Tell us, how did my brother fair during your journey home?" he said coolly.

Her tone full of false cheer, she said, "I will have to let you know when he returns me back to my home in Mōsa, your highness. If you ask about our journey to Sundom, he was seasick and insisted I dine with him."

Laughing at the latter statement, the King replied, "Yes, my sweet brother can be quite persistent! He gets that from our mother, you see."

On her many encounters on the Radiant, Rivian shared how his mother, Queen Penelope, died the day he was born. He explained how difficult her death had been for his father. Her death led his father to grow distant from Rivian and to believe his second son would be the downfall of his family and Sundom. For Rill to bring this up here and now made Sole's magick boil.

Interrupting Sole's thoughts, the king said a bit louder than she would have liked, "Tell us about what it was like to grow up in Mōsa. We have heard so much about how your people lived, but we'd like to hear it from Mōsa's official queen."

The whispers sailed across the room like a flood. Nisa placed her hand on Sole's knee and whispered, "Calm yourself. Your eyes are glowing again."

Internally counting to four, Sole answered, "I would have to say that Mōsa indeed came most alive at moonrise. That was when highlights of the bioluminescent bay created a soft, serene sea with its gentle hues of pinks and purples consuming one glaze. Since we were children, Lady Nisa and I raced up and down the pink beach with—" Her voice cracked at the memory, "With my sisters and her brother."

She took a deep breath to calm her emotions before she continued, "To be honest, it wasn't the sea or the moonrise that captivated me. It was our people and our community's pride. My parents, King Axel and Queen Lygia, raised their daughters to never identify as first, second, or third. We were just their daughters."

"That's ridiculous," Selah said absently. "To be raised by one's parents as equals when all of Transea will never see you that way is cruelty. No?" Selah asked between bites of the delicious mini cakes Nisa had grown so fond of.

Her voice clipped and eyes glowing, Sole answered

the question by keeping her eyes focused on the king. Replying to Selah's questions without taking her gaze off the king was sure to anger Selah.

"If by cruel, you mean that my sisters and I could freely love each other with no competition or threat of war, then yes. Our parents were cruel."

Turning to face Selah, Sole said, "I am sure Princess Selah knows exactly what cruelty looks like given her second daughter status in Sundom."

Suddenly the court was buzzing as if Sole had just swatted a beehive from its tree. But Sole didn't care. They would never take her seriously if she allowed them to mock her.

Interrupting the chatter amongst the guests, King Rill proceeded to bombard Sole with questions, "Please tell us, is it true you do not know how to swim?"

Turning to Rivian with her steely purple gaze, she hoped he could read her face and the look of utter betrayal that was written there. How could he share that secret with his brother? she thought.

But what surprised Sole was that Rivian appeared just as surprised at his brother's question. She didn't fully understand what was going on with her or what they intended to do with her, but she agreed to hold her composure, if not for herself, then for the people of Mōsa. The last thing she wanted to do was start an unnecessary war.

With a soft voice and gravely, she turned her gaze back to the king, saying, "My sisters were excellent swimmers, as is Nisa. I, on the other hand, spent my time reading in the library of Mōsa." Then, she gave Selah a side eye. "I was too caught up in those dreadful prophecies and such," she said, echoing the words Selah said earlier as she referred to Rivian. Her jaw tightening, Selah stared at Sole with her grey eyes as piercing as tiny silver daggers.

Rivan shifted in his seat, saying, "The princess and I agreed that once in Sundom, I would teach her to swim, and she would teach me to fish."

"To fish?" the King repeated loudly. "Oh brother, you will not have time for that as you prepare for your mating ceremony, and Princess Sole becomes reacquainted with my new Mōsian ambassador."

Her eyes on fire, Sole stood as the room grew silent. Rivian couldn't help but to stand with her. Then, turning to his brother, the king said, "All shall be revealed in due time."

"Your highness, I must ask. If your father, the king, has succumbed to the Darkness, why do I remain here when I should be making my way back to my people?" she asked with her fists balled tightly and her eyes filled with a dark rage.

"Princess, be seated," he demanded. "Once you have done so, I will tell you why you are here."

Once she sat as commanded, the king continued. "There are many things you don't know. For example, before my brother went to bring you here to heal our father, I met a Mōsian who was willing to do anything to save their people. Even assist me in overthrowing my father, the king," he recounted.

Rivian looked just as surprised as Sole. And that perplexed her. Willing the anger out of his voice, Rivian gently asked the king, "Brother, why is this the first I am hearing of this?"

Lips pressed into a fine white line, King Rill's sharp slivery eyes locked on Rivian, letting him know he had overstepped. "I am the king, little brother. My decisions are final. Last I checked, the king doesn't need to notify his counsel about anything, because he is king!" He banged the wooden table, causing a pitcher of blood red wine to spill all over the white linen.

All eyes were on Rivian. Elbowing Sole under the table, Nisa reminded her to settle herself. She hissed, "Not now. We don't even know what they have done with the Misa warriors. Be still, queen. Save your rage for another day."

Gently, Selah put her hand on Rivian's shoulder, drawing him back to his seat. Sole hated seeing that sly bitch touching him, but she appreciated getting Rivian to sit down. Maybe they had been closer than she initially thought. Shaking that thought out of her mind, Sole addressed the king, hoping he would take the focus off Rivian. "King Rill, may I speak?"

Shifting his silver eyes to Sole, Rill gestured that she could continue.

"Your Royal Highness, you mentioned that you would tell me why you still need me here."

He glared at her. "There comes a time when a king needs to make a tough decision to save his people. That is exactly what I did by bringing you here. I made a vow. Rivian was sent to secure your passage here."

"A Mōsian helped you overthrow the king?" she asked hesitantly, turned, and looked at Nisa. Nisa's eyes told Sole everything they needed to know. They had been betrayed. But by whom? Surely no Mōsian in their right mind would ever align with Sundom to secure anything. Sure, some had considered leaving Mōsa with their families from time to time. Luce's family went to Mōsa a couple of generations back, but aligning with Sundom to secure their throne was unheard of and reeked of betrayal. So, who would be desperate enough to journey here?

"I would like to see this Mōsian for myself, for I cannot believe that any of my people would do such a thing."

"Yes, Queen Sole, one of your very own made their way to Sundom in the dead of night a little over a year ago. They came with one plea, save my people, and we will give you whatever you ask. Little did that person know that you would become the savior of Mōsa." Standing, he stepped closer to Sole.

"Over the last year, we have become close, collaborated, and constructed a plan that would work. Learning every day more and more about you, your people, and your ways. How do you think my brother knew so much about what you liked, how to win your affections? That's how we learned tangible information about you, like the fact that you didn't know how to swim."

He placed his hand on the small of her back, signaling Sole to rise from her seat. His touch was enough to raise the hairs on the back of her nape. As Sole stood from her golden seat, her magick demanded to rise to the surface. It was as if her magic was becoming its own personality and way of responding to the crisis. She would have to deal with that later. She willed her magick to stand down as the king took her hand, placed it on the crook of his arm, and walked her to the center of the marbled dance floor. As the courters parted like the Serena Sea, Sole began to feel a sense of uneasiness.

Gravely, he motioned to Rivian to join them on the marbled floor. "Come, brother, this surprise is as much for her as it is for you." rising to his feet, Rivian almost ran to make it to her side. He knew how conniving his people could be. Rivian knew that whoever the king was bringing to meet her would be shocking. He would stay here with her. Leaving her alone with whoever would come through that door would never be an option.

"And so, we devised a plan to bring you here and create the Sundom Rivian and I always dreamt about."

Motioning to Luce, the king professed, "Luce, please bring in our guest of honor from Mōsa." His jaw tightening and eyes steely, Rivian was under the impression that tonight's Mōsian guest of honor had been Sole. She was not. And worst of all, Luce had known all along. Rivian didn't charge Luce because he knew it would mean leaving Sole alone. He would find Luce later, and they would figure out what the fuck was really going on around here.

The guest accompanying Luce had aged some. A dark stubbled beard made him look wiser. His grey eyes were no longer a deep-set black void. But it was his hands. His hands told Sole precisely who stood before her.

It was her mate, Nasir, who had been dead for more than a year and a half.

Sole couldn't move. She couldn't breathe. His light mahogany skin, in contrast to the grey skin he held the last time she saw him, froze her in place. His silver eyes locked on hers. Then, hearing Nisa scream, everything faded to black as Rivian caught her in his arms.

CHAPTER 19

Back from the dead

"People assume I died a year ago. But, to be completely honest, I am not sure I didn't die."

Sole was sure she was losing her mind. How could Nasir be here before her? He was dead. Her heart began to pound in her chest. She felt like she would surely die. Suddenly she saw his hands again. Hands that were no longer gray and pale but with fingertips that appeared dipped in black ink. The realization set in that this could be him. Her Nasir. Her mate. But something in him was incredibly different.

Sole knew something was wrong when she looked into Nasir's grey eyes for the first time in a year and a half and felt no mating pull. Something was terribly wrong. Looking at him now, she realized he was more scared than she was. Internally, Sole was frantic. Biting her nails, she sat on the settee and wrapped her arms around her legs. Why was she shivering? Standing, she began to pace. He was here, and no amount of pacing would help her understand how they had gotten to this point. The one thing she couldn't do was lock eyes with him. Those same eyes haunted her dreams for the last year and a half. And yet, here they were. She was afraid. Afraid she would be lost forever if she looked into those eyes. And she needed to understand what happened to him. Where had he been all that time, and how did he get to Sundom?

"Look at me," he whispered in that low tone that made her stomach queasy. Stopping in her tracks, she didn't know what to say.

"Sole, look at me." Closing the space between them but not getting too close for fear of scaring her off, he kept his distance. "So." There was that damn nickname that she hated except when he said it. "Will you please look at me."

She stopped the pacing and wrapped her arms around her midsection. Why was it so fucking cold in here? She slowly turned to face Nasir.

"You died," she whispered as her voice trailed off.

"Please look at me," he said, voice cracked and raw.

She looked up at him with her lavender eyes staring blankly.

"Your eyes. What happened to your eyes, Sole?" he

asked as he reached out to touch her face. Flinching at his touch, Sole took a few steps back, startling herself at her reaction to a touch that once comforted her.

Her tone was weary and detached when she said, "I awoke from the Darkness in this state." He had no idea how much she had changed. The lavender eyes weren't the only difference.

"How have you been?"

Willing the anger out of her voice, she said, "How have I been? Where have you been, Nasir?"

"That's hard to explain," he said, flinching.

"I don't care how fucking hard it is. I need to understand how you got here. How you are alive standing here? What the fuck happened?" she demanded as her voice cracked.

"Minutes before the Darkness consumed me, I lay in our bed staring at you."

That got her attention.

"I was prepared to lose all the sleep the Holy Mother offered me to be in that bed with you, watching your naked body take long, languid breaths. Laying there beside you, a chill entered the room. I was about to stand close to the windows when my entire body froze. I couldn't move my arms, legs, or blink. Laying there with my eyes shut in complete darkness, I was petrified, and all I wanted to do was call for your aid. I can't tell you how long I laid there wishing to reach out to you. It seemed like a lifetime.

That was when I heard you say my name. At first, it was a whisper of my name, and then terror took over your body. I couldn't see you, but I knew you were there. If only I could wake up. If only I could tell you. Then, a few hours passed and I didn't hear you near me. I thought you had abandoned me. But then, hours upon hours later, I heard your voice again. I heard it, your plea...your desperate demand for me to rise, to stay with you. I knew then that I was dead or dying."

Voice cracking and raw, he said, "I didn't want to die, but if I was going to die, at least I died in your arms."

Standing as if frozen, Sole chewed on her lower lip to keep from crying. Who was she kidding? The tears flowed freely down her cheeks as she stood there trying to make sense of everything. Nasir wanted to comfort her, but he knew she would resist. He needed to keep explaining what happened so that she could see he was the same old Nasir. Even if everything had changed.

Closing the gap a bit more, Nasir gently said, "No more crying, Sole. You should smile more."

Looking up to hear that familiar phrase he would whisper in her ears a lifetime ago made her feel warm, but it did not quell her anxiety. How could she not cry learning that he was not dead while she screamed his name? How could her bitter tears not fall at the thought of his cold body lying alone in that darkness?

"Continue, please," she whispered as she sat on the crimson settee in King Rill's study. The ornate room felt small somehow. The world felt small, and her last thirty nights a faded dream. When had her life become this mangled mess of chaos, lies, and deception?

Nasir remembered how his heart pounded, then, and how traumatizing it was to come back from the dead right where they left him. It was a trauma that lingered in him. Clasping his hands to keep them from shaking, he continued with a low and grave voice, "When they took me away from you, I felt myself fade until there was nothing. No tears, no urgency, just silence. I can't tell you how long I lay there as they tried to revive me. Then, after a long while, they brought other dead just like me... or at least, they thought. It took me time to realize that all the bodies surrounding me meant I was in the charnel house."

Mōsa buried their dead until the Darkness. That was one of the things Masine explained to Sole when she woke. Solemnly, Masine explained that the volume of deaths prevented those infected from being buried in traditional Mōsian burial rituals. Instead, they had to create the Osario houses; vaults held the piled bodies of those consumed by the Darkness. "I don't know how long I was there, entombed. Unable to move, see, or speak." Sole noticed a hollowness come over his silver-grey eyes. There's no way being locked up like that, for the Mother knew how long, he wasn't changed somehow. They had all been changed at this point. None of them would ever be the same.

"You know, I now sleep with the lights on because any form of darkness takes me back to where they left me. Waking up to nothingness is not something you can forget. I can't even close my eyes without being right back in the Osario, crawling through hundreds of corpses, using every ounce of strength I could muster to push through. The thought of getting to you was the only thing that kept me moving. So many nights, I just don't sleep."

"Nasir, I don't understand. I saw you die. They told me you died."

"In many ways, I did die that night. However, the hope of seeing you again kept me alive. Sole, I have missed you tremendously."

"Why didn't you come back?" she cried out.

"The Darkness ruined me. I knew that for me to come back to be with you, I couldn't be the monster I had become. The night I decided I needed to leave the Osario, I waited for Liara, the Misa warrior, to bring in the dead. When she arrived, I stood to greet her. There

I was, naked, confused, and Darkness covered my hands. What could she do but attack? We struggled," he said as he ran his hand through his shoulder-length hair. He's always kept it short on the sides when they were courting. Another reminder of how much he had changed.

"She almost killed me when suddenly I got a burst of energy like none I had ever experienced before and without warning, I snapped her neck. Just like that, she was gone."

Stunned, Sole sat there in silence for what seemed like years when he said, "After I laid her down, I made my way to our home. The house was dark and closed up. I pried one of our black shudders open and grabbed a pair of trousers and a tunic. Although they were huge on me now, I was at least covered."

He couldn't tell Sole that slipping on those clothes felt as if he had stepped into someone else's body, someone else's life. He knew he had much to disclose, but it had to be measured for both their sakes.

"I couldn't wait; I knew if you weren't in our home, you would be with your parents. I knew I must have changed significantly because no one noticed me as I made my way to Porte house in the dark. What I saw when I arrived broke me in a way I could not have imagined. You were lying on your mother's bed, surrounded by medics and nurses. One nurse whispered that you had fallen ill shortly after I had died. She envisioned you wouldn't last the night."

"It was at that moment I wished I had died." Jaw tightening, he spat, "I fought my way out of hell only to find that I caused your death."

"Wait, what? What do you mean you caused my death?"

"I was the first one infected and the first one to be declared dead. It was my fault you were sick."

Voice thick with conviction, she said, "I will stop you there. I will never let you take the blame for something none of us could control. Never. You were sick, as were we all. That's how the Darkness works. No human can cause the Darkness. You don't get to be a martyr here."

Making her voice soft and measured, she asked, "But why didn't you stay in Mōsa? Why didn't you stay with me?"

"You must understand, my parents were close to death, Nisa was barely breathing, and you lay there wrapped in soft white blankets as you slipped away daily. I couldn't watch you die. So, I took the last ship out to Sundom to request that the king do anything to save what was left of our people. It was when I arrived that I was brought before the king. I explained who I was, where I had traveled, and that we needed his help."

"That bastard laughed at me. He actually laughed at the pain we were in. The final straw was when he told me it was up to Mōsians to pick themselves up and save themselves. The surge of energy consumed me again. This time I managed to kill five of the King's sun guards with my bare hands before blacking out and waking in the dungeons of Sundom."

Sole put a hand over her mouth in shock listening to what he had gone through.

"After many cold nights lying in my own piss, the king's son came to visit me in the middle of the night."

In a breathy explosion of words, she blurted, "Rivian came to see you?"

Nasir couldn't help but catch the flicker in her violet eyes at the mention of Rivian's name. He would find out more about this Rivian later.

"No. Prince Rill paid me a visit. He told me of your condition."

"My condition?"

"Yes. He told me about the magick."

The way he said the word "magick" made her pause. His tone was now stiff and surly. A side of Nasir she had never seen before. He made it sound like the worst thing she could be was a mage. Flat and steady, she said, "My magick saved what was left of our people. I may have regretted it once, but I am proud of what

I was able to do for Mōsa, for Nisa. I will never regret saving them."

Anger crept into his voice "It's that very magick that left me entombed and that may have killed our parents and our friends. King Rill told me that he thought your magick could restore the order of things. He promised to bring you here to me if I agreed to help him overthrow the king. Little did we know that in less than a year, the king would fall ill to the Darkness. That was when King Rill asked that you be summoned here to court. Your job would be to heal a mad king that let our family die."

Voice low, tone uncertain, she asked, "When did the king die?"

"He was consumed by the Darkness nine moons ago."

"But that meant that Rivian was sent to retrieve me after his father was already dead."

"Rivian? I was unaware you and the prince were on informal terms," he said, his jaw tight.

"The second prince was sent on this mission by his brother. But, you see, the second prince and his father were not close. So, he was never summoned to spend time with his ailing father. He was not aware of how ill his father was," Sole was speaking to herself more than she was speaking to Nasir. "If that was the case then… What was the purpose of bringing me here?"

"I was here, or did you forget that part?" he said with a hardened voice. Then, he caught himself and apologized to her in a calm, unhurried voice. "My anger gets the best of me sometimes, after spending all that time in the dark. Please forgive me, my love."

Closing her eyes and counting to four, Sole regained control of her magick in time to ask one more question. "You say you and King Rill have become close."

"I wouldn't call it close but we've come to an agreement."

"If that is so, why did he keep you here? Why reveal your existence to me in this manner?"

"As you know, the people of Sundom don't do anything small. They have a flair for the dramatic."

Standing to her feet with eyes glowing, Sole said, "Do you not take my questions seriously, husband? I have been known to throw things when I get angry."

Just when their tempers were about to clash, Nisa suddenly entered the room, crying, "Sole, is it true?"

Then her voice faded to nothing when she saw Nasir standing there. Wasting no time at all, she ran and threw herself at her twin brother.

"I don't care what miracle brought you back," Nisa whispered tearfully against her brother's neck. "I'm just grateful you're here."

A gentle knock on the tall wooden doors startled

the group. Rivian entered the room. Eyes heavy with sorrow, rage, and confusion, Rivian uttered, " Queen Sole and Lady Nisa, I have come to escort you to your new quarters. You will be pleased to know that the Misa warriors await you in that space."

"Second born prince, are you mad?" Nisa screeched, "I have just reunited with my brother after months of believing him dead, and you want to take me, us," she said, looking over to Sole, "away from him?"

Rising to his feet, Nasir whispered, "The hour is late, and I need you all to get some rest. Tomorrow, we will have much to discuss. But for now, let us obey the king's wishes and find solace in having seen each other."

Making his way to Sole and placing his hands on her shoulders, he said, "Love, no more crying. You should smile more. The world needs to see that."

Rivian's stomach fell at the sound of Nasir's words. He remembered right before kissing her for the first time that she had mentioned that Nasir said those words to her often. Hearing them now from him made Rivian's skin crawl. He didn't want anyone touching her, mate or not.

After embracing Sole and Nisa, he whispered, "Here before, here now, and here after." Gently kissing Sole on the forehead, he motioned them to join Rivian as he left the room, closing the door behind him.

The awkwardness was palpable as Rivian moved to lead them to their new sleeping quarters. Rivian had changed out of his form-fitting dark suit and was now done up in a navy tunic that made his ice blue gaze stand out against his tanned skin. Feeling the tension in the room, Nisa made her way to the door to find none other than Zari waiting for her.

"What are you doing here?"

"I was asked to escort you and Princess Sole to your chambers. Lady Nisa."

"The second-born son will be more than suitable to escort us back to our rooms."

As the two continued to squabble in the hall, Rivian asked Sole, "Are you ok?"

"No. No, I'm not. The world has been turned upside down," she said.

"What can I do to help you?"

Her violet glare captivated him all over again. "Nothing."

Startled by her response, "I'm sorry, what did you say, my princess?"

"I said there is nothing you can do for me. Haven't you done enough?" she spat.

"Sole, I can assure you I knew nothing of this. Nothing."

"Whether that is true or not, you have lied to me

repeatedly. Forgive me if your words hold little weight with me." She knew that wasn't true, but she had to lash out at someone for how utterly fucked up this was, and he insisted on standing there looking like that and asking ridiculous questions.

"Fuck!" she spat, causing Zari and Nisa to step back into the room. Running her hands down her face, Sole paced as her eyes flickered an electric violet. Finally, Zari closed the door, granting them a bit more privacy.

"Nisa, was that him, really him?" Sole begged.

"Yes. Yes, it was him," she said a little too quickly with a nervous yet cheerful tone.

"Nisa, I don't know if it is," she said. "He is changed. Significantly."

"We have all changed, Sole."

Sole couldn't deny that. Chewing on her nails, she circled the room, eyes glowing.

Facing Nisa while the two women held hands, she said, "Nis, this may very well be a miracle or bring forth misery. Something deep inside of me tells me it may be the latter. So, promise me we will navigate this cautiously."

"I disagree with you on this, Sole. I have known my brother longer than you have and it is him," she said insistently. Then, sighing she added, "But I will heed your warning."

Locking eyes with Sole she said, "Promise me that when Nasir regains your trust, you will make things right with him."

Sole stood there as if frozen in the mountains of Andaluz, knowing Rivian was still in the room, waiting for her response as well.

Interrupting them, Zari exclaimed, "Lady Nisa, we must make haste. This is no place to be discussing what has transpired this eve. Queen Sole, there will be another time for us to connect, I assure you. Please allow Prince Rivian and I to escort you to your quarters."

As they reached the door to their new quarters, Nisa knew Sole needed a few minutes alone with Rivian, so she turned to the Sun Guard general and said, "Lord Zari, please join me in our rooms, won't you? I am sure the Misa warriors have many questions for you."

Exhibiting a crooked, nervous smile, Zari followed Nisa.

"Sole... Queen Sole," he said quickly, correcting himself, "I can only imagine how difficult this must be for you."

Difficult? She wanted to say, that would be the understatement of the year. Her dead husband is alive after dying tragically in their bed nearly two years ago. Since then, she has come to possess magick, healed her kingdom, and fucked the second born prince repeatedly, on her way to be reunited with her long-lost love. But instead, she said nothing.

Moving closer to her, Rivian said, "I know this is crazy. I know you need space to sort all this out. But I need you to promise me that you will think of your future, not just your past."

Then Rivian collected her in his arms, forcing her to get uncomfortably close to his piercing eyes and kissable lips.

"Promise me, Sole?" he whispered in her ear with that low gravely plea he often used when they mated. He was too close, and she knew it. Her body, the traitor, melted around him. But she would not cave. Not now.

"You have become too comfortable touching my body. A mistake I will surely not make again. Have you not seen what transpired tonight? My mate lives," she said, and the last few words faded to a whisper.

"How can that be? How…" Her voice trailed off, and the conclusion was inescapable. Her husband was alive, and her heart and body now belonged to another.

Rivian couldn't help but hear the desperation and fear in her voice. It angered him that he had failed at the one thing he was tasked to do—keep her safe.

"We will sort this out, no matter the outcome. I will see you safe."

"Because you have done such a fantastic job so far,

Rivian," she spat out. "Fuck you and your kingdom. Ever since I met you, you have challenged everything I thought I was. Then, when I finally cast it to the wind, you bring me here to be sequestered."

"And even now, you still trust these people? Your brother lied to you. Luce and Kia deceived you, and you misled me!" she said with a clipped voice full of dark rage. "I have no more trust or love to give you. You are a deceiver who lies without compunction."

The sharp words twisted his stomach and turned his face to stone. Sole saw how his face transformed. As if a wall went up. She knew his remorse ran as deep as his betrayal. He hadn't realized he was holding his breath when he quietly whispered. "I know I have made mistakes. You are right. So many lies have led us to this night. I have come to realize that I have no one I can trust. I am alone."

Fuck him and her heart for feeling sorry for him at this moment. But when she next spoke, her voice was soft and measured.

"You must go. There is nothing for you here. Make no mistake," the words came out with venom, "my husband lives, and he will see me safe. So I'd ask you to leave me to—"

Grabbing her by the waist and pressing her body to his, he said with a tone that was soft and full of conviction, "I may have been wrong about many things, but I have not been wrong about you. Sole, please give me time to—"

"Time to what, Rivian?" she said, trying to push him away. "Talk to your brother who has assured the court you will marry Selah, or the fact that my mate has made a promise to the High King which I took no part in? Why do men feel it necessary to tell women what to do when all they ever seem to do is muck shit up? I am tired of men telling me what to do. I am the daughter of Lygia, Queen of Mōsa, a mighty queen and warrior. I will not bow. Now please leave—"

Taking her mouth, Rivian kissed her hard, pushing her against the golden wall beside her door. His lips were still sweet with honey wine from the feast. Warmth blossomed in Sole's chest, sparks igniting as Rivian leaned in close, too close, as their lips brushed together, tentatively, for the last time. Their magicks began to weave and swirl together. The soft smell of her vanilla lavender perfume was dizzying, butterflies dancing in her stomach. His lips were warm and parted slightly, allowing his tongue to slip inside.

Breaking the kiss and pushing him off her, Sole breathlessly instructed, "Don't you ever do that again!"

Smiling that crooked smile, Rivian said, "As you wish, princess. I will not kiss you until you beg me to kiss you."

"What?" she asked as if drunk.

"You heard me, princess. I will kiss you when you beg me for it. But, for now, know this. Deep in my bones, I feel you. I was undone the moment I met you, and no matter what my brother says, I know you and I could be beautiful together. I will not rest until you are mine once more. Of that, you can be certain."

Moving one of her long locks behind her ear, he asked gently, "As you process your feeling for him, promise me you will always be honest. I know I should not ask this of you after everything that I have done but Sole, I—"

The door suddenly opened and it slammed against the wall, shaking the nearby paintings. A very frustrated Zari, sporting a black eye, stormed out of the room. Then an irritated Nisa with her arms crossed, followed him.

She saw the looks that Rivian and Sole were giving her and said, "What? I told him not to touch me."

"You kissed me back," Zari spat, coddling the eye, now forming a dark purple quarter moon.

"It's not my fault you are both a good kisser and an ass of a man!" Turning to Sole, she said, "Let's go, Sole. We have had enough of Sundom men and their surprises for one night."

Locking arms, the two ladies walked into their new

quarters, reuniting with the Misa warriors.

Staring at the door as if waiting for their return, Rivian whispered, "We are so fucked."

"Yes. Yes, we are my brother," was Zari's only reply.

CHAPTER 20

The Burden of Choices

In the skies over Sundom, two suns burned hot. For six days, Sole had avoided Rivian. He saw her often in the courtyard of his brother's gardens with her mate, Nasir. Rivian had barely slept. He was either tossing, turning, or watching Sole from his window, as she spent time with Nisa and Nasir.

Most days were wasted here in this space raging, sleeping or praying to the Holy Mother, something he never believed in. These days the Holy Mother was his only companion. Whispering to himself, "Everyone prays in the end don't they." This was the end. He had no hope left. No Sole. He never believed in the Holy Mother but wanted to. He needed her to save him from this horrid dream.

When he heard a knock on the door, Rivian rose from his bed with only his gray silk loungers and bare tanned chest. The stubble growing on his face was starting to itch, but he didn't care. Opening the door, Rivian was surprised to see his brother there.

"I haven't seen you, brother. I thought I would come to a check to see how you fair."

"I fare fine, my king."

His silver glare appeared perplexed. "Please, no need to be so formal when we are private, brother. I worry that you have not returned as yourself, Riv."

Rivian wasn't sure his brother's tone sounded much like the kind brother he loved.

"So," he began as he sat on Rivian's golden settee as if it were a royal throne. Looking around Rivian's suite, the king took in the shambles his rooms had become. Clothes tossed onto the ground, the bedsheets were unkempt and needed changing, but it was Rivian's wrecked appearance and attitude that bothered him the most. Gently, he asked, "What ails you, brother?"

"Do you truly want to know what ails me?" he asked, hoping his brother wasn't lost forever but truly cared about Rivian's needs and losses. Rill had been his best friend most of his life, and although his father did his best to keep them separated, Rill never stopped writing his brother while he was at the Sanctum.

"I will always want to know what ails my brother. Sit, let's talk like we did when we were young."

Not sure if he could trust his brother as he once did,

Rivian wasn't sure if he could tell him that he is deeply in love with Sole and that she is his mate. Mate? Well, yes, she was. He couldn't breathe without her. She consumed his every thought, and when she spoke, he was undone.

Sighing deeply, Rivian made his way to his brother. Sitting, he asked, "What are your plans with Queen Sole?"

Looking at him suspiciously, the king responded, "I see. Luce told me you two had become close. I don't blame you, brother. She is a beauty." Just the mere mention of Luce's name tightened Rivian's jaw.

"I know you and Luce have had a bit of a falling out, but I assure you, what he does is for Sundom and your protection. And all under my instruction."

That took him aback and he wondered what else Luce had done due to his brother's bidding. But then, he said, "I do not want to talk about Luce, brother. I want to understand what your plans are."

Shifting on the bed to face his brother, the king's dark gaze took in Rivian's distress. At that moment, Rivian realized his brother's eyes were different. His eyes were once a gentle grey, as the soft grey of a sea gallies wings. Now, hooded grey eyes stared back at him. They were cold, steely, and metallic as they stared back at him, making Rivian think of poisoned armor.

Something had seriously changed in his brother while he was away. But what?

Worried, Rivian voiced, "Brother, tell me more about your connection to Nasir. I see that you have both become quite close. How does this all connect to the Queen of Mōsa?"

Standing and making his way to the tall window, he faced the lush desert garden that provided medicine and food for the people of Sundom. The gardens were calming and breathtaking. The gem of the dessert was what he heard his father call it many times.

"I remember Mother taking me for walks in that garden when she carried you in her womb." Rivian relied on his brother for beautiful memories of his mother since he had never met her. "Chasing me around the ash tree, we would run until I'd fall in exhaustion," he shared. "I wish you knew her. She was the smartest of our Alacor Royal House. She beat father at the hardest games, and he would laugh so hard he would make himself cry. I wish you knew our family then. Before the kingdom, the loss and the lies. I wish she was here now. She'd know what to do."

"Do about what, brother?" Rivian explored.

"There are many things you don't know. So many things have changed since you were last here."

"Tell me about those changes? Are you in danger,

brother?" he questioned. "Rill, whatever it is, I am here now" Rivian reached for his brother's hand.

The king looked frail; how had Rivian not noticed it before now? It wasn't just his personality that changed. It was his whole being. Surely becoming king was not what changed him so.

Grabbing his king's face, Rivian demanded, "What has happened, Rill? Let me help you!"

"Father was right. You will kill me," King Rill proclaimed as he rose from the bed and began to walk away.

"Kill you? What? I would never; you are my family. My only family. You are my king, and I love you, brother."

"Once I tell you what you want to know, there will be no turning back," the king said. "Shortly after you left, father became progressively worse. I knew that it was a matter of time before he perished. I decided I needed to speed up that time."

His brother's words stopped Rivian from responding. Was he telling him that he murdered their father? He murdered the king? That was impossible. Rill was the light in his father's eyes. He was the future. Not Rivian.

Continuing Rill shared, "That was when Nasir offered to end his pain and madness."

Rivian felt his power shift through his body. He hadn't felt his magic in a while, but now, it burned like a raging fire. Not here, not now, he thought to himself. Why would he be upset about a father who never loved him being murdered by Nasir? No matter what his father wasn't to him, he was still his father. He never wished his father dead.

Controlling the raging magic burning inside, he said, "How did he do it? How did he kill our father?" The words came out bitter and with more bite than Rivian would have liked.

Surprised at his words, Rill continued, "He is a powerful beast. Luce believes that whatever he experienced in that vault destroyed the man he was. Initially, I thought his power was because he was a Mōsian. It wasn't until I saw him crush our father's head... there was blood everywhere." Then, looking into his brother's eyes, he said, "Riv, he never touched him with his hands."

"What are you saying to me?"

"We both stood there, blood everywhere." His eyes filled with tears. Swallowing hard, Rivian clenched his hands, fighting his magick as he realized Nasir was not who Sole thought he was.

"Is he a danger to Sole? Brother, I need to know."

"He is a danger to us all."

Standing, Rivian looked at his brother with the rage he could no longer control. "You are king. A living symbol, a star upon which Sundom's future is held. You have betrayed us all. For what?" Rivian shouted. Raising one's voice to the King of Sundom was a clear desire to go to the gallows but Rivian didn't fucking care. His brother had risked everything at the cost of his people.

Whispering, Rill said, "I have danced with a demon, and I fear that if we don't give him what he wants, he will doom us all. His magick is a darkness that I can't explain. Surely you have noticed that since your return, Sundom is different. Storms come in faster. The suns last longer in the sky, heating our vegetation. After he crushed our father's skull, I realized he was not what I expected. I called the guards. In an instant, he glamoured them with his dark eyes. He made them kill themselves. Some took their own swords to their guts. Others attacked their brothers. When it was all over, he stood in front of me. Someone must have cut his arm because he was bleeding. But the blood. The blood was thick and black. He then fed that blood to my dead Sun Guards. When his blood falls, things come back to life."

"What does he want?"

Exhausted, the king continued, "There are only two things he wants. He wants Mōsa and all the western isles. He wants to rule it free of Sundom's tyranny. Secondly, he wants her, but not as his queen. He wants to take her magick for himself. Once he has that, he says he will leave Sundom. Rivian, you must know by now, after reading all the books I sent you through Luce…"

Rivian closed his eyes, knowing full well what his brother was getting at.

"Rivian, do you understand now the true power of the dagger?"

"It has power over the life and death of magick. It can take magick and give it," Rivian said, saying it out loud for the first time, "Same goes for a life."

Rill nodded and said, "Nasir will use the dagger to transfer Sole's power to him, and this exchange will kill the princess."

"That's your burden, brother. Save the princess, and let this demon ravage our kingdom. Save our kingdom, and sacrifice the princess to the demon. For my part in this, I am so very sorry, little brother."

Rivian could feel his magick raging now, pulsating through his body.

"Rivian, your eyes, they are glowing."

Eyes glowing amber, Rivian said, "Sit down, brother. I have much to tell you."

Then he reached back and with one fist full of his electric energy, he threw Rill across the room, smashing the large, gilded mirror as he crashed into the book case toppling it and all its contents onto the ground.

Brothers shouldn't fight each other for the throne. But he would fight for her.

And here they were. On opposite sides, swords drawn.

After clashing swords and Rivian's swirling magick, the brothers were panting from exhaustion. Then, sitting on the floor as they did as children, Rivian explained everything. His unfathomable love for the Queen of Mōsa, his newfound magick, and why Sole can't forgive him. Rill looked at his brother, lost in thought, and whispered, "Forgive me. I will use whatever power is at my disposal to make this right."

CHAPTER 21

Twice Lost

There was sadness on Sole's face as she told Nasir he looked a lot like his father. And yet, he hadn't had the response she would have expected from someone so close to his father as Nasir was. It wasn't that his eyes didn't share her sentiment but rather that his eyes didn't give her anything except that same darkness she saw the night he died.

It had been weeks now. Weeks during which she hadn't spoken to Rivian. Why did that bother her? Why did dreams of him interrupt her sleep while she laid beside her mate? Sleeping with Nasir again was a dream she prayed for. When he was gone, she had a recurring dream. Nasir was waiting for her in front of her parents' home. She'd run to that doorstep and jump into his arms. His grey eyes would love her and remind her that she was safe. But that was not what this felt like. Nasir was not interested in being intimate, which she was happy about. This pause gave her time to think about what had happened with Rivian, and how it make her miss him.

Sometimes, when she spoke to Nasir, she couldn't shake the feeling that she was annoying him.

This evening, Nasir, Sole, and Nisa played cribitach, a game they often played as children. Nasir and Nisa were always competitive and squabbled in jest. Tonight had been different.

Nisa won the round, and like she did when they were kids, she shouted, "I am the queen!" When they were children, they would all laugh. But tonight, Nasir stood, and with a cold glare slapped Nisa. The slap rocked Sole to the core and dropped Nisa onto the floor. His grey eyes went black, and the women knew two things; Nasir had magick, and the Nasir they knew was dead.

Sole ran to Nisa's aide. Nasir's cold, hard eyes attempted to hold her in place with a power she didn't recognize. The dark mist captivated his hands and tried to stop her. But, believing she was being attacked, Sole's blood began to electrify with pure violet power and pushed back, hard.

Her magick took a hold of the powerful dark mist trying to stop her breath. It surrounded Nasir and tossed him across the room. Landing on his feet before he crashed into the wall, the two held each other's gaze.

One not of love, but of rage.

Suddenly, Luce and Zari were at their door responding to the commotion. Sole reached for the door with her magick, locking them out for fear they would be harmed.

She made her way to Nisa, who still held her face in horror. Her brother, her protector, had hit her. As Sole lifted her to her feet, Nisa whispered, "I don't know who that man is, but he is not my brother. Crush him."

Nasir's black magick swirled around his dead hands. He traversed towards Sole with a devilish grin splitting his face. Then, while showing too many teeth, he said, "Sole, you should smile more."

"Did you think you were the only one blessed by the Holy Mother with magick? Oh, you were always so naive. So gullible. It's what he always loved about you. It's what I despise the most."

His voice low and gravely, Nasir said, "How I could ever love a second-born daughter is beyond me."

"I thought you loved me," Sole said, not clearly understanding who stood before her.

"Maybe he did. But maybe you were also the easiest target on his way to being the king of Mōsa. Luna is too set on her ways and Lola is too wild. You, however? You were easy pickings."

Sole thought her heart couldn't break any more, but it did just now.

"You see, queen. I know his heart. And his heart had always had flecks of black, even before the Darkness. But did you honestly think you would let them throw him in the charnel house with all those dead, and it wouldn't change him? It created me. He lay there for months as the bodies piled up. Finally, he died while you slept amongst our people, and I took over," he whispered bitterly.

Her voice cracked and raw, she said, "I didn't know. How could I?"

"Typical." His tone walked the line between bitterness and incredulity. "Leave it to you to continue to play the victim. I wonder if you ever get tired of demanding attention when you haven't earned it. Even obtaining magick came easy to you. You should be grateful."

His words cut deep.

How could her dearest friend, first lover, her husband say these horrible things? Her heart broke, again. But she would not let him see the pain he was causing her. She was standing, but this battle took too much out of her. The warm liquid dripping from her nose told her she had pushed too far.

Another dark wave wrapped around her waist, lifting her off the ground. This dark magick was corrupting her very soul. She had to do something, or she felt she would die here and now.

"What do you want?" she asked.

"I want you," he whispered in the way Nasir would say sweet words of love and lust. But this was not Nasir, just a thief wearing his skin. "Well, I want your magick. You, not so much."

"The new king and I have made a deal. He would give me you and all the islands surrounding Mōsa if I killed his father, the king. I kept my end of the bargain, and tonight we set sail for Mōsa," he said, releasing her from his tight, hellish grip.

Flat and steady, she whispered, "Two kingdoms…" Her voice trailed off; the conclusions were inescapable. Nasir would usher in the Dark Throne. He would be the end of all things good. He would be the end of her, if she let him.

She was tired of being perceived as weak, protected, and underestimated. Today, the world would see her mother's daughter. Her fierce, violet eyes told him she was done with this conversation. Her hands began to itch, and she knew she was close to letting her magick speak for her. She just needed to buy herself a little more time.

A bang at the door shifted Nasir's focus. It was Zari and Luce, demanding entrance.

"Sometimes, you look the same. Like my Nasir. But then you look at me, and I know. You could never be him. So I will cut you down and watch you bleed for Nasir and the people of Mōsa, but mostly for me."

Standing on her feet, her magick raged to the surface. Nose bleeding and with a voice full of conviction, Sole said to her once mate, "Here before, now, and after."

Her magick left her body and passed through her brown fingers, firing its way to Nasir. She began to move as if possessed. Her magick controlling her body. Lifting her hands, palms up, a raging violet fire surrounded her. The room now pulsed with an overwhelming purple aura. Turning to Nisa with a voice full of urgency, she said, "Run!"

With his tone stiff and surly, Nasir stretched out his hand, "Oh, Sole, you have no idea what I can do." His black mystical power surrounding her. The pressure choking her, crushing her, making it difficult to catch a breath.

The panic fought to rise to the surface. She aimed her hands toward the dark mist as if trying to silence the storms of Sudom.

Closing her eyes, she remembered her father's saying, "Magick lives in you and in me," and her mother's gentle words, "You were born to do great things." The violent violet fury in her eyes surprised Nasir, but he was unmovable.

Her wrath raged. Nasir's dark shadows rose, his magick clashed against her own. Nasir charged. Sole lifted her hands once more. Her violet fire burned through Nasir. His mist consumed her flesh. She could feel it burning into her bones. Into her soul. She didn't know how, but her hands felt like they were engulfed in flames.

She closed her palm. Her violet wave pulled back before setting the room on fire. His dark mist melted to the ground. Suddenly, she felt Nasir behind her.

Turning, she swung her palm in his direction. Shoving her hands forward, flames of violet and a familiar electric amber raced towards Nasir, tossing him forcefully against the wall and onto the hard stone floor.

The room went quiet.

He laid there, lifeless.

Turning to see where the amber magick wave came from, she saw him standing there.

Rivian had come for her.

"Riv," was all she could get out before everything grew dark.

***

The sunlight woke Rivian. It was the third moon rise since Sole had battled Nasir.

Sitting here with her now, he was sure of two things. First, she was his mate, and he would do anything to protect her. The king had visited every day since the battle. Sitting in silence with his brother, Rill realized his brother loved this woman. Which meant Rivian may never forgive him for his treachery.

Nisa refused to leave her side, no matter how many times Rivian offered to watch over Sole. Nisa didn't care. Her place was here, with her, which meant Zari was in Sole's room, often trying to be close to Nisa. The two weren't speaking yet, as Nisa was still angry with him. Her perpetual eye rolls every time he said something were a clear sign she was still reeling over the betrayal.

Luce and Kia brought food in every day in hopes that Rivian could find a way to forgive them. But Rivian couldn't bring himself to eat or speak to anyone. He didn't care about anyone's feelings. He just wanted her. Once she woke, he would take her away from this place.

Into the silence, for the first time in days she spoke. "You should all smile more." Turning to face her, Rivian kissed her. He couldn't care less about who saw him. She was his, and he would never allow anyone, including himself, to keep them apart.

Looking into her eyes, he whispered, "Hey."

"Hey, blue eyes," she whispered back.

"Everyone out," he commanded.

Reluctantly, they all left the room except for Nisa, who lingered. She made her way to Sole. Kissing her on the forehead, she whispered, "You did the right thing. I love you." With that, she walked out of the room, closing the door behind her.

Leaning in closer, Rivian offered her water.

"How long was I out?"

"Almost four moon rises."

"That explains why you look like shit."

Chuckling, Rivian smiled. "There's my girl. All of my memories of you feel like magick. I know I fucked up with Selah and my brother. I want you to know you are my home. You are the future. You may want me to leave after the shit I have done, but please don't make me. I couldn't survive. I don't want to. I want you. So, if you let me make it up to you, I can promise one thing. I will never leave you. I just don't know how."

She sat up with help from Rivian, saying, "I'm not afraid anymore. If this isn't what you want, I under…" Grabbing her face, he kissed her once more. Passionately taking her mouth, he whispered, "You are magick to me."

CHAPTER 22

Making Amends

It had been a week since Rivian told her what happened after she fainted that night in the study. Nasir's body was kept in the Charnel house, as was Transean custom and tradition. Once someone died, the body belonged to their kin. In this case, Sole was the only one who could say what to do with his body.

"Is he alone?" she asked.

Reaching for her hand, Rivian knew precisely what she meant. If Nasir woke, she didn't want him to be surrounded by dead bodies. He assured her that although he was in the charnel house, he was not alone.

"I have seen to it myself," his tone soft and low.

Continuing "I have checked on Nasir daily and have placed three sunguards to safeguard his resting place."

Even after everything he had done to her, she still worried about Nasir. That is what Rivian loved most about Sole. Her ability to think of others before herself.

He loved her, and he told her as much. Finally, when she hadn't said it back, he understood.

She had to process so much pain over the last several days that he wanted to give her time. That didn't mean he wasn't with her every waking moment. Mornings were spent on his terrace overlooking his desert garden. Evenings were filled with all her favorite foods while Luce and Zari argued over who was better with a sword. Laughter, joy, and sometimes tears filled the great hall. But they were together. Looking around the room, sipping on his honey wine, he knew that no matter what happened beyond this moment, these people were his family.

Giving her space meant they had not been intimate since the Dark Wilds. The agony of being unable to be inside her sometimes made it difficult to breathe. But his body would need to wait for her. There was no time to think about touching her rich, full breasts. Although he thought of it often. He loved her and knew that when she was ready, she would tell him.

Seeing Kia approach Sole, Rivian and Nisa rose to their feet as if preparing for war. Then, placing her hand on Rivian, Sole told him with her eyes that it was fine.

Scratching the back of her head, Kia said, "Sole…." Nisa coughed loudly, signaling that Kia had not addressed the queen correctly, and after everything the bitch had done, she didn't get to be so informal with Sole. Clearing her throat, Kia continued, "I mean, Queen Sole, may I have a word?"

The room felt small and grew immensely quiet.

Standing to her feet, she said, "Of course."

Together they walked to the gilded terrace facing the sand dunes of Sundom. The moonrise was near and the pink skies seemed to be never-ending.

"What did you need Kia?"

"I've tried to make things right. But, unfortunately, in that, I have done some serious harm."

"Continue," Sole said with arms crossed.

"You see, I have known Rivian most of my life. At one point, I thought we might even be mates. So when Selah was presented as his betrothed, I was livid."

"Do you plan to continue telling me how much you love Rivian? Or is there a point to this discussion?" Sole said impatiently.

"The moment I saw him watch you board the Rivian, I knew then."

"Knew what?"

"That he loved you."

Startled by her frankness, Sole turned to face the dunes once more.

"You don't put up with his shit and you demand respect. Being the prince of Sundom means he gets whatever he wants when he wants it. But not with you. With you, I saw a side of him I had never seen before. A soft, gentle, loving side. As much as I struggled to see you both grow closer, I was sure of one thing. You are his equal."

Sole never really saw herself as anyone's equal. She saw herself as a scholar, a friend, but never an equal. To hear this from Kia now revealed to Sole that the tragedy of losing her family made her the woman she is today.

Kia continued, "When Selah approached me about destroying what was between you and Rivian, I agreed, and I was wrong."

Turning to face her, Sole spoke with violet eyes flashing. "You were wrong for many reasons. You wanted me to feel small. Bravo, you succeeded. Many before, you have done the same. I learned long ago that the Holy Mother's plan for my life may not make sense to many. The blessings that would come would make small people want to inflict their low worth on me. You made it your point to hurt, isolate, and ridicule me. Even when all I have ever done is try to befriend you." Violet eyes easing to a soft lavender, Sole asked, "So I ask you now, what do you ask of me?"

A silence grew between the two women. After all that had happened, how could they move forward?

Breaking the silence, Kia said, "I wish we could start

anew. Rivian and the boys are my only family. I've never had sisters. I fear it has made me a bit rough around the edges.

"You and Nisa have found a way to see us all for who we are and what we are not. I ask... no, I beg" she said with her jaw tightening, "that you forgive me for the harm and allow me the opportunity to be a part of this family once more."

Stunned, Sole never thought Kia would say such things, and the silence between them grew deafening. As Kia awkwardly played with her pink pixie cut, Sole understood how difficult this conversation was for her.

"I am not saying that we are friends or that it is all forgiven. I am saying I heard you and that maybe one day it won't be so awkward between us."

"That's all I ask. For a chance to make this right."

They both turned to return to the great hall when they saw five sets of eyes peering back at them from the tall gilded glass doors. The group scattered. As they walked to rejoin the group, Kia said, "One more thing, I hated every fucking minute I shared with Selah. She's awful."

Making her way back to the doors, with a smirk revealing her deep dimples, Sole simply stated, "I know."

***

Sitting in the vast ornate hall with her newfound family, Sole knew it would be hard to say goodbye to them. She and Nisa both agreed that it was time to return to Mōsa. Earlier this morning, she had an audience with the king. When the lanky, white-haired Sun Guard told Sole that King Rill asked for an audience with the Queen of Mōsa, she told Rivian it was best if she went alone.

Since the battle with Nasir, Rivian refused to leave her side. And she loved that. When he told her that he loved her, she cried. Yet she couldn't say it back. Too much had happened. His lies, manipulation, and ultimately his love would all take time to digest. She knew telling him that she needed to meet with King Rill alone was going to be a challenge.

"Fuck that!" he shouted. "I love my brother, but I will never trust him with you. Never."

Gently touching his face, Sole said, "Rivian, if I am ever to rule Mōsa on my own, I must be able to hold an audience with any king on my own. Besides, it's time he and I have a long chat about Mōsa's future."

He went on to say more but was interrupted by a gentle kiss on the lips. Then, locking eyes as their foreheads touched, she whispered, "I will be fine. I will bring Nisa with me. After all, she is my highest counsel."

"Now you must go," she whispered. I must be queenly when I meet with your king," she said.

Kissing his mate one last time, Rivian walked Sole to her quarters. Before she entered her room, she turned to Rivian and said, "Would you meet me here at moonrise? I think it's been far too long, don't you think?"

Stunned, Rivian replied with a nervous "Yes, yes, queen. I will bring the honey wine and…"

"And nothing else," she said as she quietly closed the doors to her quarters.

CHAPTER 23

The Queen of Mōsa

"I know what I am doing!" Nisa exclaimed as she chose what Sole would wear for her meeting with the king.

"I don't think black is a suitable color to wear. It's not very me," Sole said apprehensively.

"I have been dressing you since we were young, and I know what looks good on you. Now, relax and let me do this."

"Always so demanding," Sole said with a wink.

Slowing down long enough to lock eyes with her best friend, Nisa said, "Forgive me. The days in this forsaken land are long. We have lost much only to lose more upon arriving here."

Sitting in silence, the women held hands. Taking Sole right back to the day she had healed Nisa from the Darkness. It was a miracle the two women were here now. Ready to return home but not before Sole met with King Rill.

***

Sole didn't recognize the woman staring back at her from the gilded mirror. The black velvet dress left her toned arms uncovered. It was supported around her neck and flowed down gracefully cinching at the waist and billowing out just as it touched the floor. It was a tight fit that gracefully focused on her breasts.

"This is a great choice. This velvet against your skin forms the perfect combination. You are an ideal blend of grace and style. As every queen should be," Nisa said, standing behind Sole as they stared at Sole's reflection in the full-length mirror. Nisa always had a way with fashion. Sole trusted her judgment when she wanted to look her best.

But now, she looked like her mother. A lot like her mother. And she didn't know how she felt about that.

The dress's waist was slim and adorned with a thin snug golden belt.

"And the final piece," Nisa said as she took Sole's fathers's crown out of a black box. It was no longer tarnished, revealing a bright golden spiked sunburst halo crown.

"Now, you look like a queen. The Queen of Mōsa."

"I shouldn't be queen," Sole said. She didn't recognize the woman in the mirror staring back at her.

Turning Sole to face Nisa's grey gaze reminded Sole that what she was about to say was serious.

"You are the Queen of Mōsa. You were destined to be our queen. Now go do what only you can do. Save our people."

Her voice was soft and measured. Sole said, "Damn, you are good at that."

"Good at what?" Nisa asked.

"I swear you could motivate the Holy Mother if given a chance," Sole said, smiling. "I know we have been through unspeakable losses. But I am glad we survived them together."

Nisa seemed about to speak, but the thread eluded her. Instead, tears filled her eyes. Losing Nasir for the second time made her feelings more complicated. It was more brutal and tragic than when he first died. Sole couldn't help but stare at Nisa's neck, still red from his magick trying to take her life.

Wiping her tears from her eyes, the two women embraced after Nisa said, "Enough whimpering. We have a king to address."

***

Modest braziers attached to one side of each of the ten basalt columns lit up most of the throne hall that evening. The shadows played and danced where light could not reach. The milky marble stone of the domed ceiling danced in the flickering light, while grand statues taking refuge in hollows passed judgement on those passing through the refined hall.

A crimson rug flowed from the foot of the throne before ending several meters away, while matching banners with the gilded family crest hung from the walls. Between each banner, brilliant flames flickered from torches, illuminating sculptures below.

Immense glass windows were enclosed by drapes colored the same crimson hue as the banners. In addition, the curtains had been adorned with impressive needlework and gilded linings.

It was the throne that took Sole's breath away. She had never seen anything like it.

A radiant throne of gold sat amidst two giant statues adjoined by two similar but smaller seats for visiting royalty of other nations.

Sole observed several luxurious and comfortable alder benches lined up perfectly for those waiting for an audience with the king. But today, there would be no audience. Today, Sole would speak to the king as one royal to another.

"Entering Lia Soleidae of Porte house, the second daughter of Mōsa, risen healer of the Serena Sea, the blessing of Sundom, the unbreakable yielder of magick, Queen of Mōsa, and the last of her name."

Hearing it took her back. Queen of Mōsa was not at all what she had expected to become, but it was what she was destined for, whether she felt ready or not.

Standing there for a brief moment, Sole knew there would be no turning back after this step. Then, taking a deep breath, Sole placed her black satin slipper on the throne room floor and made her way to King Rill.

Sitting on his throne, Sole couldn't dismiss how much Rill and Rivian looked alike. Although their personalities couldn't be further apart, one thing was true; Rill and Rivian would make any girl swoon. Rill's shoulder-length white-blonde hair and crystal blue eyes were intimidating, but she would be unmoved today.

"Let me be the first to formally congratulate you on your title, Queen Sole Porte of Mōsa."

Bowing graciously, she said, "Your Highness."

"I ushered you here this night to discuss the future of Mōsa."

"I would like to discuss the future of Mōsa as well," she said, her eyes unwavering.

"Now that we are allies, I think it best to join forces to build one new world."

"I beg your pardon, King Rill. May I call you Rill?" she asked with a devilish smile. "I wouldn't call us allies. I would call us acquaintances, because of your missteps."

His jaw tightening, the king continued. "Our fathers' mistakes will not be our own."

"You forget yourself, King Rill. My father was a great ruler. He was fair and honest and loved his people. Your king took many missteps, causing harm to his people and his sons. Please never compare the two in my presence," she said. Her eyes flickered with violet fire.

Shifting in his seat, he said, "Your father, just like mine, divided Transea and their fathers before them. Our generation can restore what has been taken from us."

The silence in the great hall was deafening.

He broke the silence, "I will make you a promise here and now. I will give you all of Mōsa and the surrounding kingdoms to rule at your behest."

Laughing out of disgust, Sole said, "Your highness, you forget yourself. Wasn't this the same promise you made to my fallen prince? How did that turn out for you?"

The echo of the king slamming his hand on the arm of his throne permeated the room. Although startled by his moment of rage, Sole would not let him see how fast her heart was beating or how her sweaty hands consumed her interlocked fingers.

Walking towards the massive windows facing the

dunes of Sundom, Sole saw the two moons in the horizon. "Last I heard, you were not the king of Kingsguard Reef, Grimerg Rise, or the Sanctum. So why do you offer their lands so freely?"

"Princess, I mean, your majesty, many things have changed since the Darkness. Mōsa was hit the hardest, but we have now received word that many in Kingsguard Reef and the Sanctum have fallen ill to the Darkness. When your mother and father passed on, many who felt protected by their alliance with Mōsa turned to Sundom, asking for refuge and support. That is what we did."

Surprised that only Mōsa had been left undefended while she slept, Sole knew that an alliance would make the most sense. She wanted her people to feel free. She remembered what her mother always told her. "To live in freedom, you must learn to walk in forgiveness." She would have to forgive this king. Forgive him for Nasir, for Rivian, for all of Transea. But she didn't know if she could do that.

"What's the catch?"

"I beg your pardon?"

"What do you want in return?" she asked again, her tone void of emotion.

"In return, you will work on healing all who fall to the Darkness. Then, once a year, you will come here for a season to show your allegiance to Sundom." Shifting in his seat, looking a bit uncomfortable with what he was about to say next, he continued, "You will be betrothed to a Sundom royal."

As Sole attempted to speak, the king raised his hand, still covered in bandages from the altercation with Nasir, and said, "Before you protest, know this. The only way to keep our people safe is to unite forces. Magick has returned, and soon the Dark Throne will rise. We must face the Darkness together."

It seemed as though she had been pacing for an eternity. The king looked bored as he waited for a response. Finally, she said, "I will agree to your terms."

Smiling, Rill rose to his feet and said, "That's wonderful!"

Raising one hand, she said, "Before you agree, I must tell you what my terms are."

Sitting down on his throne with his jaw tight, the King waved his hand, ushering her to proceed.

"I will heal as many as I can from the Darkness. But I will never again leave my people unprotected. I will need funds to recruit new Misa warriors from King's Guard and Grimerg Rise, and rebuild Mōsa. I am sure your coffers haven't suffered the losses we have experienced on the west coast. The coin you provide us with now will be received as a gift in our partnership."

"Very well. I can sense another detail coming."

Sole swallowed hard before continuing, "I want our kingdoms to begin talks on how best to rehabilitate Sanctum. I have had enough of families across Transea tossing their second born children to the Sanctum to be trained for war, or some other use, while believing they cannot be loved beyond their usefulness."

"You know the Sanctum will not agree to such terms."

"It is made up of children. Those children belong to families, powerful families. I am sure you can persuade them with your dashing eyes and riveting conversation," she said coolly, between bitterness and incredulity. "I know that one is a little tricky so I will allow you more time to think and plan for it. I only ask that you think of Rivian while you think about how best to go about changing the Sanctum."

Rill said flatly, "Why, thank you for your graciousness, Queen of Mōsa."

She gave him a small smile and continued, "Additionally, you will be betrothed to a Mōsian royal or citizen of your choosing. You will travel to Mōsa once a year during our harvest, where you will purchase our wares. And finally, you will grant me a vessel to return to Mōsa tomorrow, where I will rebuild and begin my travels to the other regions."

Calling for a squire, the King of Sundom and the Queen of Mōsa entered a treaty. Both hoped it was the right thing for their people. As Sole prepared to head back to her quarters, she turned to the king and said, "Your mistakes in trusting the wrong person could have cost you your kingdom and your brother. If you do anything to hurt Rivian again, treaty or not, I will end you."

"I wouldn't expect anything else," he said with a smirk.

With that, she walked out of the great hall and led her Misa warriors to her quarters.

CHAPTER 24

Ghosts of Lovers Past

Sole slipped into her silk white nightdress. It was the same one Rivian first saw her in on the Radiant. The lights were low and the scent of lavender permeated the room and her moonstone skin. She was ready to tell Rivian everything, but first, her desire to be close to him, to feel him on top of her, took center stage.

Tonight would be the first night they would be intimate since the Dark Wilds. Even though they had made love before, she was nervous. What if he wasn't interested in her? What if he decided that Selah was the woman he should mate with? What if—?

A knock at the door startled her out of her toxic thoughts. He was here. Her heart beat faster. He had come for her. There was nothing that could stop them now. Glancing at herself one last time in the mirror, Sole adjusted her long locks to one shoulder, revealing her soft neck. Making her way to the door, she saw him there.

"I brought the—" He stopped to gawk at her. Then, composing himself, he continued, "I brought the honey wine."

Opening the door wider, Sole invited him in with her eyes. That was when she noticed his blue eyes started to flicker amber. His magick was alerted, and Sole smiled at the idea that he still didn't know how to control it.

"You look beautiful," he said as he closed the gap between them. "Fuck, you are beautiful. I will never understand why they told us the women of Mōsa were not lovely creatures. You are captivating. When I see you, I am undone."

"You aren't too bad looking yourself. I almost told your brother the same thing when I met him today."

"What the fuck?" Smiling, he pulled her closer and said, "I will fucking kill him or anyone else that touches you. You are mine alone." His voice grew deeper as his amber eyes flickered.

Taking her mouth, Rivian didn't know how he had survived all these years without her. As he kissed his way down her neck, he gently pulled on the string of her white nightdress. As it floated to the floor, she stood before him, naked, in the soft light. Bare, breathless, and his. She was his, and he would do everything he could to make her happy and keep her safe. He loved her. He hoped she felt the same. Tonight, he would do everything in his power to show her how much he loved her.

His kisses lingered on her breast, and with every suck, bite, and lick, she found herself gasping for air. It had never felt like this with Nasir. He was gentle and loving. Rivian was passionate, confident, and caring. The connection she felt now told her one thing. Rivian was her fated mate. She has never loved anyone like this before. Suddenly, the orgasm that woke her from her dreams every night since arriving in Sundom reached her. Screaming his name, Rivian gently covered her mouth. "Shush! The warriors will think I have harmed you," Rivian said with a laugh as he laid her on the bed.

"They know better than to interrupt their queen when she is entertaining her mate," she panted.

Lifting his head from her breast, he looked up at her and said, "Mate? Say it again." He began raining kisses all the way down to her navel.

"I don't know what you are talking about," she whispered as she guided his head down below.

"You know what you need to say. Say it again, my queen."

"Why did you have to say 'my queen' with that fucking sexy tone?" she asked, whimpering with need. Then she yelled, "Fuck!" when a second orgasm reached her. She knew he loved it every time she came because his eyes, those fucking eyes, flickered amber until they stayed that way. She could grow to love those eyes. Looking up at him as he pressed his hard body over hers, she knew. She could never give this up. Never.

His eyes flickering, he spread her legs, looked at her glistening pussy, and groaned. He knew he had to be inside her. Standing to pull off his black trousers, he released his hard cock. Panting harder, Sole knew what came next, and she was ravenous.

Pressing his hard body onto her, Rivian whispered, "You should smile more, Sole."

"What?" she asked, thinking she had misheard him. He began to laugh when suddenly his laughter erupted into something dark, evil. Sole knew something was terribly wrong.

"You should smile more!" he yelled with a voice that could cut glass. Facing him, Sole could see Rivan's eyes were fully amber now. Not one blue fleck remained. Sole rose to her feet, using her magick to throw him across the room. She attempted to summon her warriors, but Rivian held her back. She knew she would have to face the man she loved alone.

"Rivian, I don't want to hurt you," she said as she reached for the navy robe that sat on her settee. "If your magick has caused you distress, we can figure it out. We can talk to Rill, and he can—"

"Did you always whine this fucking much when you were with Nasir? No wonder he chose to die on his mating night. You are insufferable."

Stunned, Sole couldn't believe what she heard came out of his mouth. What began to rise to the surface wasn't her magick. It was her tears.

"What? Why are you saying this, Rivian?"

Pushing a wave of his amber magick at her, knocking her into the wall and shattering her mirror. A sticky warm liquid began to drip down her forehead and onto her hair. The smell of lavender and blood permeated the air.

Closing the distance between them, Rivian continued, "The master was right. You are garbage, not fit to lead. You are not unique, Sole of Mōsa. Maybe you were to your father before he passed on, but not to me. I regret the day I ever met you."

Looking up at him, Sole could see the rage in his eyes and something else. There were tears streaming down his face.

She realized that somehow, Rivian was being controlled.

"Riv, who has done this to you?"

Once again, he struck her with a wave of his magick, causing her to crash onto the floor. Sole attempted to stand, but something was wrong with her leg. Looking down, she knew it was broken. Rivian made his way toward her and knew if she didn't do something, he would kill her.

Pulling from her healing magick, Sole sent a wave to Rivian. She knew she couldn't hold it for very long. The damage he had done to her body was taking a toll. Suddenly, as the magick consumed him, Rivian's clear blue eyes returned.

"I can't stay long. I love you, Sole. Nasir lives, and he will destroy you. You must call the warriors now; I don't know how long I can hold him back!"

"Hold who back?!"

"Nasir," Rivian said it too fast and too loudly. She knew he would soon fade away. She couldn't help the tears streaming down her face. Rivian couldn't either. Placing her on the soft bed, he kissed her hard, and then his hands wrapped around her throat. Unable to catch her breath, Sole faded and let the Darkness consume her.

CHAPTER 25

Sisters

It was their laughter that woke her from her deep sleep. Lola's wet, wavy hair laid flat against her deep brown skin. The more the women splashed water, the faster Sole found herself running to reach them. But her legs grew heavy.

Suddenly Luna's hazel eyes—her mother's eyes—stared back at Sole. Standing next to Luna, Lola reached out her dainty hands toward Sole, saying, "When will you come to us, sister?" Grief attempted to accost her once more.

Pushing back the tears, realizing she had cried enough, Sole whispered, "I want to be with you. There is nothing left for me there."

The three women embraced; Sole couldn't help but believe this was where she was meant to be. Maybe, she had finally died. Perhaps she could finally find peace. She would do anything to stay in the pink ocean she loved with her sisters. Lola held Sole's face in her gentle hands when her eyes changed from hazel to forest green as she whispered, "Find me."

In a calm, unhurried voice, Luna held her sister's hands as she said, 'When the dark throne rises, the three shall bring forth an era of magick and sorrow.'

A concerned weary voice shouted, "Your Highness, you must wake. We need you. Wake!"

As quickly as those words were spoken, Sole awoke to a pool of blood dripping from her head. Looking around, Sole saw a strange, beautiful golden room with flowing silk burnt orange curtains. Attempting to sit up, Luce and Rory pushed her back to lie on her settee.

Sitting upright, Sole's violet eyes took in the destruction that was her geodesic dome room. Wondering how her mirror was broken, the memories flooded back, drowning her in the words Rivian last said to her.

Realizing she was half naked, one of her warriors grabbed her a black tunic and travel leggings. "We must make haste; our people's lives are in danger. We are taking you home, Queen Sole, or all will be lost," her trusted warrior Rory exclaimed. Sensing the urgency, Sole's weary voice was cracked and raw. Reaching for her neck, she could feel the swelling circling her neck. Her voice, what had happened to her voice?

Looking up at Luce, he answered the question Sole

asked with her violet eyes. "Your highness, we believe Rivian did that to you. He did everything you see here. We must make haste, as you are in grave danger."

Speaking in a quiet tone as her voice cracked, Sole asked, "Where is Nisa?"

It was the silence that gave them away. No one, not even Luce, would answer that question. Finally, flat and steady, she asked again, "Where is Nisa?"

As Luce finished lacing her travel boots, he helped Sole stand on her feet. Then, whispering to her, he said, "Before I tell you what has happened, you must remember you are the Mōsian queen. What I am about to say to you will change everything. You must hold it until a more suitable time."

Her tone could have frozen Sundom. "Where is Nisa?"

"Earlier this moonrise, the King received word that the three Sunguards guarding the charnel house where Nasir laid dead were decapitated. When the guards entered the space where Nasir should have been, he was gone."

Steading herself with the chair by her study, Sole asked, "Where is he now?"

Luce nodded as he took a moment to find his voice, "We believe he is on his way to Mōsa."

This couldn't be happening. She needed to find Nisa

and leave immediately. Her fists balled tightly, eyes staring blankly, she said, "Continue."

"After Rivian left you here, he made his way to the throne room in search of the king. Nasir met him there. The two men entered the throne room to find the king in the company of Zari and Nisa. Ensuring the king's safety Zari opened the secret compartment that leads to the Sundom tunnels. The king entered the tunnels and later was found in his room."

Luce continued, taking a moment to find his voice again, "Zari and Nisa stayed behind to ensure Nasir never left that room. A battle ensued. A guard outside the throne room saw when Rivian stabbed Zari in the chest."

Luce's voice was weary as tears threatened to escape. Then, he said, "That was when Nasir enveloped Nisa with dark magick and extinguished her last breath. She is gone."

"Gone where?" Sole questioned, not realizing that she had been holding her breath.

"Your majesty, Zari may not survive the night, and Nisa... Nisa is dead."

As if in a trance, Sole made her way to her secret drawer, unlocked it by pressing the key slot, and pulled out the blade she and Rivian had found in the Dark Wilds.

Eyes flashing amethyst, tears streaming down her face, Sole said, "Take me to her."

***

The light of the two suns shimmered down on Nisa's body. Her beautiful face was blue, tilted to the side. She met her stare and waited for her glazed-over grey eyes to move. They didn't. Sole's tear-filled eyes wandered down her beautiful face and stopped at her throat.

Her arms and legs were bent at awkward angles. A heavy sigh left her as she stared at her best friend's body devoid of the grace it had recently held.

"Leave us," she whispered to no one in particular.

"Your majesty, we must make…." Luce exclaimed

"Leave us!" she shouted as the echo of her grief permeated the castle.

Closing the doors behind him, Luce stepped outside the door.

Sitting down beside her dearest friend, Sole caressed Nisa's soft hair. Whispering, Sole said, "I have been blessed with many blood sisters. For many years, I thought no one could penetrate that relationship, until you. You did it so graciously that my very territorial sisters adored you. That's what you do, Nis. You capture hearts."

As tears fell like waves onto Nisa's hair, she said, "There are no words… just slashes to describe how hard the future will be. How bitter it will be. How angry I will be. I will simply be lost without you. You have helped me grow into the queen that I am. I will miss you putting others in their place and refusing to tolerate their fucking bullshit."

Caressing the cold hands that once held her back was heart wrenching. Hot tears streaming down her face Sole remembered the last words Nisa uttered "You are the Queen of Mōsa. You were destined to be our queen. Now go do what only you can do. Save our people."

Lighting up her wave of healing magick she sent a wave to her best friend. Over and over again Nisa lay lifeless.

"I know I will see you again. But, for now, know this. You were beautiful, brave, and bold, and I will try my best to be that on this side of eternity. As the years come and go without you, I want you to know this...I will make them pay. I will avenge you and everyone the Darkness has stolen from us."

"Rest easy, my sweet friend. You fought so well, inspired many, loved so profoundly, lived so loudly, and can never be forgotten."

Rising, Sole left the room where her friend lay to find

Luce and Kia waiting for her outside. Turning to Kia, a composed Sole said, "I need to arrange a crypt here in Sundom to place Nisa in."

"The king has arranged for Nisa to be placed in the crypt for the Royal House of Alacor."

Mōsian tradition demanded that a deceased Mōsian be laid to rest immediately. The morning she woke after almost being murdered by her mate Sole had to bury her dearest friend.

Sole turned to Luce and Kia. "Take me to the king."

CHAPTER 26

A New Captain

The throne room had lost its luster. Distress, loss, and grief were palpable. Yet, Sole was determined to hold her resolve. As they waited for the king to join them, Sole didn't pace or play with her hair. She was simply stoic. A queenly vision refusing to let the recent tragedies define her at this moment. She was battle-born, the daughter of Lygia and Axel, and she would not be defeated.

Rill entered the room. Gone was his elaborate gilded attire. A crimson tunic and fitted black trousers made him real somehow. Allowing his vulnerable side to be visible to the allies in this room. It was obvious he loved his brother, and he may have been the very person to lead to his demise.

"Status report," he asked Luce, his tone firm and slightly shaken.

"We believe they have made their way to the

Valiant—the vessel the King once promised to Nasir." For a brief moment, Sole saw a look of terror consume Rill.

Speaking to no one in particular, the king said, "That vessel was stocked with gold, goods, and grain. Where do we think they are heading?"

"We found notes in Rivian and Nasir's rooms where Mōsa was mentioned repeatedly. So, we believe they journey southwest to Mōsa."

Breaking the formality, Sole walked up the stairs leading to the throne. Sitting on his gilded throne, Rill stared as if heartbreak was about to undo him.

"Leave us!" The Queen of Mōsa shouted.

Luce knew better than to challenge her and decided it was best to usher the group out of the throne room.

Turning back to face Rill, Sole embraced him as his tears of guilt, remorse, and rage consumed him.

"What kind of king allows his enemy to take his brother?" he asked brokenly.

Refusing to pardon Rill for his actions, Sole whispered, "We have all made critical mistakes."

The silence consumed the space.

"How could I let him kill Nisa and take my brother if he is not already dead?"

"Take a breath, Rill." Clasping his hands, Sole whispered, "We have all lost much this night. I visited Zari this morn and healed his wound. While with him, he explained what happened. He told me how, right before he stabbed him, Rivian uttered, 'I am sorry, I am lost, brother. Please protect her.'"

Zari also heard Nasir say they would be off to Mōsa immediately. They walked through the corridor, and then they were gone. He thinks they set sail a few hours ago."

"It will take them thirty moonrises to make it to Mōsa."

"I plan to be there when they arrive. But I will need your help. After all, we are allies, are we not?" Sole replied with a slight grin.

"Whatever I have, it's yours. Just make me one promise. You will bring my brother back."

"I will crush whoever gets in my way. I will bring him back if I have to burn down the world to do it."

Surprised at her harsh statement, Rill said, "My, my, Queen of Mōsa, be careful. You are starting to sound like a Sundonian."

Reassembling the group in the throne room, Sole and Rill shared the plan to rescue Rivian and kill Nasir. They didn't even notice the miracle of Sundonians and Mōsians working together to save two kingdoms.

Rill had agreed to provide Sole with a hundred Sun Guards, gold, grain, and a vessel to carry them over the sea. When asked what size vessel she wanted, Sole simply asked, "What size is the Radiant?"

There was no other ship she would trust to get her back home.

A group of Sun Guards barged into the throne room, Selah at the helm.

"What is the meaning of this?" Rill shouted, sounding more kingly than he had since the incident.

Saleh bowed in her golden armor set, a metal, mohawk-like ornament affixed to her helmet, a row of feathers inserted into it. Her masterfully crafted vambraces were adorned with an impenetrable dragon jaw on either side. She wore a tiny skirt of several layered metal sheets reaching just below the groin. It was Selah's upper thigh that had Luce transfixed.

"We have come to save our second-born prince from the Mōsian army."

Rory couldn't help but burst out laughing, causing Selah's jaw to clench.

Rolling her eyes, Sole made her way to Selah Grado, her mate's former betrothed. "Let me make one thing clear. We all love Rivian, but he is my mate, and I will crush anyone that gets in the way of that. Including you. Now, shut the fuck up and listen to my orders."

Flustered, Selah turned to her king for assistance. With a crooked smile, he said, "Princess Selah, have I introduced you to the Queen of Mōsa? Meet Lia Soleidae of Porte house, the second daughter of Mōsa, risen healer of the Serena Sea, the blessing of Sundom, the unbreakable yielder of magick, the last of her name, Queen of the Western Isles, and my beloved brother's mate." Pausing briefly, he added, "It would be best if you bow now."

Bowing, Selah edged out a bitter "I beg your pardon, your majesty. Your wish is my command, Queen of the Western Isles."

***

"We know that the fastest way to Mōsa is not the Serena Sea," Sole explained as they all gazed at the map in the war room. But unfortunately, the group knew this all too well. "This moonrise, we will sail to the foothills of Grimberg Rise, make our way through the Sanctum to reach Mōsa on the twelfth moonrise. It will be dangerous and require much of us. So, If you want to change your mind, the time is now."

Immediately Kia raised her left fist in the air, a Sundom hand gesture signifying unity. It was the words she repeated after that shocked Sole.

Kia shouted, "Here before, here now, and here after." Next, Luce joined her. The Misa warriors slowly raised their fists, reciting the Mōsian motto. Selah's Sun Guards did the same as she reluctantly joined in. When

King Rill rose to his feet chanting the Mōsian oath, she knew they had changed Transea forever.

In this hall of misfits, Sole knew one thing—to save Rivian's life, she would have to learn to kill.

EPILOGUE

It was the scent that woke her from her deep sleep. Lilies, fish, lavender, and grass permeated the air. Her face was lying in the dirt and snow. Unfamiliar trees in every direction surrounded her. Bewildered, she wondered how she had gotten here. Looking around, she tried to get her bearings. Rising, she felt strange. Something seemed out of place.

It wasn't until an odd smell hit her nose that she realized she couldn't hold off the inevitable. Slowly, she stood. Immediately she knew something was very wrong. The place was quiet and soothing. And yet the woman couldn't shake the feeling that something was terribly wrong.

"How did she get here?" She whispered to herself. One moment she was in her room after a big party. Running her fingers through her long coiled hair, she looked around again. For her life, she couldn't remember what party she had attended. But she knew it was special.

She had to think.

She had to remain calm.

Panicking would get her nowhere.

Taking a good long look around her, there was nothing really to see but trees and ground. Occasionally a rabbit would bounce by her, and a bird would fly over her head, and she would shake.

As overwhelmed as she was, she couldn't help but appreciate the beauty surrounding her. Somehow this place reminded her of somewhere extraordinary—her home possibly.

"But where is my home?" she pondered out loud.

Suddenly she noticed something that shocked the breath out of her. The leaves on the trees were turning colors right before her very eyes. She sat bewildered and watched as they shifted from pink to blue to purple and back to pink. She couldn't make any sense of it. Maybe she hit her head at some point. She knew that trees weren't supposed to do this. She remembered someone telling her a story once about magickal trees. But magick hadn't been around for generations. She wished she knew what had happened!

Making her way towards the tall glowing oak, she reached out her hand to touch it. It was as if a fresh wave of water and magick touched her. Somehow she knew this power did not come from the tree but from her. Removing her hand from the oak, she saw her fingertips continue to glow while the tree's light faded away. Then, testing her theory, she touched the leaves, which glistened and shimmered like an ocean in the moonlight. Somehow the closer she got to the tree, the more the leaves reached out for her.

Bewildered and amazed, she knew one thing for sure. She had magick. She remembered being a child and someone, a tall man with a warm smile, would often tell her stories of old when magick was alive. Standing in this forest, she could feel the woods calling to her. The whispers grew as her fingers tingled with warmth the further she entered the field of large trees. Fleeting images crossed her mind. A beautiful woman was eating marbled pie with her. The man with a warm smile was dancing with her at a party. But, it was the two girls sitting together reading a book that captivated her most of all. The way they all loved her was magick. "Where are those people?" She said out loud as she looked around, trying to make sense of where she was.

The moonrise was quickly approaching. She would freeze if she didn't find shelter soon. Then, feeling her hand tingle, she lifted it and studied the green flame flickering on her fingertips, promising to light her way.

Her heart beat as if coming out of her chest. This magick excited her. She wondered what else it could do before hearing twigs snapping to her left. She knew she had to hide and hope for the best. Whatever came near her would be in for a rude awaking, when suddenly she blasted it with a wave of her magick.

Surprised and shocked that she could do such a thing, she walked up to a beautiful man that lay unconscious. What had she done! She was going to run from here. But instead, she just killed someone! Coughing loudly, the handsome man opened his eyes. So, she did the only thing she knew to do…she hid behind a tree and waited quietly.

"Greetings, My Lady," She heard the stranger's deep voice as he coughed to catch his breath.

She peered from around the large trunk of the tree and there he was, a beautiful man with dark, thick hair curled at the nape of his neck. His cheekbones were high and wide, his nose surprisingly straight for a guard. At least she thought he was a guard, given his armor. His square jaw and well-formed mouth turned the knots in her stomach.

"I will not harm you. Are you in distress? It doesn't seem you are, given how strong you are. How did you do that?"

His smile did her in; had she ever seen a smile more pleasant than his? But, the way the right side of his lip curved up, which made his deep dimples appear, would be the death of her. Unless she just died, and this is heaven. Sometimes, dimples appear on both cheeks when he is freely smiling and able to show his fangs.

"You have fangs?" She asked.

Smiling, he said yes. I didn't always have them, but I guess many things have changed since the Darkness." His very tall stature, roughly larger than six feet, forced her to look up at him as he spoke.

"Darkness?" she wondered. Had she ever seen a man that was this tall? She couldn't remember, but it wouldn't surprise her if she hadn't. His captivating eyes were a pool of gold and honey. They scared her and, at the same time, let her know she was safe with him. He smells of chocolate, cinnamon, and pine.

"Are you joking?" he asked.

"About what?"

"About the Darkness? I fear you may not be well."

Not wanting to tell him about her newfound magick, she disclosed her second secret. She was lost.

"I…I am not sure how I got here," She whispered.

Bewildered and concerned, he said, "My name is Kingsley Do'Ramos. But you can call me King. All my friends do."

"Friend? We just met, how could we be friends?" She asked as he stared at her full lips.

"Of course we are friends? My dear lady, I just saved you from being eaten alive by the bears in these woods. So I can assure you I am no stranger. Besides, I believe a beautiful woman should flirt with a King at least once in their lifetime, don't you?" He asked with that adorable, crooked smile.

King couldn't understand why he was flirting with her. She was distressed, but he couldn't resist. Her brown copper skin was like a windfall autumn leaf. Her smoldering, doe green eyes and queenly figure showcased her curly hair as it plunged over her shoulders in waves of midnight black. Her pouting lips looked as soft as suede. But it was her smile that electrified him.

"Well, that settles it; for us to be friends, I must know your name, miss."

Palms sweaty, she said, "I think my name is Lola." It was as if saying her name jarred her memories free. Excitedly she exclaimed, "Yes, my name is Lola Sirena Porte, and I'm from Mōsa."

"Are you joking, my lady?" The gorgeous man asked her.

"I'm sorry. What do you mean? Am I joking?"

Looking at her doe eyes, he could tell she was serious. Closing the gap between them, he reached for her hand, kissed it, and bowed, saying, "Princess, it's just that you are supposed to be dead for over three years. Where have you been all this time?"

ACKNOWLEDGEMENTS

Writing a book is harder than I thought and more rewarding than I imagined. None of this would have been possible without my husband, Jade. I could have never done this without his creative genius, late-night chats about characters, world-building and consistent editing. He has been my greatest support from reading early drafts, designing the original book cover, and keeping the kid and pups out of my hair so I could create this novel. He is just as crucial to this book getting done as I was. Thank you so much, honey. Thank you for being my real-life Rivian.

To my Jaden, who taught me that I could create a new world full of science and magick! His energy and creative soul helped me visualize a world that was living in my mind. I am thankful every day for his creative soul and that I get to be his mom.

To my Papi, Felipe took me to every fantasy movie with a backpack full of Snickers. That time with you taught me to dream big.

In many ways, this novel is my family's story and how they faced the complexities of entering a new world full of prejudice and loss. But, it's also about resilience, power, and immense love. The people of Mōsa represent my deep roots and love for my Dominican heritage and people.

Yvette, Jenny, Debbie, Alex, and Genesis, I am eternally grateful to be their sister. The authentic sibling relationships found in these pages are because God gave me them.

To Melissa, my best friend. Every part of Nisa Asha is Melissa. She stood by me during every struggle and all my successes. Rest easy, Amiga.

I'm eternally grateful to my Mami Ligia, who taught me that I was born to write and inspired the character development of Queen Lygia. You will always be a queen in my eyes, mami.

To my creative team, mil gracias! Without the experiences and support from the creatives in my life, the visual aspect of Rise of Dark Throne could not be possible. MoonPress Cover Design, thank you for taking our book cover vision and making it a reality. A million thanks to Starkey Author Services for making sure this novel made sense. Mariana, thank you for sitting with me to plan a fantastic book launch, even when it was hard. Kseniya Bocharova, your illustration of many of my main characters brought this world to life. I have told you before, and I will say again, that you are brilliant. Finally our amazing map artist Cartographybird Maps .

Writing this novel has been a dream come true! I hope you find yourself in this novel as I did.

xoxo,

Ligia

ABOUT THE AUTHOR

Ligia is a Dominican American writer. Born in New York City. She spent many summers falling in love with the warm sandy beaches and Mangú of the Dominican Republic. All while reading exquisite fantasy romance novels.

Those experiences inspire worldbuilding in her novels. Graduating with two master's degrees in counseling and human services drives how she brings her characters to life. Ligia is located in Tampa, FL, where she enjoys brunch and travel with her husband, son, and their two Mini Aussies, Jake, and Ollie.

THE GREAT LANDS OF TRANSEA

- SANCTUM
- GRIMERG RISE
- THE VENTANE WOODS
- HOUSE OF DO'RAMOS
- KINGGUARD'S REEF
- GALAMEDA BRIDGE
- HOUSE OF PORTE
- MENELIK ATHENAEUM
- MŌSA
- IRIS EXPANSE
- THE SANCTUARY